Headline: Murder

Headline: Murder

a mystery

April Lindgren

Library and Archives Canada Cataloguing in Publication

Lindgren, April, 1959-

Headline: murder / by April Lindgren.

ISBN 978-1-897187-41-8

I. Title.

PS8623.I515H42 2008   C813'.6   C2008-900489-2

Edited by Doris Cowan
Cover and text design by Melissa Kaita
Cover photo by istockphoto/Nuno Silva

Printed and bound in Canada

*Second Story Press gratefully acknowledges the support of the Ontario Arts
Council and the Canada Council for the Arts for our publishing program.
We acknowledge the financial support of the Government of Canada through
the Book Publishing Industry Development Program.*

 ONTARIO ARTS COUNCIL
CONSEIL DES ARTS DE L'ONTARIO   Canada Council   Conseil des Arts
for the Arts   du Canada

Published by
SECOND STORY PRESS
20 Maud Street, Suite 401
Toronto, Ontario, Canada
M5V 2M5
www.secondstorypress.ca

For Tolya

Chapter One

THE TELEPHONE RANG just as Pia settled down to write for the evening. A languid warmth had replaced the day's heat, luring residents in her downtown neighborhood out of their homes. The high-pitched singsong of children playing drifted through her window, dancing like a disjointed melody over the restrained murmur of gossiping adults. Pia's elderly Italian neighbor, Maria, was one of the old guard who had resisted the wads of money pressed on them by young urban professionals hoping to unleash renovation fever on the small, tidy homes built by previous generations. In winter, the survivors of the upscale onslaught vanished: they turned up the heat, closed the drapes, and hibernated inside their homes. But on summer evenings like this, they were all out on their porches, watching, trading news, and inadvertently showing their uptight, worka-holic neighbors how to transform a city street into a village square. Every evening, two or three gray-haired women – some in trademark widow's black, others in the colorfully patterned housedresses that sold for next to nothing on nearby Bloor Street – would join Maria on her front porch. Together they would observe the world go by and discuss what it all meant.

The patio doors that led to the back garden of Pia's house were open, admitting the night air and the disembodied sound of Maria loudly exchanging greetings with passersby. The ambient racket was a reassuring sign that all was right with the neighborhood as Pia tapped away at her computer.

She still had a day job, so work on the book had to be done on evenings and weekends. Pia preferred to write a little bit each day, if possible, so that she didn't have to rush at the end to meet her publisher's deadlines. Experience had taught her how time evaporated, making life miserable for the world's procrastinators. *Too Young to Die* was the fifth in a series of mystery novels featuring the lovely and brainy Cleo Leone. The previous books had been moneymakers, so much so that Pia had been able to buy and gradually renovate her crumbling Victorian house – an investment she'd made contrary to all the advice of family, friends, and real estate agents.

The day job was a temporary gig as entertainment editor of the *Gazette*. It was blessedly undemanding – a break from all the years of relentless deadlines and pissed-off politicians Pia had dealt with as a political reporter. She had intended to quit the daily newspaper business completely and live off the surprisingly significant proceeds of literary murder and mayhem.

But when she'd offered her resignation three months earlier, her publisher, Perry Alton, had panicked at the prospect of losing a big part of the paper's political brain trust.

"You want some peace and quiet?" he'd mused. "Well, the entertainment editor is going on a leave of absence for a year. Could I talk you into taking over for him? The biggest decision you'd have to make is which movie star to put on the front page of the section."

Pia guffawed at the suggestion. "Perry, I'm a pop culture illiterate. I can't tell one movie star from another. I've only seen *Oprah* once in my life and that's because I couldn't get the channel changer in a hotel room to work."

"You can learn," Perry had insisted. "James Nowt is the assistant editor and he knows everything. He'll help you."

Pia recognized the trap. After all these years, she knew how Perry's mind worked. He was betting that her contacts would still call her with the sort of news tips that generate front-page stories. He figured she would succumb to old habits and jump back into the political fray. And maybe he was right; maybe after a few celebrity-saturated months she'd be too bored to resist.

She accepted the offer, thinking the change might be the break she craved. As it turned out, Pia enjoyed the new job and she'd kept her distance from major political stories as they erupted on the paper's front pages – until now.

Some people can ignore calls. But after twenty years of conditioning in the news business as a reporter and columnist,

Pia found a ringing telephone irresistible. You just never knew when it would lead to the next big headline. And so, even though she was immersed in her villain's latest machinations, old habits prevailed. Pia absentmindedly picked up the phone. It took her a moment to figure out that the voice on the other end of the line belonged to Bill Walterson, a senior security guard at Queen's Park, site of the provincial legislature.

"Pia, I think you'll want to get over here right away," he said, his voice sounding low and strained. "We've just discovered May Gatway murdered in the fifth-floor attic."

May Gatway? The culture minister? Pia was instantly alert, feeling the familiar rush of adrenaline as Walterson's words sank in.

"You better get here quick. She's all cut up," Walterson urged before slamming down the phone.

Pia grabbed a notepad and tape recorder from the desk in her study. One part of her mind was processing what Walterson had just told her. The other part was analyzing her reaction. There were studies suggesting that this mixture of anticipation, horror, anxiety, and excitement – combined with a serious dose of will-I-make-the-deadline angst – could be addictive. Some researchers had even gone so far as to suggest the adrenaline hit made it difficult for reporters to give up the thrill of chasing news for a living. Pia felt like an addict falling back into old habits. But this was a sensational story.

Bill Walterson was gruff and blustering, but definitely a "reliable source." Pia knew him from the days when she'd worked out of the *Gazette*'s bureau in the pink sandstone legislature building that was the center of Ontario's political life. He'd come by her office on his evening rounds, usually just after she filed her column. For Walterson, a chat with Pia was a break from the tedium of a job that once in a while involved riot control, but more typically amounted to regular walks through the legislature, checking to see if doors were locked, shutting off lights, and ensuring that nobody who was working late smoked in the building.

For Pia, the chatty encounters were a pleasant enough end to the day, and the information she had gleaned from them had occasionally proved downright valuable. It was Walterson, for instance, who had told her about the delivery of thousands of dollars of lavish new furniture for the office of a minister who'd just announced that the government planned to save money by slashing welfare payments. He'd also gossiped about the many late evenings the short, fat Speaker of the Legislature – responsible for decorum during debates and daily Question Period in the parliamentary chamber – spent in his office with the tall blond secretary who worked for him. This time, however, there was no confiding, mischievous overtone in Walterson's voice as he delivered the news about May Gatway.

In her old life as the *Gazette*'s senior political columnist, Pia had occasionally written about Gatway. The minister, a brittle brunette of the thinnest, richest variety, was bright enough. She'd used some of her family's ample money to start what became a successful advertising business. Then, some years later, she had jumped into politics, first as a fundraiser and then as a successful candidate for elected office. She was appointed to the provincial cabinet almost immediately and quickly began making headlines. As minister of culture, she displayed signs of grit by announcing that one of her priorities would be to encourage, bully and, if necessary, legislate art collectors into returning any works of art stolen by the Nazis during the Second World War. Her stand grabbed the attention of Toronto's arts community and made international headlines.

But Gatway was also one of those unforgiving neo-conservatives who, despite a private school education and money-drenched background, honestly believed her success was due solely to hard work and determination.

"Gatway should spend less time pressing hot buttons and more time on the real issues," Pia once opined in a year-end column in which she graded cabinet ministers on their performance. Her assessment of Gatway was based on more than just her activities on the cultural front. The minister had also been in the news for suggesting that expectant mothers on welfare shouldn't receive any additional financial support during pregnancy, because they would just "spend it on drugs." She'd argued that singing the national anthem at the start of each day in the classroom would improve school discipline. And she'd called upon federal immigration authorities to cancel the visa of a foul-mouthed American rap star scheduled to play a gig in Toronto. It all added up to a less than impressive mark of C in Pia's opinion. Which isn't to say that Gatway deserved to be "all cut up," as Walterson had put it, in the dingy attic of the legislature building.

Pia's sporty silver BMW, purchased with book proceeds, was parked in the garage at the back of her garden. She called the *Gazette*'s front-page editor on her cellphone as she wheeled onto the street, filling him in on what she knew and asking that a photographer be sent to the scene. In less than ten minutes, she was pulling into the legislature's parking lot. Three police cruisers were already there. Others were on the way, the urgent wail of their sirens ripping through the evening's peace. Pia went to the back entrance where Walterson was on duty, his face the color of newly dried concrete.

"This is really, really ugly," he said softly, motioning for her to enter.

Pia nodded, said a quiet word of thanks, and slipped into one of the building's stairwells. The five flights of stairs were a relatively easy climb for Pia, who diligently offset the effects of good wine and food with at least a few three-mile runs per week. A tall, dark-haired, young police officer stood at the bottom of the final rise of steps, halting her dash.

"Pia Keyne from the *Gazette*," she gasped, interrupting him as he announced that nobody was allowed into the attic. "Just let me up there for one minute and I promise I won't bug you again. Just one minute." The corporal was in the midst of his third refusal when Pia heard a familiar voice echo wearily down through the stairwell.

"It's okay, let her in. I'll be responsible."

Pia felt a rush of relief. One of her first jobs at the paper had been as a junior police reporter, the lone female in a press corps of tough-talking cynics who thought women were good for one thing only – and it wasn't covering the news. Detective Nancy Morton, who back then was also on her way up in a world where women were considered an unwelcome nuisance, had decided that "girls should stick together." They had gone out for the occasional drink and meal, and Pia began inviting Morton, as well as her girlfriend of the moment, to her annual Christmas party.

In those early years, Morton fed Pia enough scoops to earn the young reporter the grudging respect of her male competitors. There was also plenty of gossip about the two women among both the cops and the press corps. Admittedly there were moments in the beginning when they both knew that Morton's interest went beyond sisterly solidarity. But Morton, a six-foot-tall blond with short, badly cut hair, was no fool despite her weakness for sassy, curvaceous redheads in high heels. She concluded correctly that Pia liked men if and when she was in the mood to like anybody, which wasn't all that often. In the end, the two women settled on friendship.

Since she'd started writing mysteries, Pia had often needed help with information on police procedures, and Morton was always willing to oblige, providing the briefing took place over a good home-cooked meal. When it came to helping out with news stories, Morton was not always so forthcoming, but they had an understanding: Pia reserved the right to be pushy and press Morton for insider information on crimes, and Morton reserved the right to say nothing when she thought it necessary. Pia thanked the newsprint gods that this was not one of those moments.

"We're going to walk through here," Morton said, stepping aside to let Pia into the fifth-floor corridor. "You will not touch anything, you have to be out of here before the rest of the media horde arrives, and when you see what you are going to see, you better not throw up. Understood?"

"Understood."

"And you are going to owe me one. A big one."

Pia nodded without hesitation.

Morton opened a door and the two women entered a space that looked like little more than a warehouse. Pia knew they were directly above the legislative chamber, where she had so often made notes as government and opposition politicians worked hard to score points off each other in daily Question Period. As a reporter, she had developed a love-hate relationship with Ontario's legislature building. Opened with much pomp in 1893, the pink sandstone structure, nicknamed the Pink Palace, sits like a grand matron on University Avenue looking south toward Lake Ontario, a massive expanse of fresh water cut off from the city by a wall of cookie-cutter condominiums and the much loathed elevated Gardiner Expressway. The legislature's architect, a Brit by the name of Richard A. Waite, had been inspired by the Romanesque style, that is to say he had a fondness for arches and rugged stone. The building's towering windows and skylights were deliberately designed to bring in lots of natural light. But with the light came the hot sun, which turned south-facing offices into sweat tanks that resisted all attempts at air conditioning. The elevators were still a novelty when they were installed at the end of the nineteenth century. Back then, on opening day, amazed members of Parliament and the public rode them up and down until they broke. As Pia was fond of pointing out, they still didn't work very well.

She had spent many, many hours in the Pink Palace. On good days she admired the rich wood, marble, and gleaming glass that gave the building its sense of permanence and tradition. On bad days – when she was marooned in a creaking elevator; giving a giant cockroach a wide berth in the hallway; or sweating, freezing, or dodging the heavy metal fire doors that had been known to go berserk and slam shut of their own accord – she fantasized about working in less idiosyncratic digs.

Love it or hate it, she'd made a point of getting to know the building, with all its secrets and hidden passageways. The basement, for example: its dominant feature was a hallway in *haute* institutional style that led to a cafeteria, mailroom, security offices, and other mostly mundane operations. One innocuous door, however, opened into a dark, narrow vestibule and four damp, barren jail cells, each just barely wider than the span of a man's outstretched arms. In the past, when criminals were still held in the building, double doors on each cell would shut the incarcerated off from the rest of the world. The inner door had a small screen near the base, so guards could see what was going on inside. The heavier outer door was held shut by massive metal drop-locks.

Some people thought there were ghosts in the building, and were certain they haunted the jail cells. In Pia's imagination though, the fifth-floor attics were the spookiest part of the old building. After work one evening a few years earlier, Walterson had taken her on a tour, showing her everything from the big, open spaces with soaring ceilings and high wooden catwalks to dank, steamy closets filled with jumbled wires leading to electrical panels and ventilation pipes. Raised metal-grille walkways carried them through some rooms. In other areas there was simple wooden plank flooring. Walterson pointed out a caged area covered in green indoor-outdoor carpet. At some point, he said, it had been used as a driving range by political staffers. Another section of the center attic was filled with dusty sofas and chairs, old light fixtures, ramshackle crates, and other cast-offs. Some rooms, those with mahogany trim and spectacular views, had once been offices.

Pia had been most intrigued – and repelled – by a long, narrow room with three small square slits cut into one wall near the soaring ceiling. Years ago, members of the Ontario Censor Board had spent hours in the windowless room watching films and deciding if their content was fit for public consumption. She couldn't shake the image of board members shut up in the bleak space, forced to watch pornographic or violent movies projected from behind the slits. It was as if the walls, painted a dull, bilious green, had absorbed the most disturbing of the giant film images projected on their surface. She wasn't sorry when Walterson's tour had moved on.

Now, on her second visit to the building's upper reaches, Pia's uneasiness returned. Morton led her through an area full of gleaming, space-age air ducts, and bristling winches that raised and lowered the legislative chamber's elaborate chandeliers for cleaning. They entered another long room, lined on either side with haphazardly piled chairs, desks made from heavy, dark wood, and other discarded furniture.

Near a table off to one side, dozens of old plaques and photographs had clearly come off the worst in some sort of struggle. Pia stopped for a moment to study the muddle. One framed photograph lay face up on the floor, its glass broken and scattered. "Members of the Ontario Federation of Agriculture, 1964," the caption read.

"The trouble seems to have started here," Morton said, pointing to the scattered frames, a chair that had been tipped over and, most ominously, a trail of blood drops on the battered wooden floor. She led Pia through the maze of office castoffs. May Gatway, it soon became evident, had been running and fighting for her life. As she fled, she had tried to knock obstacles into the path of her pursuer. The debris acted as a road map for the chase. But the bloodstains on the old floorboards made an even better guide. Drops, at first intermittent, appeared more often as the detective and Pia entered the old film censors' viewing gallery.

Pia saw May Gatway in the distance. At first, she couldn't

understand why the honorable minister of the Crown appeared to be standing. Then, as they got closer, she saw the black, iron fireplace poker protruding from Gatway's chest. The murderer had struck with such force that the pointed metal rod had gone straight through her slight body, pinning her to the pillar like a butterfly in a collector's display case. The sleeves of Gatway's blue silk blouse were in shreds, her hands and arms streaked with bloody cuts, including one across her right wrist that had dripped blood into a pool on the floor. Another deep gash ran down the length of one patrician cheek. Blood from the wound had washed down her neck, staining her pale skin. May Gatway's eyes were wide open, staring down at a yellow-handled box cutter near her feet. It was one of those run-of-the-mill tools that people buy for run-of-the-mill household projects. This one, though, was coated with blood.

"God, Nancy, who could have done something like this?" Pia gasped, stepping back and almost tripping over a tangle of fireplace tools. The detective grabbed Pia's arm to prevent her from falling but didn't answer the question

"Time's up. Let's get out of here," she said.

Chapter Two

PIA WOKE THE NEXT MORNING from a restless sleep and the sort of nightmare that her unconscious really should have apologized for. Lying in bed with her eyes closed, she tried to banish the dream, the horror of being chased down, hunted, trapped by an unknown evil. But even as she struggled toward wakefulness, she felt pinned down, suffocating, unable to erase the images of May Gatway's ugly fate. It was a huge relief when she realized that the dead weight on her chest was just warm, furry, fourteen-pound Winston.

"Get lost," Pia grumbled, as she raised her head to stare into the big orange tabby's yellow eyes. He purred blissfully while she scratched him behind the ears, and mewed in protest when she pushed him away so she could get up. It was eight o'clock, too late to do any work on *Too Young to Die*. Leone, intrepid investigator, would have to wait until tomorrow for the big break in her latest murder case. Pia crawled out of bed, threw on an emerald-colored silk robe that set off her green eyes and copper hair and went downstairs to retrieve the newspapers from the front porch.

The story she had filed last night was the main event on the *Gazette's* front page. The Gatway murder was also the lead item in the *Spectator*, but Pia was pleased to note that the competition's coverage didn't have the same depth. *Gazette* subscribers could read in grisly detail how the minister's body had been pinned to the post with the black fireplace poker, how Gatway's right wrist had been slit, how the blood had pooled at her feet, how the killer appeared to have taken the time to wash up in an old, unused bathroom located just off the film censorship room. And that was just for a start.

The night before, after leaving the attic with Nancy Morton, Pia had stopped to talk to Bill Walterson. He'd filled in the details about the young security guard who found Gatway during routine rounds. Earlier in the evening, Pia's story reported, the minister had hosted a reception attended by Jewish community leaders and nearly three hundred prominent members of the arts establishment. Jasmine Assad, one of the *Gazette's* arts reporters and Pia's best friend at the newspaper, had covered the event and was able give Pia additional background. Speaking to the crowd gathered in the legislature building's main foyer, Gatway had made an announcement that put an end to widespread speculation. Laws and regulations would go into effect in the next six months, she told the assembled guests, requiring all provincially funded art galleries to review their collections to ensure they did not contain Nazi plunder. The minister also appealed to major private collectors to examine the provenance of their own artworks for suspicious gaps in history or unaccountable changes in ownership around the time of the Second World War. To drive home the point, the minister said, officials in her department were drafting a new law that would make it easier for victims of past crimes to recover their possessions from both public institutions and private collectors.

"Some people in the crowd didn't look too happy about that," Jasmine had observed the night before, while Pia frantically typed the information into the final-edition account of the murder.

Gatway, Pia reminded her readers in a quickly sketched bio of the victim, had been a member of the provincial legislature for six years, and the lucky heir to millions of dollars from her father, one of the city's most successful real estate developers in his day. Voters in Gatway's riding had elected her to a second term just two years prior to her demise.

The minister was forty-four years old when she died. Two decades earlier, she'd married Paul Stark, a University of Toronto business graduate who had dabbled unsuccessfully in the retail electronics business before reinventing himself as an entrepreneur specializing in educational software for children. Early in her first elected term, Stark had caused his wife considerable embarrassment when he was stopped by police for driving erratically. He'd been charged with drunk driving and for drug possession after the officer noticed a bag of white power lying in plain view on the passenger seat of his Jaguar.

The cocaine and booze incident made headlines, but it hadn't hurt Gatway much politically. She'd played the role of supportive spouse, determined to help her husband kick his addiction. Stark received a suspended sentence and was ordered to enter a treatment program. The story went away after that, though it resurfaced whenever journalists reviewed Gatway's political career.

Pleased that she had seriously beat up on the competition, Pia set aside the papers and made coffee in the kitchen, noting with satisfaction the sunlight streaming into the house. The windows overlooking her backyard garden stretched from the hardwood floors up to the high ceiling. They had been added in the latest of many home improvement projects. Pia hated the dust, the noise, and the disruption of renovations, but she loved the results. The main floor of the house, once a warren of small, dark rooms, now consisted of a kitchen, her study, and a wide, open salon with the original elaborately carved oak fireplace as the central attraction. A bay window, the top one-third filled with rich green and gold stained glass, illuminated the front of the room; a similar window allowed light in through the side. Pia had furnished the room with an eclectic mix of new and old, much of it acquired during the ten years she'd spent on foreign postings in Europe and the Middle East. Two sleek white leather sofas sat on either side of the fireplace. An old oak coffee table with an elaborate flower pattern carved deeply into the legs and edges sat between them on a carpet Pia had bought while on assignment in Damascus. The walls of the room were pale green. Doors sparkling with beveled glass opened off the living room into the study, a book-lined retreat with dark green walls and double doors that led to the garden. Pia's bright yellow, blue, and white kitchen, with its wall of windows and glass doors leading to a deck overlooking the garden, made up the rest of the main floor.

Coffee in hand, she walked out onto the back patio to observe the garden created in the years since she'd bought the place. A bird sitting in the old pear tree, the centerpiece of the lush retreat, rejoiced in the morning sun. The dahlias she'd experimented with this year were starting to bloom, promising a burst of late-season color. Winston, after following her outside and pleading for breakfast, rolled around on the deck, collecting a light covering of dust, twigs, and leaves on his fur. The garden usually made Pia feel at peace. This morning, however, her mind was racing with the implications of Gatway's death. And even the garden's serene beauty couldn't shove the images of the minister's limp body out of her mind's eye. Pia sighed, turned toward the house, and prepared to face the day.

The deputy arts and entertainment director, James Nowt, was at her office door within seconds of Pia's arrival in the newsroom.

"Amazing story this morning," he said effusively. "The *Spectator* looked pathetic. I can't believe you got all that detail."

"The whole thing was pretty awful, James. I had no idea a body could even contain that much blood. I can't get rid of the image. And I keep thinking about how terrified May must have been."

James looked more carefully at his boss, who now sat at her desk behind a mound of papers and used Styrofoam coffee cups. He marveled at how a woman with an immaculately kept house and impeccable dress sense could spend hours quite happily in the workplace equivalent of a garbage heap. She'd arrived looking fantastic in a chic, cream-colored silk suit, but there were faint dark circles under those green eyes that had melted the hard-bitten hearts of even the paper's toughest editors.

"You look a bit done in, so I'm sorry I have to bring this up," he said. "But the arts community fundraiser is today and the paper is the major sponsor. The publisher's secretary sent down a reminder saying he is expecting you to join him at his table for the luncheon."

Pia groaned.

"And while I have your attention," James went on, "Linda Epsony has already called four times for you this morning. She wants to write an opening night review of the Chelsea Community Theater's production of *Little Shop of Horrors*. What do I tell her?"

"Tell her to forget it," Pia said impatiently. "Tell her we've got a new policy that says we won't review every little local production that comes along. We have to draw the line somewhere and this is it. The answer is no, and I don't care how many times she calls."

"She's not going to give up easily," James warned glumly as he turned to leave.

Back on the day he'd sold Pia on the idea of taking over the arts and entertainment section, Perry Alton had extolled James Nowt's knowledge and professionalism. He had been dead-on. James, a slim, fair man with two published poetry collections to his credit, had at least twice in the past refused to take over the editor's job himself. At thirty-eight, he was intent on devoting the better part of his energies to producing another collection of verse. In the meantime, his judgment on entertainment matters was impeccable.

"People care much more about where stars get their fashion advice," James insisted to his skeptical new boss one day when she toyed with running a story about the troubles of mariachi bands in crime-ridden Mexico City on the third page of their section.

Pia felt a pang of misgiving about her stand on amateur theater reviews. A few weeks earlier she'd decided to flex her editorial muscle by decreeing that a major metropolitan daily newspaper should not feel obliged to review every theater production in the city when space in the paper was at a premium.

James agreed but he warned her that bringing in the change would not be easy. "I think this is a decision that will come back to haunt us," he predicted.

"Either the reviews go or I go," Pia joked in her version of a dramatic stage voice. James rolled his eyes.

Pia used the time before the arts fundraiser to select a long feature on Hollywood stars and their plastic surgery as the main story for the next day's entertainment section. She scribbled a note to James urging him to run as many before-and-after pictures as possible. Then she sauntered through the newsroom to the city editor's desk to ask if there was anything new on the Gatway murder. Tall and lanky, Craig Linde was nicknamed Einstein because of his thick thatch of uncontrollably frizzy gray hair. Nothing yet, he said, but the police reporter was following developments. Pia retreated to her office. There were definitely other angles to pursue. After thinking for a few minutes, she sent an e-mail to Jasmine Assad, asking her to check on the identities of the city's major private art collectors.

"I'd like to find out more about their response to Gatway's request that they comb their collections for stolen art. Would any of these pillars of respectability have been angry enough with the minister about this new law she was proposing to do her in?" she asked half seriously before signing off and heading to the luncheon.

The rubber-chicken crowd was out in force for the event in support of young artists. Pia spotted Perry Alton in the distance as she walked into the hotel ballroom. She smiled wickedly at the thought of spending a pleasant hour trying to provoke the *Gazette*'s rotund, balding proprietor. I'll tell him I'm publishing pictures of nude women on the front page of tomorrow's section, she thought idly. Artistic pictures of nude women, as befits a family newspaper. A moment later she noticed Perry's companion and her step faltered. "*Shit, shit, shit,*" she thought. But it was too late to melt back into the crowd: the two men had spotted her and the publisher waved her over.

"Pia, glad you could make it. Do you know Martin Geneve? He'll be sitting at our table."

"We've met," Pia said, smiling uncomfortably at the tall, dark-haired man in front of her. He was as attractive as ever, if one liked the cold, calculating type, she thought, her mind trying to work out the social niceties of dealing with someone she'd deliberately – and obviously – been avoiding for nearly a year.

"Yes, we've met," Martin said sardonically. "But we haven't kept in touch."

Perry cut short further conversation, urging his guests to take their seats for lunch. Pia walked to the far side of the large round table assigned to the *Gazette*, trying to put as many chairs as possible between herself and Martin Geneve. But she wasn't going to get off that easily.

"I'll join you, shall I?" Martin asked, pulling out a chair for Pia and then folding himself into the one beside her before she could answer. "It will be a chance for us to catch up."

Pia glanced at him, annoyance beginning to overcome her initial embarrassment. He was impeccably dressed in a dark suit, a crisp white shirt, and a tie that matched his dark gray eyes, eyes that reminded Pia of Lake Ontario on a stormy day. Or of ice on a frozen river. Noting that the chairs on either side of them were still empty, she decided to make the most of the momentary privacy.

"Look, I'm sorry I didn't return your calls," she said, keeping her voice neutral. "Work has been incredibly busy. I've changed jobs and I haven't had a moment to spare, what with the learning curve and all."

She flushed slightly under Martin's cool scrutiny, sure that he was recalling the night last year when they first met at a dinner party thrown by a mutual acquaintance. Pia had been vaguely aware that Martin's telecommunications firm was one of the most successful in the country. She'd noticed that he was attractive. It was impossible not to, especially since he'd made a point of coming over to chat with her before dinner was served. Pia had left the party early because she had to rush back to the paper to deal with a breaking story. Her instinct told her he would call and he did, the very next afternoon. But by then she'd checked him out in the newspaper's archive: two divorces and a string of supermodel dates highlighted in the society pages. Trouble, in other words.

"You are not your mother, who fell for every good-looking jerk who came along," she'd reminded herself. "Two divorces and those lingering looks? This guy is in the Don't Go There zone."

Martin had left a message, inviting her to dinner and asking her to call him back. Silently rejoicing when she got his answering machine, Pia said she was too busy with work but thanks for the invitation anyway. He called several times after that, but through diligent monitoring of the call display on her telephone she managed to avoid speaking to him.

The truth was, she *had* been busy with work and her latest book. But she'd also been preoccupied with the baby decision. At forty-three, Pia had been toying with having a child on her own. Someone to love who could be counted on to love her back. Someone she could trust. She'd been immersed in researching sperm banks even as she absorbed the statistics, provided by more than one doctor, about the odds against a woman her age getting pregnant.

A year had passed and to her relief so had the worst of the child-bearing frenzy. Too old. Too risky. Too complicated. Tests just a month ago had confirmed the doctors' prognosis: her hormone levels were so low it was unlikely she could conceive. Pia didn't allow herself to indulge in regrets. There had been plenty of men, but she had never let any of them get close enough to count. Her career had been her baby – the travel, the foreign postings, the excitement of a ringside seat at everything from the collapse of the Berlin Wall to meetings of world leaders in glittering capitals. And now she had her books to absorb her. She could live with the disappointment as long as she didn't think about it. So she made herself not think about it.

Pia realized Martin Geneve was still talking to her.

"Well, you certainly wouldn't get an A for good manners at the school I went to," he was saying quietly as other guests took their places. Thankfully, the introductions around the table prevented him from saying more. The conversation soon shifted to May Gatway's death. Pia was peppered with questions as her table mates speculated wildly on motives for the murder.

"Maybe it was the Liberal opposition leader," Perry joked. "Didn't somebody say recently that he looks like the crazy killer in *Psycho*?"

When the chitchat drifted to city politics, Martin Geneve again turned to Pia.

"Personally, I think the police should be looking at Paul Stark," he said quietly. "The guy's in big financial trouble, and I hear the marriage was on the rocks – which says to me his wife wouldn't have been all that keen to bail him out."

Forgetting that she intended to be cool to Geneve, Pia leaned closer and asked in a low voice, "Her husband? That's interesting. How do you know he's in trouble?"

"He recently came to me asking for new financing. I took a look at his operation and decided to stay as far away from it as possible. But when I told him to forget it, he practically begged me for help. Said his wife was a bitch who wanted to leave him high and dry. He said she wanted a divorce and that he'd get very little out of it because she'd be entitled to keep the money left by her father all for herself. Apparently it was money she'd inherited before he latched on to her. If you ask me, Stark is between a rock and hard place."

Pia took a moment to absorb the information. "Thanks," she said. "I'll look into it."

"Are you grateful enough to have dinner with me tonight?"

"No. I mean, no, thank you," Pia said, caught off guard. "I make it a policy not to mix business and pleasure."

"Come on, Pia. I might have a redeeming quality or two or even three. I'm not asking you to marry me. It's just a date. Surely you can fit me into your schedule."

Pia had had enough. The guy oozed charm. But then so did many of the men who had wandered in and out of her mother's bedroom. She felt a panicky need to escape.

"Excuse me, please," she said, drawing her companions' attention away from the chocolate mousse that had just been delivered. "I'm sorry, but I have to get back to work to meet a deadline. It's been a pleasure meeting all of you."

Perry Alton looked up, surprised. It was a graceless exit and Pia knew it. She glanced quickly at Martin and felt his eyes on her as she made her way out of the room. She'd reached the door when the idea came to her. Maybe she shouldn't be so hasty. Maybe she should just take a chance. The doctors said it was highly unlikely she could become pregnant. But that didn't mean it was impossible. She struggled to put the thought back into the dark, unworthy corner of her mind that had spawned it. But before she could manage the feat, she found herself turning and smiling at Martin Geneve.

Chapter Three

BACK IN THE NEWSROOM, Pia slammed the door to her office, dropped into her chair, and stared at her desk. An abandoned coffee cup vied for space with piles of newspapers and movie posters. The mess, she thought, resembled her state of mind. A jumble of old, useless, unpleasant stuff.

"Pia, not every man is a variation on the guys who flitted in and out of your mother's life," she remembered Dr. Gabriella Garcia saying gently one day. "Are you going to keep them all at arm's length forever?"

"Yes" had seemed a reasonable response back then. And it didn't seem like such a bad idea now, Pia thought, recalling the tears, the hysteria, and the wasted days her mother had spent shut up in dark bedrooms mourning the departure of another Prince Charming who failed to rescue them from their hand-to-mouth existence. Of course, all that was before Max entered their lives and stuck around, changing things forever.

Pia looked out the glass walls that made her office feel like a fishbowl and saw Jasmine Assad coming across the newsroom with a piece of paper in her hand. Jasmine was short and delicate with dark eyes and spectacular, thick, wavy black hair, though you wouldn't know it these days. For the last two months she had been wearing a brush cut that accentuated her fine features and made her eyes seem enormous.

"It's very economical," Jasmine told her appalled Muslim parents the first time she visited them with her shorn head. "I can get it trimmed down at Mike's Barber Shop for ten bucks plus tip."

Pia smiled at the determined look on the face of the young woman who had, over the last four years, become her closest confidante. Jasmine was an unusual mix – a painter who wrote to make a living, an artist with her feet planted firmly on the ground, the quirky, determinedly secular daughter of conservative Muslim parents. Pia, well known among her friends for her astonishing grasp of political minutiae and her equally astonishing ignorance of popular culture, was in the absurd position of being Jasmine's boss – Jasmine, who soaked up culture, high and low, the way a sponge absorbs water.

"Quick," she would say to Pia after they'd had a few glasses of wine, "who is Madonna married to?" Pia almost always flunked such tests in the days before she got her new job. She had more of the correct answers these days. Professional pride demanded it and she *was* the arts and entertainment editor. But the years she'd apparently wasted immersed in politics and

28

literature could not be easily recouped. She still often resorted to wild guesses during Jasmine's impromptu quizzes. The incorrect answers left her friend doubled up with laughter. "Where have you been all your life, girl?" she'd gasp.

"Jasmine," Pia would protest, "one day when I was seven my mother told me the television was broken and it never got fixed. Then when I was fifteen and went to live with Aunt Margaret, she disapproved of the sort of trashy magazines that obviously polluted your brain. I'm still trying to catch up, so give me a break."

Jasmine bustled into Pia's office, lifted a pile of magazines off the chair facing the desk, and sat down.

"You were wondering who among the private collectors in the province might stand to lose if there were questions about their art collections? I drew up a list and then checked to see who was at the reception in the legislature the night of the murder. I've got a few interesting names."

Jasmine paused dramatically, then continued, waving the piece of paper. "I, suggest to you that any or all of these six people are our top suspects. They had motive. They had opportunity."

Smiling at her friend's drama queen tendencies, Pia grabbed the paper but got no further than the first name on the list. Wilson Scott was a member of the provincial legislature and a colleague of May Gatway's in the Conservative Party.

"Wow, Wilson Scott. I knew he collected art and always wanted Gatway's job. But I didn't know he played in the big-time art league," Pia said. "What's he collect?"

"Mostly Canadian stuff," said Jasmine. "But he also has some early-twentieth-century paintings too. He's loaned pieces out to museum shows, so we know about a few of them. If the provenance of everything he owns was thoroughly checked, who knows what we'd find? Is he the type who would do the right thing and give back a piece of art if he found out it was stolen sixty years ago?"

Pia remembered when Scott was first elected at age thirty-three. The tall, good-looking blond MPP with impeccable conservative roots caused a stir among young female political staffers in the parliamentary precinct.

"I'm not sure. What I do know is that he was furious when Gatway was named minister of culture and he got stuck being the parliamentary assistant to the minister of agriculture," she said. "That had to hurt. There was a story going around that he had a few drinks the day the new cabinet ministers were sworn in and at some point loudly suggested that Gatway had money but no taste. Even I've figured out that that's a big insult in artsy circles."

"You're learning. When Gatway started pushing hard to get collectors to double-check the origins of their artworks, maybe it put him under the gun. I mean, he's a public figure and it would look very bad if was hanging on to something that rightfully belongs to some Holocaust survivor or the family of a Holocaust victim. I guess the question is, was he worried enough to kill?"

"He doesn't strike me as the type, but I think I'll go talk to him. At least I can try to find out what he was up to after the reception last night."

They were silent for a moment and then Pia spoke again. "It was awful the other night, Jasmine. I can't get what happened to May Gatway out of my head. I know it sounds melodramatic, but when I saw her dead like that, I had this horrible sense that I could still smell her fear."

The words hung in the air between them. Jasmine suddenly remembered the story a sobbing Pia had told her one boozy night a year earlier. She looked more closely at her complicated friend. Had Pia's own experience of being helpless and cornered magnified her reaction to Gatway's fate? Pia had escaped alive, but in many ways she was still scarred. About the only good thing to come of that trauma, Jasmine thought, was that the teenaged Pia had gone to live with her Aunt Margaret.

Perhaps sensing the direction of Jasmine's thoughts, Pia hurriedly began recounting what she'd heard earlier in the day about Gatway's husband. "So that makes two potential suspects," she continued. "Wilson Scott and Gatway's husband, Paul Stark."

Turning back to Jasmine's list, her eyebrows shot up when she recognized another name. "Martin Geneve! He's the one who told me about Stark over lunch today," she said. "Strange that he didn't mention that he was actually at the reception."

"Does he strike you as the murderous type?"

"Again, I really don't know. But he's probably worth checking out. In the meantime, I'll try to talk to Gatway's husband as well."

"I'll put together whatever background I can find on everybody on the list," Jasmine said, looking wary as she tried to chart a safe route out of the office. "Cripes, Pia, why don't you clean this place up? It's a health hazard."

"It's all important, essential information that I'm going to study so I can be an informed member of the arts community." Pia laughed as her friend, shuddering with disgust, picked her way out of the office.

Left alone, Pia pressed the play button on her answering machine.

"Pia, dear," Linda Epsony's well-bred voice began, "you are so new in your job that I don't think you quite realize the significance of this production of *Little Shop of Horrors* for the local theater community. We really should meet so I can explain to you how important it is that we review it. I, of course, am available to write the piece." Pia angrily jabbed the erase button before she had to hear any more.

Then she looked up the address of Paul Stark's firm, scribbled it in a notebook, and headed out. Gatway's husband was probably at home, but she decided to check his office first. It would be worth the trip just to get a first-hand sense of how the business seemed to be doing.

Twenty minutes later, she walked up the steps of a renovated building in what used to be a semi-abandoned downtown warehouse district. Now it was a fashionable address. Educational Software Inc. was a stylish operation, she thought, admiring the gleaming wood floors and bare brick walls of the building's reception area. Off to one side, a brass plaque near a set of ornate glass doors invited her into Stark's company offices. She told the receptionist she wanted to see the boss regarding his wife's death and, much to her surprise, was quickly ushered into a gleaming white space with high ceilings. Towering windows that looked out on out-of-service railway lines dominated one side of the room. A huge glass and chrome desk sat in front of them. The only color in the place shouted from two large paintings on the walls. One was a splash of red, the other a disciplined pattern of yellow-toned bars set against a purple background. Pia liked them both, if only because they were a welcome sign of life in a room that otherwise felt bright, cold, and devoid of humanity.

When Paul Stark walked into the room, she realized she'd seen pictures of him with Gatway. He wore black pants and a black turtleneck that accentuated his tall, thin body. The dark clothes contrasted dramatically with pale blond hair that was thinning on top and a little long at the back. Stark's skin had an unhealthy pallor, his eyes were slightly red-rimmed.

"I'm sorry to keep you waiting," he said, approaching Pia with his hand outstretched. "There's a media circus outside at the house, so thank you for meeting me here. I've never organized anything like this before so I'm really going to be depending on you people at the funeral home for all sorts of guidance."

"Actually, Mr. Stark, I'm Pia Keyne and I'm from the *Gazette*. I apologize. I gather you were expecting someone else."

Stark looked ready to show her the door.

"Please, give me a moment. I'm sorry about your wife's

death; I knew her from covering the legislature. I want to talk to you because I'm hearing some pretty damaging speculation on the street about who killed her, and I thought you might want the chance to put it to rest." Stark's shoulders stiffened; he paused for a moment, sighed, and then motioned to a chair near his desk while he went to sit behind it.

"Why don't you tell me what on earth you are talking about?" he said coldly as he picked up a tiny silver box from his desk and began toying with it between long, pale fingers. Fingers, Pia noted, that were trembling slightly.

"The rumor I'm hearing is that May wanted a divorce and you weren't too happy about it. Is that true?"

"Christ," Stark said, halting his fidgeting. "People are vicious." There was a long pause and then he looked up. "For the record, May wanted to have a baby. Does that sound like a woman who was looking for a divorce?"

Pia was momentarily taken aback by the image of May Gatway as a mommy. She noted, however, that Stark hadn't directly answered her question.

"Were you at the reception at the legislature last night?" she asked, calculating that she had, at most, about five minutes before Stark threw her out.

"I was," he replied dryly. "And to answer your next question, I went straight home – alone. May, as you probably know, was a workaholic. She stayed at the office.

"The police found me at the house. Officers came to tell me about what happened. But really, I don't have to answer any of these questions. People can think what they want."

"They can and they will, Mr. Stark, so it makes all the more sense to get your side of the story out."

Stark slouched back in his chair and studied Pia thoughtfully. Then he straightened up, apparently having reached a decision. "Okay," he said finally, "I'm going to tell you something that may be of help in finding May's killer. But then you have to leave me alone. Is it a deal?"

Pia nodded, her eyes fixed on the file Stark picked up from a pile on his desk. He pushed it across to her.

"I was up all last night after they made me identify May's body and answer questions at the police station. When I got home, I went to her study to look around her desk and I found this."

Stark hesitated and then spoke more slowly. "Being married to someone means understanding their good and their bad points. I always knew that," he said slowly, "but this reminded me all over again how ruthless my wife could be when she felt the need. If you are looking for her murderer, Pia Keyne, then I suggest you follow up on this, because I think she was using it to get her way about something."

Pia opened the file and found herself staring at a photograph of Wilson Scott. The Conservative MPP stood at a bar in a dimly lit club. Wearing a dark suit and tie, he looked as if he'd come directly from Question Period in the legislative chamber. His behavior, however, was anything but parliamentary. The honorable member was leaning over, passionately kissing a young man in jeans and a white T-shirt. The youth, who looked as if he should have been home doing his high school homework, was sitting on a stool with his back against the bar. One of Scott's hands was buried in the boy's long blond hair. The other was planted firmly on his companion's crotch. Pia was stunned.

"Turn the picture over," Stark instructed before she could say anything. Pia obliged and discovered a handwritten note on the back.

"Back off," the message said, "or everybody in town will get a copy of this. Mommy, daddy, and the premier won't be pleased." It was followed by a date from a few weeks earlier with the word "sent" beside it, heavily underlined.

"Is this May's handwriting?" Pia asked, finally recovering her voice.

Stark nodded.

"You think she was using this to put pressure on Scott?" Stark stared coldly at Pia. "What do you think?"

"But what did she want from him?" Pia's words came slowly as she tried to assemble possibilities.

"I don't know for sure what she did with it. Maybe it was self-defense because I think he had something on her. Or maybe he was just being annoying. He never liked May, you know."

"Have you shown this to the police?"

"Not yet. But I will if they keep asking me questions about what I did after the reception. I'll make you a copy so you can discuss it all with Wilson Scott. Ask *him* about his activities last night. Then I want you to leave because I really do have to see someone about a funeral."

Chapter Four

WITH JASMINE'S HELP, Pia worked on a follow-up front-page story for the next day's paper. She started with the information from Paul Stark about Gatway's desire to have a baby and went on to describe in detail how the dead woman had planned to help the owners of plundered art treasures recover their lost property.

Jasmine hung up the phone after interviewing an expert on the law and art ownership. A number of other countries, she reported to Pia, had already adopted new laws making it less onerous for people to prove that paintings, sculptures, and other works of art had once belonged to their families. Governments in Canada, the expert also pointed out, were big financial supporters of public art galleries and could use that clout to force the institutions to review the history of everything in their collections. Gaps in the ownership records or suspicious-looking documents often provided the first hints that something was amiss, he said. While the directors of major museums around the world had all committed, several years ago, to conduct such reviews, there seemed to be a marked lack of enthusiasm for actually getting the job done.

Pia and Jasmine held back on Gatway's apparent attempt to blackmail Wilson Scott. There were just too many unanswered questions.

"We don't even know absolutely for sure if Gatway wrote the note," Pia said as they stared at the photo, trying to figure out what bar Scott was in when it was taken. "Maybe somebody else dreamt up the plot and just gave her a copy. We need to talk to Wilson Scott to find out what was going on before we can even hint he has a role in all this."

Pia repeatedly tried to contact Scott as the evening deadline approached. She needed to ask him about the photo and the note, but she also wanted to know how he felt about Gatway's art recovery initiative. He had an art collection himself. Should the government pursue the dead minister's pet project? Her calls to Scott's office weren't returned.

"He's too busy cruising the bars for pretty boys," Jasmine muttered as the minutes to deadline ticked by. In the end, the paper's lawyers had the final word – to publish speculation about a possible blackmail scheme without hearing Wilson Scott's version of events was to risk major legal trouble.

"Let's nail it down tomorrow," Pia said wearily as she pressed the button on her computer, sending the story off to the editors. It was just after 8 p.m.

When she got home, Winston wasn't immediately at her feet making his usual pitch for dinner. Pia threw down her purse and went to the kitchen where she saw the big cat staring, mesmerized, at the narrow space between a dish cabinet and the wall.

"It's a mouse, you dope," she said, peering into the opening. The creature was dead in the trap she'd laid a few days earlier after hearing the familiar pitter-patter of little invaders. "If you were a real cat, I wouldn't have to do this," she grumbled as she grabbed a broom, pushed aside the cabinet, and swept the death machine, victim and all, into a plastic bag. Pia set another trap and then reached for a piece of paper on the refrigerator door. Under a column with her own name at the top, she scratched out the number 7 and scribbled in 8. Under Winston, she scribbled the usual 0. Oblivious to the humiliation, the cat meowed, purred, and worked at tripping his mistress as he wound himself around her legs.

"You should be ashamed," Pia complained as she fed him his dinner.

A few minutes later she was dressed in her running clothes. Pia had discovered the joy of exercise in high school. The hours she spent training with the track team or in the pool meant hours she wasn't thinking about her mother, or Max, or what happened to them. These days, she relied on running to clear her head and keep off unwanted pounds.

Pia's route took her west for a few miles along nondescript side streets lined with small, tired-looking houses. After lingering through the long summer evening, the sun, having decided it had had enough, plummeted in the western sky. Darkness spread over the neighborhood like spilt ink. Mothers with lined faces and harried voices that testified to their exhaustion rounded up the last of their children, stragglers who were allowed to play outside until late because there was no school the next day. The early part of the run wasn't scenic, but Pia did it anyway because it took her to High Park, the crown jewel of Toronto's green spaces.

It was too late and too dark to go into the park alone, so she ran beside it for a while, resisting the urge to take one of the winding paths into the forest, an oasis for city dwellers seeking relief from concrete, glass, and traffic. Instead, she headed for a nearby high school track, and ran some laps while two teams of teenagers clad in opposing colors played out the last minutes of a lively soccer game on the brightly lit field. Life was good, she thought, tripping happily up the stairs to her house nearly an hour later.

The next morning, she went in search of Wilson Scott. The sign on his office door at the legislature building reminded all who entered that he was the parliamentary assistant to the minister of agriculture. The reception area, however, made few concessions to rural life and Pia smiled, trying to imagine the reaction of visiting farmers in the city to discuss the latest crop crisis.

At least half a dozen paintings decorated the walls. To Pia, some were incomprehensibly abstract. Others she found quite lovely, including a vibrant winter scene that sparkled with the boisterous spirits of turn-of-the-century skaters in long skirts and woolen jackets. Twin sofas made of soft burgundy leather sat on either side of a black marble cube that served as a table. A young man in a sleek suit and expensive-looking loafers greeted her when she came in. He said hadn't heard from Scott yet and wasn't sure when he'd be arriving. Pia sat down to wait.

When the door opened a half-hour later, however, it wasn't the member of Parliament who entered but a tall, slim man with chestnut hair and lively brown eyes framed by a trendy pair of horn-rimmed glasses. Pia didn't catch his name when he spoke to the receptionist, but he too seemed prepared to bide his time. Settling into the other sofa, he glanced at her, then nodded in recognition.

"You're Pia Keyne?"

"That's right," she said, taking in his well-tended appearance. The oversized art book he laid on the coffee table also caught her eye. "But you don't strike me as a farmer."

"I'm Jack Cleary, curator of the legislature's art collection. And this," he said, motioning to the book that had obviously attracted her interest, "is a book of nineteenth-century Canadian art."

"How did you know who I was?"

"I recognize you from when you were still up here writing about the goings-on in this place," he said, smiling. "And I sometimes go to High Park on the weekend for a run. I think I've seen you there once in a while. You usually look preoccupied."

"So I guess I've never said hello."

"Oh, I don't blame you. I'm sure your mother warned you not to talk to strangers."

Pia laughed. If only you knew, she thought, recalling the list of strangers who came and went from her mother's life. They chatted about different running trails in the city for another ten minutes, but when there was still no word from Wilson Scott, Cleary announced he would come back later. Then he asked Pia if she would like to join him for a coffee.

"What exactly does a curator do around here?" she asked as they walked over to a café on Yonge Street. For the next hour, Cleary told her about the legislature's art collection and how for the last three years it had been his job to keep track of all artworks, ensure they were in good repair, and rotate the paintings on display in public spaces and in politicians' offices.

The thin, pale artsy types had never much appealed to Pia, but Jack Cleary was making her reconsider. He was funny and smart. And he didn't seem to mind that she didn't know her dead artists from her live ones.

"Wilson Scott is a big fan of the legislature's permanent collection," Cleary continued. "All the paintings you saw in his office belong to it. He exchanges them for others quite regularly. I'd hoped to catch him this morning to discuss what he wanted next because, God knows, there's a lot to choose from. Only about fifteen per cent of the collection is up on the walls at any one time. The rest of the paintings are in storage, waiting for their moment in the limelight."

"Where is all this stuff kept?"

"We have a building in the north end of the city. I'll take you on a tour sometime if you want to see it."

Scott was still nowhere to be found when they returned to his office. Pia left her card and told his aide she wanted to set up a meeting as soon as possible. Then she suggested to Cleary that they go for a run together some evening.

"If there are two of us, we can go into the park even if it is getting dark," she said quickly, suddenly feeling shy as they exchanged phone numbers. "I don't like to go alone after the sun goes down."

James Nowt was watching for Pia and loped over to her the moment she set foot in the newsroom.

"There's trouble in your office," he said anxiously.

"Is it the health and safety committee again?" Pia joked.

"Pia, I'm trying to give you a heads-up. This isn't funny. Linda Epsony is in your office. It's about *Little Shop of Horrors*."

Pia groaned. Approaching her office, she saw that a small gray-haired woman was indeed waiting for her, distaste written all over her face as she surveyed the chaos around her. Epsony had installed herself in Pia's chair, behind Pia's desk. She did not get up when Pia came through the door.

"You must be Pia Keyne," Epsony said in the same raspy, well-bred voice Pia had come to recognize from the numerous telephone voice-mail messages. "I've been trying for days to reach you. We really do need to chat, my dear."

Stunned by the little woman's audacity and her unapologetic hijacking of the office desk, Pia was momentarily speechless. Out of the corner of her eye, she could see James Nowt and Jasmine shamelessly watching through the glass wall.

"There's been a terrible misunderstanding about coverage of the little-theater community," Epsony plunged on. "Now I know you are just a beginner when it comes to the arts, dear, so I don't think you realize what an error it is to abandon coverage of the amateur theatricals. I've been the department's freelance reviewer for years, so I know what I'm talking about and, for the record, little theater is the heart, the life, the soul of the community and the *Gazette* is part of the community. So I'll do the review, shall I? The usual deadline?"

Pia struggled to control of her temper, although Jasmine would later tell her that even her lips were white with anger.

"Linda, we've discussed this before. We will review some little-theater productions but not all of them. We need to expand our arts coverage to other events, and space in the paper these days is at a premium. We just don't have room for reviews of every single show so we're being selective. We won't review *Little Shop of Horrors*, but we will get to others."

Epsony, her eyes narrowed to cat-like slits, rose slowly to her feet. With studied deliberation, she picked her way around the piles of paper on the floor, glaring at Pia as she brushed past her.

"This," she hissed, "is not over. We will fight for our rights."

Pia wondered what rights those might be, but held her tongue. It was all she could do not to shove the woman out of the office. Being accused of single-handedly destroying the city's amateur theater community was enough of a headache. She didn't need an assault charge, especially with so many eyewitnesses. Einstein, a few copy editors, and a stray reporter or two had by now joined James and Jasmine to watch the show. Pia cursed the corporate brain trust that opted for the glass-walled offices so that editors could look out and see what was going on in the newsroom. What they hadn't considered was that everyone in the newsroom could also observe what was going on in the offices. She composed herself, waited until she was sure Epsony was gone, and then walked out to confront the voyeurs.

"Don't any of you have work to do?"

Her colleagues greeted her snarl with shouts of laughter. "Having a wee bit of trouble with the ladies who lunch and run little theater, I see," observed Einstein. "We could use you back on the political beat if you can't handle them."

"Don't tempt me," Pia said morosely, as she contemplated the tedious day of departmental administration and correspondence that awaited her. This plan went out the window a few hours later when Wilson Scott's lifeless body was discovered in a shabby east-end motel.

"These right-wingers are falling like flies," Einstein observed in the tightly controlled voice he reserved those days for when a big story broke and his organizational skills were put to the test.

Pia, drawn out of her office and into the newsroom by the buzz of excitement, immediately volunteered to go to the scene.

"Great. You knew the guy right?" said Einstein, his hair standing on end. "We'll start putting together background on him here. Call us with whatever you get. So far there's no indication whether he killed himself or somebody else did the job for him."

The Highway Inn, where Scott spent his last moments, was a bleak place in a bleak part of town. The inn itself was actually a drab motel of twenty-five rooms stretched out along Kingston Road. Once a main thoroughfare, the road and the dozens of motels along it were casualties of progress as Toronto's expressway system evolved. They had long ago given up relying on tourists and business clients and instead provided temporary housing for hundreds of homeless families dependent on government support. Many of these families consisted of children and single mothers who were down on their luck and dependent on local social service agencies for housing. In other cases, authorities used the motels as quarters for refugee claimants, people who had made their way to Canadian borders and then pleaded for asylum. The motel strip had grown to resemble something of a mini United Nations for the desperate as their applications slowly wound their way through the system.

Police cruisers jammed the motel parking lot by the time Pia arrived. Leaving her car on the street, she walked slowly across the cracked pavement in front of the building, noting the child's bicycle abandoned near the screen door of one room and the two battered green lawn chairs outside another. Every window in the place was grimy with city dirt. Someone had put plastic containers for plants on either side of the entrance to the motel reception, but the flowers had long since shriveled up and died. In their place, cigarette butts littered the hard brown soil.

Pia decided to start with the reception, though the action was clearly down around room 11. A balding man in a sweat-stained T-shirt looked up as she came through the door. He appeared to be in his fifties with skin that approximated the gray of his grubby shirt. The odor of old cigarette smoke clung to the lobby, and the man behind the counter was doing his best to reinforce the stench, contrary to city and provincial laws that declared smoking in public places the next best thing to attempted murder. A cigarette dangled from his fleshy lips, the replacements stashed in a pack that was pushed up one sleeve of his T-shirt. Pia introduced herself and found out that Reg Wizinski managed the Highway Inn.

"So what happened here?" she said, checking her annoy-ance as Wizinski looked her up and down, eyes lingering on her chest.

"The dead guy – well, he wasn't dead then – checked in around eight last night," he said. "He registered as Richard Rankin. He wasn't our usual sort of customer, if you know what I mean. We don't usually get the clean-cut business types with the cellphone and Gucci shoes. But he paid cash and his money was the same as anybody else's. I figured he was maybe going to hire some local talent for an hour of two, get his jollies, and get out. It happens. So he goes into his room and I don't think any more about it until around two-thirty this afternoon when I see the Do Not Disturb sign still on his door. I realize he hasn't checked out, so I start looking for him to leave or pay up for another night."

Pia nodded encouragingly.

"I called the room but nobody answered, so I got a little bit worried. I went down there, opened the door and saw the guy all curled up in a ball on the bed. He was naked and his skin was white as this," Wizinski said, motioning to a napkin on the counter next to the discards of a McDonald's meal. "It scared the shit out of me and I called 911 right away."

Wizinski said he hadn't seen any visitors to the room, but he acknowledged he spent most evenings with his eyes glued to the little TV at the end of the counter. "So I wouldn't really know if somebody came by and killed the guy. Anyway, I don't think that's what happened. Before the cops got here, I noticed an empty pill bottle on the table beside the bed. And a letter, too. I didn't touch anything though – learned from the TV how you shouldn't be touching stuff in these sorts of iffy situations, in case there's more to it."

Pia wrote it all down in her notebook and then headed to room 11 where she was pleased to see that Nancy Morton once again seemed to be running the show.

"Thought one death a week would be enough for you to handle, Morton," she said sympathetically when she caught the detective's eye.

"Yeah, and I thought you'd given up reporting because you wanted a cushy desk job," retorted the detective. "Seems to me you're pretty hard at it."

"Some stories are too good – or bad, I guess I should say – to resist. What happened?"

Morton sighed. "You'll have to call me later for more information, but so far it looks like Scott decided to kill himself. I'm here because I think he also decided to solve the Gatway murder for us." Smiling wryly at Pia's astonished look, Morton told her there was a suicide note.

"It's a full confession. Says he followed Gatway into the attic the other night because she was threatening to tell the world he was gay. I don't know what his problem was. Who cares these days? Anyway, he said he tried to talk to her but apparently the talk didn't go well, so he grabbed a box cutter that happened to be lying around and went after her. He chased her through the attic and finally killed her with the fireplace poker. In the note, he says he couldn't live with what he'd done and then he goes to great lengths to apologize to her parents and to his constituents – and even to the premier, for chrissakes. They're supposed to be making laws up there in that place, not contributing to a crime wave. No wonder the country is falling apart. And Pia, if you print that last bit we're through."

At an impromptu press conference a few minutes later, Morton told reporters it did not appear that foul play was involved, but insisted no final conclusions could be drawn until the investigation and autopsy were complete. She then stunned reporters by revealing that Scott had confessed to May Gatway's murder, and that he'd provided enough detail to suggest the confession was credible.

"So the preliminary indication is that we've got the suicide of a thirty-six-year-old man, Wilson Scott, on our hands. It also appears, at least so far, that the dead man and May Gatway's murderer are one and the same."

Morton did not go into the details of Gatway's blackmail attempt but Pia had no qualms about reporting what she knew in the *Gazette*. It wasn't often that a story came along involving murder, suicide, blackmail, homosexuality, a sleazy motel, and the gruesome demise of two high-profile politicians. The press was consumed with obtaining the details in the days that followed. There was no shortage of material.

Gatway's autopsy results were released. It made for grisly reading but in the end, the experts concluded that their findings were consistent with Scott's description of events on the night of her death. The minister, the report said, drew her last breath between 8 and 8:30 p.m. She died from massive blood loss caused by two major wounds. Her murderer, either during the initial struggle or at some point during the chase through the attics, had slashed major blood vessels in his victim's right wrist. The life was draining from her body even as she ran. The fireplace poker just finished the job.

"I'm told it pierced a main artery," Morton told Pia. "Not nice."

Wilson Scott had chosen a much tidier death for himself.

"He took enough drugs to do in an elephant," Morton confirmed with her characteristic sensitivity a few days later. "This stuff was a codeine compound, just about the strongest available. It was described to me as a modern-day morphine that acts as a good painkiller but is lethal if you overdose. That makes it real popular for suicide attempts. It has the added advantage of being easily available on the street."

The Gatway family insisted upon a private funeral at the Anglican church they had attended for years. The media were shut out of the ceremony and her relatives refused to speak to reporters afterwards.

Scott's family announced that he would be buried in a private ceremony in his hometown of Thunder Bay. Pia, who with Perry Alton's blessing had temporarily abandoned her editing duties, volunteered to go – but not before making her apologies to James Nowt, who'd been overseeing the arts department in her absence.

"This is it, James, I promise," Pia told him. "I'll just go up north for the funeral and then it will be back to movie stars and the like. Just please get us through the next few days."

Thunder Bay is a port city that clings to the northern shore of Lake Superior, the largest of the Great Lakes. The view flying into town is a spectacular reminder that, outside of the crowded south, many of Ontario's communities are still small islands of urban life in a sea of forest. As the plane circled before landing, Pia saw the Sleeping Giant in the distance. What appeared from shore to be an island was really a peninsula shaped like a man lying on his back. According to an Indian legend, the Sleeping Giant was really the god Nanibijou who was turned to stone and condemned to sleep offshore forever after one of his aboriginal followers betrayed the whereabouts of a sacred silver mine to white intruders.

Pia heard the whole story from Eric Paivanen, the well-dressed young man who manned the reception desk in Scott's office. He'd barely stopped talking since they encountered each other in the airport lounge.

"I worked on Wilson's election campaign up here, and when he got elected he offered me the job as his assistant," Paivanen said, settling down next to her on the plane. "I've been with him ever since. He's a great guy." Paivanen paused. "I mean, he was a great guy."

"Except that he murdered one of his colleagues," Pia said, unable to help herself. "Would it really have been so bad if people found out he was gay? I mean this is the twenty-first century and gay people even get married."

"It it shouldn't be a problem but some politicians are still nervous. I think guys who kept quiet about their sexuality and then got elected sometimes feel trapped. They worry that if they come out publicly – or if somebody outs them – that some voters will have a problem with the gay part and others will just be pissed off about being left in the dark about it. This might have been part of it for Wilson. But I think a bigger part was that he wanted to protect his mother. She knew he was gay but I got the feeling she was uncomfortable about having her friends find out. So let's just say it wasn't something he was eager to have advertised."

"What do you think Gatway wanted from him that she would resort to blackmail?" Pia asked, posing the question that had been puzzling her for days.

"I've been wondering about that myself," Paivanen said. "The boss was pretty mad when he wasn't named minister of culture. Everybody knew that. He's been building an art collection for ages and really got into it five or six years ago when his granny left him a pile of money. I mean, he actually knew something about art and culture. He always said May Gatway was the sort who would buy a sofa and then look for color-coordinated art to go with it. We were under orders to tell him any dirt we heard that could get her into trouble."

"Was there anything?"

Paivanen was quiet for a moment and Pia was surprised to see his fair skin flush a deep shade of pink.

"I guess it doesn't matter if I tell you now, does it?" he said, staring down at the coffee cup on the tray in front of him. "I don't know if this had anything to do with what happened, but about two months ago I heard that Gatway was very, well, interested, in somebody in her office – somebody who maybe didn't want to be involved with her, if you catch my drift. I told Wilson about it."

"May Gatway was sexually harassing one of her aides?" Pia said, leaning forward to get a better look at Paivanen's face. "Male or female?"

"Male. You don't have to believe it. I'm just telling you what I heard," he said defensively. Pia could not get him to reveal his source or the victim's name. In a desperate bid to change the subject, he launched into the long, elaborate tale of Nanibijou and the silver mine and gods being turned to stone and other local lore that Pia only half heard.

Scott might have confronted May Gatway with the sexual harassment charge, she mused while her companion droned on about local history. Perhaps he thought he could use the information to pressure her into resigning. Maybe she fought back with the picture of Scott and the kid in the bar. If she was desperate enough, Gatway had the money to pay somebody to follow and photograph him as he sampled life in the big city.

They were both ambitious politicians and capable of dirty tricks, of that Pia had little doubt. What she found more difficult to imagine was Wilson Scott impaling somebody with a fireplace poker. Interrupting the native mythology lesson, Pia bluntly asked Paivanen if he thought his boss capable of murder.

"If you'd asked me that a few weeks ago, I'd have said absolutely not. During the election campaign, his brother Ron told me that when they were kids, Wilson made a huge scene when he realized the bugs in Ron's butterfly collection had been deliberately killed and stuck with pins for display purposes. Murderous rage just doesn't seem to fit. But I guess the facts tell a different story, don't they?" he concluded gloomily.

The conversation was still bothering Pia later in the

afternoon while she waited outside a funeral home in the city center for Scott's brother to deliver a statement to the media. It was a spectacularly sunny day, with a cool breeze drifting in from the lake glistening in the distance. The glorious weather seemed to fade, however, when Ron Scott emerged from the stately stone building and slowly walked toward the dozen reporters gathered on the sidewalk. He was shorter and heavier and less blond than his brother. Pia couldn't help but think he had a nicer face, one that was more suited to easy smiles than the grief that had so brutally – and publicly – invaded his life.

"We will miss the Wilson we knew, the kind of guy who gave to his community and his family and his friends," he told reporters before his eyes filled with tears and his voice cracked. "I'm pleading with you all, now that this is over, please leave us alone so we can dwell on the good memories."

Back in Toronto the next day, Pia met Nancy Morton for lunch.

"Well, even if Gatway was hitting on somebody on her staff, it doesn't really change anything," the detective observed after Pia recounted what she'd been told. "We've got Scott's confession in the suicide note. We have a motive: he was afraid of being outed. And nobody in that fleabag motel saw anything suspicious the night he died." Morton paused to take a bite from her sandwich and then her face brightened.

"Maybe it's time you stopped picking at this mess and went back to, what is it, entertainment?" she continued. "I'd like to know when the next big lesbian sex scene is going to happen on prime time television. I'm single again these days and it would give me something to look forward to."

Chapter Five

BY THE FOLLOWING MONDAY, the sensational deaths of Gatway and Scott had finally ceased to be front-page news and the case, as far as the police were concerned, was closed. Pia's thoughts, however, kept returning to stray bits and pieces of the real-life drama. The possibility that Gatway had been sexually harassing an employee nagged at her. Then there was the improbable transformation of the Wilson Scott she knew into a ruthless killer. He'd always been bitchy about his colleagues, willing to share damaging gossip ands shred reputations from behind the scenes. But in her mind he'd always been a lightweight. There was nothing to suggest he went in for cold-blooded murder. Blackmail, yes, that fit. But actual blood on his hands? Years of journalism experience had taught Pia that a few extra calls could pay off big time. She resolved to make the effort. It would satisfy her curiosity about human nature.

And she'd had an idea during the flight back from Thunder Bay when she'd been thinking about May and Wilson and the volatile cocktail of emotions that had destroyed their lives. Sex, jealousy, ambition, murder, suicide, politics, blackmail: they were the makings of a book. She had the political and the police contacts. She knew the personalities involved. And she was almost certain there was more to the story.

Bill Walterson was first on her list of people to talk to. If anyone knew whether May Gatway was spending inordinate amounts of time with one aide or another, it would be the legislature's senior night-shift guard. Pia was driving to work, mentally outlining questions to ask him later in the day, when she saw protesters around the front door of the 130-year-old red brick building that had housed the *Gazette* since it first began publishing. About twenty women, most of them middle-aged or older, all of them well dressed, paced back and forth chanting and waving placards. Pia slowed down at the sight of the crowd and also because the street was crowded with haphazardly parked BMWs and luxury sport utility vehicles. She narrowly avoided slamming into a gleaming silver SUV as the slogans on the placards sank in.

"*Gazette* kills local theater," declared one protest sign carried by a matron in an immaculately pressed linen pantsuit. "Little theater is great theater – ignore us at your peril!" said another. "Honk if you love little theater," urged a third. Pia did not honk. Cursing silently, she did, however, roll down her window to hear what the women were chanting.

"We won't go away until you review our play," they shouted like aging but highly disciplined cheerleaders.

Pia parked, rushed into the newsroom and found a local theater newsletter on her desk, probably hand-delivered by Jasmine or James. They've gone into hiding, she thought grimly, looking down at the publication. Her face, with a big, black X through it, was on the front page. Above the photograph, a headline screamed "Arts enemy Number 1." Underneath she read how the *Gazette*'s new entertainment editor, "a former political reporter with no known love for or knowledge of the arts," had decreed that little-theater productions in the city would henceforth be reviewed only occasionally. "She must be made to change her mind," the text warned ominously.

Pia wondered whether she should quit or if Perry Alton would fire her. It would be too bad, really. She was kind of getting to like the job. As if on cue, the telephone rang.

"Pia?" It was the publisher, sounding breathless and rattled. "Tell me why I had to sneak into my own newspaper past those crazy women? Is there some good reason we aren't reviewing *Little Shop of Horrors*? I'm really hoping so, because my wife tells me the girls in her bridge club – some of the same lunatics out in front of the building – refuse to speak to her and that it's all your fault."

Pia decided she had little to lose by going on the offensive. Linda Epsony, she told Alton, feared that her freelance opportunities at the *Gazette* were drying up so she had been fostering unrest among little-theater supporters. "Perry," she continued, "there's so much going on in the city that's interesting – more interesting than the old standards the blue-rinse crowd puts on. This play is about a bloodthirsty giant plant and a sadistic dentist, for God's sake. I told them we would review some of their productions, just not all of them. They won't be completely ignored."

"I don't doubt that Linda bloody Epsony's behind this. She's been leaving me four messages a day. I've ignored them. But we have got a problem, Pia, now that she's got that whole gang so riled up. It seems like every little-theater supporter in town is after me. My secretary says there have been thirty-three calls already this morning and it's not even ten o'clock. We need to make them stop," he concluded abruptly.

In the discussion that followed, Alton, who made his domestic peace a priority, wanted to cave completely and let Epsony do the review. Pia balked, even as she wondered at her need to take a principled stand over the review of a horticultural horror story. In the end, they agreed to send a critic on opening night, but that it would be someone other than Epsony.

"I'll find another reviewer," Pia insisted. "And, Perry, you can tell your wife it's safe to go back to her bridge club."

"First I'll go out and tell the ladies on the front steps the good news," he said, sounding relieved.

Pia went in search of James. She found him in the cafeteria, staring nervously out the window at the protesters. After insisting indignantly that he had not been hiding, he agreed that compromise was a good idea. He proposed sending one of the paper's student reporters to do the review on the weekend.

"There's a girl who is a summer intern who might do a good job. She's interested in writing for the arts department, plus she's Perry's wife's cousin's daughter or something like that, so you'll win points with him by giving her a break," he said, acknowledging Pia's grateful look with an easy smile and graciously forgoing the temptation to tell his boss he'd warned her. "I'll arrange it."

By late afternoon the protesters were long gone, and details of the next day's arts and entertainment section were settled. Pia left, determined to track down Walterson. Twenty minutes later, as she was hurrying toward the main entrance to the legislature, the curator, Jack Cleary, emerged from the building.

"Heading out?"

"Yup, I've done my duty for the day. What are you up to?"

"Oh, I'm just trying to sort out a few things left over from the Gatway mess," she said vaguely. Jack looked curious but said nothing. Glancing past him through the doors, Pia spotted Walterson at the security desk and said she had to go.

"I think Jack Cleary has a thing for you," Walterson teased when Pia was standing in front of him. "He lit up like a police cruiser on a high-speed chase when he saw you. Are you going to go out with him?"

"Mind your own business or I'll start thinking you are jealous," she said, laughing. A moment later, she was all business. "Bill, I know the investigations into the death of Gatway and Scott are officially closed but there are a few things that still bother me."

Walterson raised his bushy eyebrows and leaned back in his

chair, gazing indulgently at his favorite reporter and admiring the way coppery tendrils had escaped from her pinned-up hair.

"Do you think May Gatway might have been playing around with somebody on her staff – some guy?"

"You have a nasty mind, girl," he said slowly. "But then I guess I do too, because I wondered something along those lines myself. Last winter she started spending more and more nights working late with a young fellow in her office. Tall, dark-haired, good-looking guy by the name of Alex, Alex Juarez. What got me thinking that they were up to something besides work was that when I did the evening rounds, the door to the office was often locked, even though they were both inside. You know how it is around here. If people stick around after hours, they usually leave their doors wide open so everybody will see how hard-working and important they are."

Walterson tapped into the security computer and confirmed that Alex Juarez worked for Gatway. "Now that she's gone I don't know if he's still got a job," he added, "but feel free to go see for yourself."

A young couple was leaving Gatway's office just as Pia came around the corner. The woman, about twenty years old, was a tiny blond with big blue eyes, pale porcelain-fine skin, and an extremely short skirt. Her hand rested lightly on the back of the young man beside her as he struggled to lock the door and simultaneously deliver a kiss. Alex Juarez, a few years older than his companion, reluctantly pushed the door back open after Pia introduced herself and asked for a few minutes of his time.

"Chris, will you wait for me?" he asked the girl before leading Pia into what used to be Gatway's inner sanctum. "This shouldn't take too long."

They entered a large room with thick, pale blue carpeting. A sofa and chairs, upholstered in a rich navy and silver striped material, filled one corner. A large desk in dark wood sat in front of the office's gracefully arched windows, while a gleaming mahogany boardroom table with a dozen chairs around it took up the remaining space.

"I thought you might be able to help with a few of the questions about May Gatway's death that still haven't been answered," Pia said, settling into the deep cushions of the sofa. "For instance, the theory is that Wilson Scott followed her into the attic after the reception here in the building. But why on earth was she up there in the first place?"

Juarez, who had remained standing, abruptly straightened up and nervously brushed back the lock of dark hair that hung down near one eye. "I have no idea. I went out with Chris after the reception and we met some friends. You can ask her, she'll tell you."

"Heavens, I'm not accusing you of anything. I was just wondering if you knew why she went into the attic. Had she said anything about her intentions beforehand?"

Juarez shrugged his shoulders and remained quiet. Pia knew from experience that people hated silence in a conversation and would almost always try to fill the void if she held out long enough. She hoped the man before her, conditioned by both youth and good manners, would do just that. She'd almost given up hope when they heard a low, angry voice.

"Tell her what was going on," Chris said, pushing the door open further and stepping into the room. "Please Alex, people should know what she was like, how awful she really was." Juarez stared at the girl, a red flush starting at his neck and slowly rising to engulf his face. Chris, her blue eyes snapping with fury, seemed oblivious to his distress.

"She was after him, always keeping him working late, suggesting they go for dinner, touching him," she burst out. "I used to work in this office too, answering the phones. But she fired me when she found out we'd dated. That's what the disgusting bitch was really like. She was old enough to be his mother, for God's sake."

"Enough, Chris," Juarez said, finally recovering. "Just go home. Please, just go home." The girl took one look at his distressed face and burst into tears. After she ran from the room, Pia looked at Juarez again. And waited.

"Yeah, May was definitely interested in more than my political services," he admitted.

"Did she get anything more than political services?"

"Are you going to put this in the newspaper?"

Pia shook her head. It was obvious she was going to have to convince him to talk, so she got creative.

"I'm just trying to figure out what happened between May and Wilson Scott and why. You know I write mystery novels?"

He nodded.

"Well, to write a good mystery you need to know what drives people to kill. I'm a journalist but I'm also a writer who spends a lot of time thinking about murder, and that makes me curious about Wilson Scott's state of mind. To understand that I need to understand what May was up to."

"But for sure this is not going in the paper?"

Pia reassured him again.

He sighed. "Well, she was my boss. And the way she dealt with Chris showed she was willing to fire me too, if I didn't, you know, live up to expectations. So a lot of nights when we were in here supposedly working, I was, uh, performing other duties," he said, in a voice that combined bravado and embarrassment.

"Why didn't you quit or file a harassment complaint?"

"I'm a guy. If I'd complained about some woman forcing sex on me, I'd have never heard the end of it. And, well, you know, she wasn't ugly. A little skinny, but not ugly. Most guys my age would love it if a woman wanted lots of no-strings-attached sex. Besides," he said, shrugging, "I have car payments, and when this all started six months ago, I'd just bought a condo. If I'd walked away for no clear reason, I'd never have found another job around here, and it's not so easy out there in the real world right now, especially if you don't even have a reference."

"So you chose the path of least resistance?"

"Like I said, she was the boss. You really want to know why she was up in the attic?"

Pia nodded.

Juarez avoided looking Pia in the eye. "She – May – liked doing it in different places," he began. "Once we went to the Speaker's apartment to do it on the bed in there. Other times we'd screw around here in the office or meet at a hotel. A few times she had me come to her house. Now *that* was creepy, because she wanted me to chase her around the house as a warmup. I kept worrying that her husband would come home."

Pia was grappling with the idea of May Gatway as sexual predator. Cripes, the Speaker's apartment? It contained sleeping quarters for the member of Parliament chosen by his peers to referee debates and proceedings in the House. The current Speaker lived in the city and went home to his own bed each night. That meant the apartment was used for formal luncheons and dinners only when visiting dignitaries were being entertained.

"And were you supposed to meet her the night she died?" she asked.

Alex looked worried for the first time since the conversation began. "She was one weird woman. Wanted me to meet her up in the attic. Said it would be fun to play around up there – apparently there are a lot of big mirrors or something. But she only gave me my orders near the end of the reception – the one that was being held here the night she died – and I'd already promised to have dinner with Chris and some friends. To tell you the truth, I'd just had an interview for another job that had gone well. I thought it was going to turn into an offer and I

66

was pretty fed up with May's demands. So I just didn't show. I went out instead."

Pia made a mental note to check out Juarez's story with his friends. Even if he had joined them for dinner, he might have met his boss upstairs first. Maybe he'd chosen that moment to tell her he just wasn't interested and she'd tried to bully him into service. He could have lost his temper, chased her down – it was apparently part of their sexual shtick – and killed her. There still would have been time to go to dinner. Of course this scenario assumed he was the kind of guy who could murder a woman and then blithely go out on the town to enjoy himself. And it certainly didn't account for Wilson Scott's suicide note and confession. He claimed he'd followed May out of the reception into the attic where he confronted her and killed her.

"Alex, did anybody else know about this tête-à-tête?"

"Christ, of course not. May was pretty clear. I had to keep my mouth shut if I wanted to keep my job."

"Well, at least now we know why she was up there," Pia mused out loud. "I wonder if she would be alive if you had kept the, uh, appointment?"

"You can't imagine how many times I've asked myself that question. I've also wondered if I'd be alive to talk about it."

Chapter Six

MAY GATWAY, NASTY IN LIFE and equally poisonous in death, Pia thought ruefully as she drove home after meeting Alex Juarez. His story filled in some of the blanks about the minister's actions the night she died. But it also left Pia feeling anxious and unsettled. The human drive for sex – the straightforward stuff and the weird kind that mixed it up with power and pain – had a lot to answer for, she brooded as she pulled into the driveway.

Alerted by the sound of her key, Winston was waiting at the door, a habit he'd developed back when he was a little ball of orange fur newly adopted from the local humane society. He did his best to wind his body around her legs, almost tripping her as she made her way upstairs to change. His antics, however, weren't enough to divert her today.

Juarez had added another unwelcome picture to the May

Gatway file in Pia's head, the file that already contained images of the woman's bloodied body. The flashes of bravado in the young man's voice had alternated with other moments when he sounded hunted. As if summoned by the rawness of his voice, dark memories clawed their way out of the locked back room of her mind – the room marked "Do Not Enter."

Pia threw herself on her bed, furious with her inability either to shed the past or to come to terms with her mother's maternal failings, even after so many years. Her father had been killed in a construction accident soon after she was born. Patrice refused to discuss him, and Pia was so young at the time of his death that she had no memories of her own to cherish. What she did remember, however, were the years her mother worked as a hostess at La Muse, one of the city's better French restaurants. Patrice took the idea of making customers feel welcome to extremes, Pia thought bitterly, recalling the many nights she woke to the sound of her mother's throaty laugh and a strange man's voice in their small apartment. The visitors were usually gone by the morning, but Patrice was always optimistic about their long-term intentions.

"I met a nice guy last night, sweetie," she said to her young daughter on more than one occasion. "I think he's a keeper – the kind of guy who will help us get out of this cubbyhole and into a decent house. We'll have beautiful clothes and you'll have a sports car when you are sixteen and we'll go to Europe together. Maybe just to Paris and London the first time because there's so much to see there. We'll go to Rome later."

Sometimes the man hung around, showing up once or twice a week for a month or two. Inevitably, though, Patrice overplayed her hand by asking for money or inquiring about when he planned to leave his wife. Then he would vanish, leaving behind overlooked white undershirts or whisker-clogged razors or half-consumed bottles of Scotch. Sometimes there would be a loud argument after one of Patrice's plaintive demands, followed by the sound of a door slamming. More often, though, he just stopped phoning or dropping by. Whatever the exit strategy, Patrice's reaction was the same.

"That bastard wasn't good enough for me," she would insist angrily as her anxious child proffered cups of tea and desperately tried to find words of comfort. "He was a big talker but, you know, I don't think he had any real money. And his manners were terrible! Did you notice the way he talked with his mouth full the other night? And he never even touched his napkin. I don't know why I didn't see him for the pig he is right from the start."

Patrice's anger, however, was preferable to what came later. Her fury spent, she would go to her bedroom, lock the door, and sit alone in the dark for hours at a time, ignoring her daughter's pleas to come out. It was during these episodes that Pia learned to fend for herself. As a precocious eight-year-old determined to prove that she was a big girl, she would carefully take the right amount of money from her mother's purse. Then, ignoring the concerned looks from neighbors, she would make her way out of the six-story apartment building they lived in and down the street to the corner store, where she would buy milk, bread, peanut butter, and jam – staples of her diet during Patrice's misery days. If there was enough money left, she would treat herself to a vanilla ice cream cone.

Pia hated all of the men who wandered in and out of their lives, but in the end she hated Max the most because he came and stayed. Like the others before him, he came home with Patrice after work one night, so Pia heard his voice before she ever saw him. That was a Thursday. She was eleven. On Sunday he came for dinner. Max was in his late fifties at that point, about a decade older then her mother. He startled Pia when she met him, because he was completely bald in an era before baldness became a fashion statement. He wasn't much taller than Patrice, but his well-cut shirt skimmed the muscular body of a man committed to physical activity. Max arrived with red roses for Patrice and white and yellow daisies for Pia, who despite herself was flattered by the attention.

"You are going to grow up to be as beautiful as your mother," he said, drawing his gaze away from Patrice long enough to examine Pia speculatively as he handed her the flowers. At the table, she noticed, Max didn't talk with his mouth full. And he used his napkin. Her mother, a tall redhead with blue eyes, white skin, and the lush figure her daughter would inherit, glowed with happiness.

"I'm in love, sweetie, and you are going to love him, too. Just give it a little time," Patrice cooed the next morning. Pia withheld judgment and watched as Patrice grew increasingly enamored of the man and of the money generated by his successful construction business. In a sign that the stars were finally aligned in her mother's favor, Max's twenty-year marriage had ended just weeks before he met Patrice, who believed men were most susceptible to her wiles just after divorce. Six months later, Patrice announced that she and Max were getting married and that they would all go to live in his house.

"It's a beautiful place in a fabulous neighborhood and it has a pool. Won't you just love that, darling? And you know what? Max is going to send you to private school so you'll get to know all the kids from the best families."

And things did go well at first. The house, with its six bedrooms, family room, music salon, library, and pool, was a stately Georgian affair decorated in a stiff, formal style by one of the city's top designers. Pia's corner room was large and sunny, with a walk-in closet and ensuite bathroom. The windows looked out over the garden and pool. Her natural athleticism helped her fit in immediately at the new school, where she was quickly recognized as an asset to the basketball and track teams. She also began working for the school magazine after it published one of her short stories. Patrice quit her job at the restaurant, took golf and tennis lessons, and threw herself into shopping and traveling, with and without Max, who spent long hours at work.

"Then my boobs started to grow, I started having boyfriends, and sex messed everything up," Pia had told Dr. Garcia. "My mother couldn't forgive me." There had been warning signs, but what did a fifteen-year-old know about warning signs? She'd felt vaguely uneasy on the occasions she'd noticed Max standing at an upstairs window staring down at her as she lounged around the pool in one of her skimpy bikinis. Patrice was away a lot in those days on extended shopping and golfing trips, so Pia and Max were left on their own for days at a time.

"You're looking pretty sexy tonight," he said to her one evening as he emerged from his study, Scotch in hand. Pia, who was on her way out the door, blushed uneasily while Max's eyes lingered on her legs.

"My mother was away as usual – this time it was Italy with a girlfriend," Pia told Dr. Garcia. "I was dating this boy who was a bit older than me – I think he was seventeen – and that night we went to a movie and then he drove me home. There were no lights on in the house so I assumed Max wasn't back yet. He often worked late or went out for dinner with colleagues when my mother was away. I invited Mark in and we went out to the pool where the lights were low and it was romantic."

They'd started kissing and soon Mark was rubbing his hard penis up against her. She let him lift her tank top so he could caress her breasts. Then he reached down and pulled her up tight against him.

"Please, please, do it for me tonight, I'm dying," he breathed into her ear. "Just try it for a few minutes. If you don't like it we'll stop."

Even as he said this, Mark was reaching down to undo the zipper of his jeans. Pia, torn between reluctance, and what she thought was the love of a lifetime, timidly nodded her assent. He pushed her hand inside his open pants, gasping as he felt it close over him. Leaning back against the cedar wall of the cabana, he gently pushed down on her shoulders until she knelt in the grass. After stroking him several times she took him in her mouth.

"Oh, God, please, *please* don't stop. I love you. This feels so good. Just don't stop," he moaned softly as he held her head and pushed himself in and out of her mouth. Pia had no intention of stopping. Mark was her first serious boyfriend and his ardent touches and kisses over the previous few months had taken over most of her waking thoughts. She was wet and excited that night as her lips tightened around him.

Then out of the corner of her eye, she thought she saw a movement in the window where Max often stood looking down at the pool. Before she could pull away from Mark, he pushed himself deep into her throat and came with a soft groan. A minute later he was kneeling on the grass beside her, telling her he loved her. Pia, however, was oblivious to the boy's caresses. There was nobody at the window now, but she was almost certain Max had seen them. If he told her mother, Patrice would be furious with Pia, who was under orders not to cause any trouble or offend Max in any way. In the meantime, there was only one thing worse than contemplating Patrice's anger and that was the thought of facing Max himself. The idea made her insides twist.

After Mark left, Pia went inside the house and tiptoed past

her stepfather's study. The light was on and she heard the sound of ice cubes being swirled in a glass. Max liked his Scotch, Patrice would observe dryly of her husband, noting his penchant for at least two stiff drinks before dinner each evening. Safe in her bedroom, Pia tried to convince herself she had imagined the shadow in the window. She undressed, crawled into bed, and eventually fell asleep, only to wake up with a start. It was nearly three in the morning. She was cold because the bedcovers had fallen onto the floor and the long T-shirt she wore to bed was twisted up above her hips. Shivering, Pia clawed her way out of sleep determined to find her covers. Then she heard the unmistakable sound of someone breathing hard, someone in her room. Just as she was about to scream, Max reached down and covered her mouth.

"It's just me, baby, good old Max. Max, the guy who watched you give a blow job to that kid tonight, you little whore. I think I'll tell your mother what I saw."

Pia felt her fear give way to dread as his words, wrapped in alcoholic fumes, sank in.

"Maybe you don't want me to do that?"

Pia shook her head.

"Ah, well then, maybe we can work out a deal," Max whispered.

There was a full moon, Pia remembered. Its light shone into her room through the windows overlooking the garden and the pool. Usually, she enjoyed the cool, gentle glow, but on this night all she could remember was the moonlight gleaming briefly on Max's bald head as he reached down to push apart her resisting legs.

"Nice," he growled as he licked one of his fingers and began probing her. Pia clamped her legs together in protest, sat up, and began pushing him away. His bathrobe fell open, revealing his erect cock.

"That's right, you sit up, my girl. If you give it away to that kid, you should be willing to put out for the guy who foots all the bills around here. Your fucking mother's never around, so you might as well do the job now that I know you're so enthusiastic." He reached behind her head, grabbed a handful of hair, and pushed himself deep into Pia's mouth, making her gag. "Oh, yeah, I can tell you've been practising," he groaned. "You're good at this. I'll be wanting more." It seemed to go on forever but finally he came, pounding into her mouth and gasping. A moment later he was gone.

It felt like hours before Pia was able to breathe normally again. She heard a sound at the door and was about to cry out when she realized it was Max putting a key in the lock and turning it. For a long while, she was unable to move, but then the first wave of nausea hit. She threw up into the garbage can beside her bed and fell back on the mattress feeling as if her guts, her soul, her heart had been ripped from her body and shredded.

That first assault was on Friday night. On Saturday and Sunday Max returned repeatedly, suffocating Pia as he crawled over her, invading her body in ways she had not imagined possible. On Monday morning, he unlocked the door and came in wearing a dark suit, tie, and crisp white shirt.

"Get up and go to school," he said, his bloodshot eyes greedily taking in the shape of Pia's body as she pulled the bedcovers around her. "And remember. You say nothing about this and I say nothing to your mother about your performance out by the pool. She'll be home this afternoon."

After Max left the house, Pia got into the shower. She scrubbed her skin red, yet still felt filthy. She forced herself to put on her school uniform and went to class, where she endured math and chemistry and English literature, oblivious to what the teachers were saying. As the hours passed, she felt something inside her beginning to stir, something she soon identified as rage. Pia examined her options. She could run away, but it wasn't obvious where she could go. She could stay and try to keep out of Max's way, but Patrice was away so much this was simply too risky. The only other option was be to tell her mother what had happened. They'd be out of the house in a nanosecond, maybe two, if Patrice stopped to kill Max on the way out the door.

She resolved to talk to her mother the minute Patrice came home. This would give them time to pack and leave before Max returned from work. In retrospect, Pia smiled at her naïveté. That afternoon, Patrice had arrived from Italy laden with shopping bags and overstuffed suitcases. Her skin and eyes glowed, the result of expensive spa treatments and surgical touch-ups from "a miracle doctor in Roma," as she put it in the burst of chatter that began the moment she entered the house.

"There's a big, big problem," Pia interrupted as Patrice stood at the foot of the stairs sorting through her luggage. In a voice trembling with a mixture of shame, outrage, and fear, she told her mother what had happened. "He kept coming back over and over again to hurt me," she concluded as tears trailed down her face.

Patrice had become progressively paler as Pia recounted the events of the last few days. Then she turned away, went over to look out the window, and said nothing for the longest time.

"We really need to pack and get out of here," Pia said, walking over to touch her mother's shoulder. "We don't want to be here when he comes home and . . . " She stopped abruptly as Patrice swung around and delivered a hard, stinging slap to her face.

"You stupid little bitch, how could you? I worked for years to get us here and now you think we should leave and give it all up? How do you think you'll be able to go to that fancy school of yours? And who is going to pay for university? In case you have forgotten, we have nothing without Max. I never, *ever* want to hear another word about this. Do you understand? The subject is closed, over, forgotten."

The angry red imprint of Patrice's hand was like a brand on Pia's cheek. Her green eyes wide with shock, she couldn't look away from her mother.

"Well, it's obvious you can't stay here," Patrice said after a moment in a hard, cold voice. Every word felt like another vicious slap. "I'll see if your Aunt Margaret will take you in.

She's alone in that big apartment of hers. And you'll still be able to get to school. I hope you haven't fucked things up so badly that he'll stop paying for your tuition." Patrice drew a deep breath, trying to get her temper under control.

"This is a good thing that I have here – that *we* have here – and I'm not going back to that shitty apartment and restaurant work," she went on, the words tumbling out. "We're not going back. If living with Margaret is the price you have to pay, then so be it. It won't be that bad and you won't be around to bother Max. Go and stay with one of your girlfriends tonight. I'll call Margaret and sort things out."

Recalling the desperation in her mother's voice, Pia's feelings of rage, shame, and betrayal were as powerful today as they had been on the day the scene had unfolded twenty-eight years ago.

"You got one thing right. I'm not staying here one more night. He's all yours," she had screamed at Patrice. "I wouldn't want to spoil your nice life by reminding you what he – your husband – did to me. How he raped me – yes, he raped me even if you don't want to believe it."

And so Pia went to live with her mother's older sister. As a little girl, she had worshiped her stylish aunt, one of the *Gazette*'s first female reporters and editors. Margaret, who had never married but always seemed to have a boyfriend in tow, once had the thick red hair that distinguished the women in her family. In later life, that hair had turned snow-white, although her face still retained a delicate beauty that belied an inner toughness and an irreverent sense of humor – qualities that stood her in good stead as she rose through the paper's ranks to become a respected editor.

Margaret was still working when Pia landed on her doorstep, but she also golfed in the summer, went on luxury ski trips in the winter, and dated. Pia remembered being uncertain about how her sophisticated older relative would adapt to the arrival of a fifteen-year-old in her life. But as it turned out, she needn't have worried.

Patrice left soon after overseeing the delivery of Pia and her four large suitcases to the foyer of Margaret's penthouse apartment, a wide, bright space with a black and white tiled floor. The wall on one side of the entrance was stark white while the other was a deep, uncompromising red. A huge painting hung on each side, the work of a former boyfriend whom Margaret described as a great artist but a "lousy sweetheart."

Margaret looked carefully at the pale, unhappy girl standing alone in front of her, then gently pulled the teenager into her arms. "My darling, I don't know what happened –and you don't have to tell me unless you want to – but I am thrilled you are coming to stay with me. It's going to be all right, Pia. We're going to be okay together in this place. There's plenty of space. You will have the guest suite; it has its own bathroom and a sitting area so you will have privacy."

It was Margaret who introduced Pia to the magic of journalism. "It's like going to the theater every day, dear. Only you never ever know what's going to be playing on stage or how it will turn out," Margaret said one evening when they were looking through old scrapbooks containing stories she had written as a young reporter. "Okay, maybe when you start out and they send you to cover the strawberry pie festival it might seem like a bit of a test. But look what happened. Covering that strawberry pie festival was one of my first assignments. And it became a page-one story because some local teenagers had a few beers, got hungry, broke into the local hall, and ate the top contenders.

"Things just got better and better after that," Margaret insisted, taking in Pia's skeptical look. She picked up another thick scrapbook. "Look, this was twenty years later and I was the Washington correspondent. Now *those* were interesting times."

Pia never saw Max again. In the months that followed, she spoke to her mother by telephone and they occasionally went out for lunch. But conversation on those occasions was stilted, just one stage removed from an exchange of pleasantries between strangers. Patrice talked about tennis and shopping and travel. Pia limited herself to discussing events at school, sports, and life with Margaret. A year after Pia moved in with her aunt, Max's actions and Patrice's betrayal still overwhelmed her with feelings of disgust, shame, anger, and loss. It was worst on the nights when she would wake up, trembling and sweat-drenched from a recurring dream where Max was again opening the bedroom door and coming toward her, erect and predatory. One Sunday morning, after enduring the dream yet again, Pia told her aunt what had happened. The lines on Margaret's face deepened as Pia, sobbing uncontrollably, blurted out the whole story as the two of them sat at the kitchen table.

"Oh, I'm so sorry. How could he? And what was your mother thinking?" Margaret said as she pulled Pia to her feet and into her arms "I have to think about what to do about this. We have to think about it. You can't pretend it never happened and neither should they. How can they live with themselves?"

It was never clear what Margaret had in mind. A week later there was a knock on the apartment door just before dinner. Pia vividly remembered looking at the faces of the police officers and knowing something was terribly wrong.

In fact, it couldn't have been worse. Patrice and Max had been driving on a highway north of Toronto when a transport truck loaded with steel beams veered to miss a man changing his car tire on the side of the highway. The driver avoided the stopped car and driver, but he hadn't noticed Patrice and Max cruising in the lane beside him in their low-slung Mercedes. By the time the truck stopped, the car was tightly wedged underneath it. The highway was closed for nine hours while police investigated and workers cut the vehicle and its passengers free. Both occupants were pronounced dead at the scene.

Chapter Seven

THE SUNSET HAD PAINTED the evening sky pink and mauve when the insistent jangling of the telephone in Pia's bedroom dragged her out of the past. Groggy and half asleep, she rolled over to answer it.

"I thought that you might have realized what a useful source I could be after our interesting discussion over lunch," Martin Geneve said, his voice containing a hint of laughter. "If I can persuade you to have dinner with me, I expect I could be persuaded to tell you all sorts of secrets."

Be nice, Pia told herself. But she couldn't quite manage it. The man was too smooth by half, and his overly confident manner made her immediately wary.

"I was serious when I said I don't date sources, Martin. Especially the kind who don't share pertinent information, like the fact that you were at May's reception at the legislature

– in other words, right there at the scene – the night she was killed. That's a little something most people would have mentioned."

"Good God, woman, you absolutely must give me an opportunity to defend myself. Please, have dinner with me on Saturday."

Pia looked at herself in the mirror across the bedroom. She was a dazed, crumpled mess, her eyes heavy with sleep and the pain of unpleasant events remembered. Under normal circumstances she'd think of her mother and just say no. Patrice had been a "bad picker" when it came to men and judging by Martin's rocky romantic past, he was definitely a bad pick. But he might also be useful. He was rich and well connected in the art world. He attended the same party as Gatway the night she was killed. Maybe he could help her understand the world of wealthy art investors. Okay, and maybe she'd sleep with him just to see what came of it.

"It's a date. But this is about research. I'm thinking about doing a book on the deaths of Gatway and Wilson Scott. Pick me up Saturday at seven-thirty."

Martin laughed at her peremptory tone. "I'll be there. We'll go to this little Italian place I know. Don't dress up."

It was dark in the city the rest of Canada loves to hate by the time Pia made a Greek salad and sat down to eat it with smoked salmon and cream cheese on rye bread. The book idea percolating in the back of her mind was starting to make more and more sense. Admittedly, everybody – including Nancy Morton – had pronounced the case closed. There were no fingerprints on the murder weapons in the Gatway case to cast doubt on Wilson Scott's version of events.

Scott's autopsy had confirmed he died from an overdose of drugs washed down with Scotch. Again, no surprise there. The pill bottle had been found in the motel room with only his fingerprints on it. They were also all over the water glasses and on the bottle of Scotch on the bedside table. The medical examiners reported no signs of sexual intercourse, which also suggested that Wilson Scott was in the motel for no other reason than to kill himself.

"Read my lips. It's over. Leave it alone and stop bugging me," Nancy Morton had said with finality after briefing Pia over the phone on the coroner's conclusions.

Okay, so maybe she wouldn't find out anything dramatically new. But then the case was already so sensational – closeted gay member of the provincial cabinet murders rich-bitch member of the provincial cabinet – it probably didn't matter. At a minimum, Pia was certain that she would be able to collect enough never-before-reported details to tempt book buyers. But that meant she had to get to work gathering those details. People forget the little things. They move on.

First, she'd go back to the motel where Wilson Scott's body was found. The residents of the Highway Inn were transient, anxious to leave behind the uncertainty, overcrowded rooms, hot plates, and bad mattresses that characterized this chapter in their lives.

In the newsroom the next day, James Nowt told her that Shawna Regent was available to review *Little Shop of Horrors*. "She's the summer intern I mentioned. She's training in the sports department right now and has already done a stint covering general news, so at least she's got a little newspaper experience under her belt," James said cautiously. "She also says she was a member of the drama club in high school, which is better than nothing, I suppose."

"Oh, let's give her the chance. You don't have to be a specialist to decide whether a man-eating plant is scary or not," Pia said, looking forlornly at the pile of unopened mail that had accumulated on her desk. Her e-mail inbox would be even more cluttered. She was sorting through everything when Jasmine came into her office.

"I've been checking on our man Martin Geneve to see what sort of art collection he has," she told Pia. "He's known as a man with money who is willing to spend it. There's precious little information out there on what he actually owns. But I've talked to people who have been to his house, and apparently the stuff on the walls is very impressive. He sounds like one of these guys who quietly acquires works of art and admires them within the privacy of his own home. Nobody is the wiser unless they get in to see for themselves. One school of thought is that collectors at his level avoid publicity about what they buy because they don't want to be targets for thieves."

"I have a date with him on Saturday," Pia confessed abruptly, wincing when Jasmine let out an astonished squeal. "I suppose

I could get him to invite me home, but he might get the wrong idea and, as you know, I'm no art expert. I doubt I'd recognize anything he has on display."

"Sister, he's one of the most eligible, handsomest, richest men in the city. There are women in Toronto who would like nothing better than to give him wrong idea. Do you like him?"

"Oh, Jasmine, please. He's a playboy. He's asked me out before and I put him off. But I'm considering doing a book on Gatway and Scott, and he might be able to help me understand the art world that Gatway was so hell-bent on shaking up."

"Yeah, right," Jasmine said, smiling knowingly. "I'm thinking you want to jump his bones."

"Don't you have any work to do?"

"Okay, I'm leaving, But you might want to check out these websites," Jasmine said, smiling wickedly as she handed Pia a piece of paper. "They're all about stolen art and the Second World War. It will give you something to talk about on your date."

Pia rolled her eyes. But after Jasmine left, she turned to her computer, typed in the first of the websites, and began reading the story of Hitler's massive art-plundering project.

The führer, a frustrated artist in his own right, had wanted to build a great museum of Germanic art in his hometown of Linz. To make the dream reality, he instructed special commando units to track down certain pieces of art from all over conquered Europe. Paintings and other artworks were also initially extorted from Jewish families in return for exit visas. By the late 1930s, however, outright confiscation was common. In France alone, the Nazis compiled a list of 203 private collections, with more than ten thousand works of art. Whole museums were plundered in Eastern Europe, Russia, and Poland.

After the war, the Allies found huge stashes of art treasures hidden throughout Europe by the Nazis. The most significant discovery was Hitler's own collection of more than ten thousand paintings, drawings, and sculptures, concealed in an Austrian salt mine. According to historians, moving the artworks down off the mountain took twelve months, and sorting through all the pieces recovered from across the continent took years. It was Allied policy to return the art to its country of origin and to let local authorities sort out the sticky business of ownership. Some countries simply put the artworks into museums. Others set up bureaucracies that proved to be nightmarish for anyone trying to recover stolen possessions. The Soviets considered the items their armies discovered to be war reparations and made no pretense of attempting to return them.

Canada had signed a treaty that committed the government to assist in repatriating illegally imported artworks, but it applied only to pieces that arrived in the country after 1972, when the law went into effect. May Gatway had been urging the federal government to change the law to ensure pre-1972 imports would also be covered, Pia noted. The minister had also championed legal changes that would make it less onerous for claimants to prove ownership. She'd even floated the idea of creating a commission to rule on claims to art made outside the courts. Public institutions, private museums, and private collections would all have been subject to the new provisions if Gatway had lived to see all her plans become law.

None of these ideas would have endeared her to major collectors, who were worried – with reason – that some of their treasures might be claimed by previous owners. So Gatway's aggressive proposals could be a motive for murder, Pia mused. Except, of course, that Wilson Scott had admitted to killing his colleague.

There was no getting around that confession. Did she believe it? Sort of. Writing the book would be an opportunity for her to reassure herself that the case's neat, tidy solution was in fact the truth.

Pia looked at the clock. It was late enough in the day that she could leave the office with a clear conscience. She'd have to fight rush hour traffic on the way over to the motel strip, but she'd be there after work and before dinner, presumably when there would be lots of people around.

The Highway Inn was indeed a busy place in the late afternoon, Pia discovered as she navigated around the potholes in the decrepit parking lot. She watched as children ran in and out of the tiny housekeeping units. Four girls had a skipping game on the go. One little boy, armed with a water gun, gleefully sprayed anyone who came near. The sound of young voices and slamming doors mixed with the clatter of dishes as mothers from Asian and African countries labored to reproduce the taste of home in an alien land. A light breeze carried the tantalizing smell of curry, onion, and garlic to Pia as she approached the far end of the parking lot where half a dozen boys of different ages stood around a wooden picnic table. Two boards were missing from the top of the collapsing structure. The seat on one side had disappeared. The group fell silent and eyed Pia suspiciously when she stopped in front of them.

"Hi, guys," Pia said. "How are you doing?" Blank stares greeted her inquiry and then a tall black boy, who looked to be about fifteen, said something in French. The group burst into laughter.

"No, I am not a white refugee from the United States," Pia responded in the same language, giving silent thanks to her aunt for insisting she spend two summers in France during high school. Her facility in Canada's other official language had also come in handy during the years Pia spent covering federal politics in Ottawa.

"I'm a reporter interested in that guy who died here a little while ago."

"He killed himself, lady. Why are you still interested?" asked the boy who had initially made fun of her.

"I just have this idea that maybe somebody visited his room and maybe one of you guys saw this visitor."

"You gonna put us on TV if we did? We'd like that, being TV stars."

"Sorry, I'm a newspaper reporter. I promise though, that I'll spell your names properly," Pia said, smiling.

"Ain't nobody interested in the newspaper, man. It's TV that counts," said the boy, who turned and began to walk away. Before Pia could say anything more, the three older boys followed him across the parking lot. The remaining two kids, the youngest of the bunch, stared at her.

"I don't supposed either of you saw anything the night that guy died here?" she inquired in English.

"That depends," one of the boys responded.

"What do you mean?"

The boy hesitated, leaned over to mutter in his friend's ear, and then straightened up. "It means we might have seen something but we need pizza from that place over there to remember," he said, smiling mischievously. The street in front of the motel was loaded with slow-moving, bumper-to-bumper traffic, but Pia could still see the Papa's Pizza outlet on the other side and the sign advertising two slices of pizza and a can of Coke for three dollars. She looked at the two boys and sighed. They probably knew less than she did about what happened to Wilson Scott. But they were enterprising.

"Okay, it's a deal. But if you two don't have something to tell me, I'm not going to pay and you will have to stay over there and wash dishes. It won't be fun because I hear that Papa is mean and ugly and really hates kids who don't pay for what they eat," she said, softening the threat with a smile.

Tariq and Mohammed were both twelve years old and from Somalia. As the three of them made their way over to the restaurant, the boys also told her that they and their families had been at the Highway Inn for three months. They'd left squalid refugee camps and made their way to Canada where, upon arrival, they'd claimed refugee status. While their claims meandered through the bureaucratic red tape that was Canada's refugee determination system, the motel was their home.

Standing under the harsh fluorescent lights of the pizza shop a few minutes later, the boys' bravado evaporated. Momentarily puzzled by the way they stared wide-eyed at the menu board above the counter and at the huge wheels of fresh pizza displayed under the blazing heat lamps, Pia eventually realized that they had no idea what to do next.

"You guys ever been here before?" They shook their heads, tongue-tied.

"Well, why don't you go sit down over there and I'll order for all of us," she said, motioning to a booth.

"Yes, please," said Tariq. He was a tall, slender boy with thick, straight black hair and skin the color of cream-laced coffee. Mohammed, short and heavy-set with curly hair and a lively, round face dominated by pudgy cheeks, enthusiastically nodded his agreement.

The boys' eyes shone as they took their first bites of steaming pizza and guzzled their soft drinks. Pia felt a pang of guilt for introducing them to junk food and its life-long perils.

"I always wanted to come here but my mom, she said we don't got the money," Tariq told Pia in between bites. "She's always working, my father too, but still, no money."

"So your parents have found jobs?"

"Our mothers, they work together in a factory where they put shampoo in bottles and stuff like that," Tariq said. "Our fathers, they are friends just like me and Mohammed are friends. They work cleaning buildings. My dad doesn't like it because he's a doctor and he says he should be looking after sick people."

"My father, he's not happy too," Mohammed chimed in. "He is a chemist but his English so bad, he can't be a chemist in this country."

"So do you guys want to be doctors and chemists when you grow up?"

"No way, man," Tariq bristled. "I'm gonna be a spy. I been practicing," he said, smiling mysteriously. "Maybe you got some questions you want to ask me about that?"

"Okay, spy, on the night the guy died at the motel, did you see anybody going in or out of his room?"

"We saw some stuff," Tariq said, all of a sudden losing his nerve. He avoided her glance and stared instead at the orange plastic table top. "Pretty funny stuff."

"It was really late – very dark outside," Mohammed said, "and we was sitting around outside thinking about going for a walk around the motel. We like to do that when our parents are at work all the time. Well, we were just going to start our walk, and this woman comes into the parking lot off the street and knocks on the door to that guy's room. My mother is a good Muslim – she covers her hair and stuff. But this woman, she was a really, really good Muslim, all in black, all covered up including her face.

"We thought it was one of the ladies from the motel but then we thought not, because the covered ladies, they don't go out much, especially at night. And this lady, she was going to a white guy's room. Her husband would be very angry."

"So she was wearing a burka?"

"Yeah, but she wasn't a she," whispered Mohammed, who looked longingly at the pizza counter. Pia leaned in toward the boys, her heart pounding.

"What do you mean, Mohammed?"

"Well, first we peeked in the other rooms like we like to do. But there wasn't much to see that night – everybody sleeping or at work. Then we got to the white guy's room. When we looked in there, we saw the burka lady pulling off her hood. But underneath it was a man, not a lady. The two guys were laughing about this, but I think it was wrong. A man shouldn't wear a lady's clothes. We watched for a bit but they were just talking so it was boring. We left."

"Guys, why didn't you tell the police about this?"

Mohammed looked horrified. "No way. Our parents would be so mad," he said, looking to Tariq for support. "Everybody was at work – our mothers were at the factory and our fathers were cleaning. We're supposed to sleep, but lots of times, it is so hot you won't sleep so we like to be outside."

"So you spend the evenings peeking at other people in the motel?"

"There isn't much to see," said Tariq, who managed to look both sullen and embarrassed. "Mostly nothing to see."

"But it is really dangerous – we have to be really quiet, just like real spies," Mohammed interjected, trying to rescue his friend.

"Okay, okay," Pia said. "Forget about whether you should or shouldn't have been spying on everybody. What did the guy in the burka look like?"

Both boys shrugged. "We could only see a little because of curtains," Mohammed said earnestly. "But he was white, that's for sure. And he was a he."

"Did you see him leave?"

Both boys shook their heads. "We needed to go to bed because we had to play soccer the next day," Tariq said seriously.

"And our mothers, they would come home pretty soon," chimed in Mohammed. Pia seized on the detail, grilling the boys about what time their parents returned from work. She finally concluded that Wilson Scott's visitor had dropped by the motel at about one-thirty in the morning.

"Will that man get in trouble for wearing a burka when he's not a girl?" Mohammed asked innocently. "I think it must be a sin to pretend like that – I mean I don't think Allah would like it because he doesn't want men and women mixed up at the mosque and stuff. He won't like it if they are mixed up under a burka."

Pia smiled and suggested the boys have another round of pizza before going back to the motel. She watched while they consumed four more slices and vaguely recalled something about pepperoni being made from pork. It was a good bet that this meal was something else that would not meet with Allah's approval. She welcomed the opportunity to speculate on Allah's list of dos and don'ts. It meant she didn't have to think about what the hell she should do next.

Chapter Eight

IF THE BOYS WERE TELLING the truth, their story raised a whole bunch of questions about the deaths of Wilson Scott and May Gatway, Pia thought as she drove home after seeing Mohammed and Tariq safely back to the motel. The same person who murdered Gatway could have arranged to meet Wilson, could have spiked his drink with enough drugs to kill him, and could have left a fake suicide note confessing everything. All nice and tidy.

But two different killers couldn't be ruled out either. Lots of people had reasons to kill Gatway – her husband, an unhappy art collector, or her reluctant young lover were possibilities that came immediately to mind. Wilson Scott might have been murdered by an angry lover who then crafted the suicide note confession based on media reports and whatever Scott had told him about the feud between the two politicians.

"You thought you could come and go in the burka so that even if somebody saw you, they'd have no idea who you were," Pia thought. "But you didn't count on those two little imps peeking through the window. And you didn't count on me finding them. Or on the power of pizza." Her gut told her the boys' story was true.

The light on her telephone answering machine was flashing when Pia arrived home.

"Hi, Pia, this is Jack Cleary. I'm calling to see if you want to go for a run tomorrow after work. Give me a call. If I'm not home, leave a message telling me where you want to meet and at what time. Hope to see you. Bye."

Why not? Pia thought. He seemed decent enough. And interesting and knowledgeable in the ways of the art world. Maybe he'd have some ideas as to who among art collectors would have the most to fear from Gatway's art-return campaign. She dialed Jack's number and when he didn't answer, left a message, suggesting they meet at her house the next evening.

Preoccupied, Pia tripped over Winston a few times before realizing he was looking for dinner, not affection. She fed him and then settled down to type up what she had learned from the boys. She saved the document and then printed a copy as a backup in case her laptop succumbed to one of its many electronic glitches.

With that out of the way, Pia shifted gears, leaving behind the puzzles, betrayals, and malevolence of the real world and moving into its imaginary equivalent. Her real-world sleuthing had taken her away from *Too Young to Die*, putting her behind schedule. Journalism had taught the discipline required to meet deadlines. Pia never missed them. She made herself a sandwich of fresh tomatoes, basil, and aged provolone and settled down in her study, determined to write another chapter before going to bed.

Her talent for concocting plots for mystery novels and the extra income her fiction writing generated had both been surprises. Pia wrote her first novel at Aunt Margaret's urging. At the time, she'd been in the grips of another cash crisis because the roof of the house was leaking and the contractor wanted ten thousand dollars to put on a new one.

"I should have gone into business and earned some real money," she grumbled as details of contractors' estimates and specifications for tar paper and shingles sank her plans for a winter ski holiday and a spring trip to Paris. Margaret was sitting at the kitchen table as Pia looked glumly past her to the pail catching the steady drip of water that oozed from around the light fixture in the ceiling. Her aunt reached down into her bag, pulled out a file, and handed it to Pia.

"You should have listened to me when I told you not to buy this dump. But no, you knew better," Margaret sighed. "So I've been thinking about ways to help you to avoid bankruptcy. The most obvious strategy would be to sell this mistake that masquerades as a house. But I know you won't do that. So here's an alternative: write one of these romance novels. I've done the research and got all the information here on what the publishers are looking for – everything from how many words to how much sex. Do this, solve your cash-flow problems, and spare your poor old auntie all this whining."

Pia opened her mouth to dismiss the idea, but the impatient look on Margaret's face made her hold her tongue. She opened the file and started reading. "There seems to be a choice here. Do you think I should try to write one that has a lot of hot sex or should I try something milder?" she said, when she finally looked up.

"Well, my dear, I've never thought of you as the puritanical type. Why not just go for the heaving breasts and throbbing organs right from the start?"

Pia laughed and got up to hug her aunt. Margaret looked her usual immaculate self in dark green slacks and a matching turtleneck. She also glowed with happiness, thanks to a new relationship with one Sergei Gagarin, a Russian who had immigrated to Canada a few years earlier. Gagarin claimed to be a relative of Yuri Gagarin, Russia's first man in space. Pia had her doubts about that and about the mysterious international security firm he claimed to run. But her aunt clearly enjoyed his company. The willowy Margaret was slightly taller than her new love, but what he lacked in height Sergei made up for in bulk. Even in his sixties, he was all muscle. Wavy white hair flowed back from a square, handsome face and his bright blue eyes were a barometer of his moods, laughing at one moment, serious or melancholy the next.

Margaret never had lacked for admirers and over the years she had introduced Pia to several of them. Sergei's attentions, however, seemed to generate something special in the older woman. Like Margaret, he loved the theater and the symphony, caviar and champagne, the south of France and good restaurants. Mostly though, he made Margaret laugh with his clever jokes and stories about the absurdities of his old Soviet life.

"Maybe I'll write my first book about a chic older woman and her roguish Russian lover," Pia suggested. "He'd ply her with champagne and sweet talk and sweep her off her feet."

"Listen, darling, your imagination can take you places I've never dared to go. You don't need me for inspiration."

Margaret was right about Pia's imagination but wrong about where it would take her. Pia never could quite manage writing a romance. Instead, she found she had a talent for murder mysteries. Her protagonist, Cleo Leone, was a hard-bitten former cop, drummed out of the police force for exposing corruption among her fellow officers. She was in her forties, a bit rough around the edges and tough, except when it came to her ten-year-old adopted daughter.

Pia loved writing the first book and was thrilled with its success. She paid off the new roof and started work on the next Leone adventure.

Too Young to Die kept her busy until nearly midnight. Dreaming up puzzles for Leone to solve was amusing, but it was also hard work at the end of a long day. Pia fell asleep the moment her head hit the pillow.

The next evening, Jack Cleary arrived right on time, looking fit in T-shirt and shorts. He in turn cast an admiring glance at

Pia in her sleeveless running top and tight black shorts that showed off her bare legs.

"You look great," he said. "I hope I can keep up with you."

They headed for one of the ravines that cut a green swath through Toronto. Although they are always mentioned in Toronto guidebooks for the benefit of visitors, the ravines are almost exclusively the preserve of city residents with the time to explore their meandering depths. Discovering one of the ravine trails means leaving behind dense downtown neighborhoods, the towering buildings of the financial district, and traffic-clogged streets. The ravine world is one of winding paths and lush forests alive with birdsong and the murmuring voices of people walking, running, or cycling.

The evening was a gift from nature. Soft yellow light from the setting sun and a gentle breeze played in the treetops. As they ran, they compared notes on the various trails they'd tried and discovered that they both loved running along the Lake Ontario waterfront. Jack moderated his pace to match Pia's, but he too got a workout as they followed streets that rose up and over what used to be the lake's old shoreline and finally brought them into the Cedarvale Ravine. Pia told him about her past glories and defeats as a cross-country runner in high school competitions.

They arrived back at Pia's house more than an hour later to find Margaret relaxing on the front porch bench.

"Margaret, I'm sorry we weren't here. I didn't realize you were coming by," Pia apologized.

"It's no problem at all, dear. I've only been here about ten minutes. It's given me a chance to people-watch in the neighborhood," Margaret said, casting a speculative look at Jack. Recovering her breath and her manners, Pia introduced them and insisted Jack come inside. Minutes later she was smiling broadly as her aunt deployed the journalistic skills that had made her so formidable back in her days as a newspaper woman. Jack, relaxed and unsuspecting, would be lucky to have any secrets left by the time Margaret finished with him.

"Cleary? The name rings a bell, though I don't think I know any Clearys in Toronto," Margaret mused as they sat around the kitchen table. Pia suspected her aunt had never heard the name Cleary in her life, but suggesting she had was an invitation for Jack to elaborate. Two pairs of green eyes looked at him expectantly.

"Well, Ms. Ritman, I don't know about Clearys in Toronto. This one in front of you is originally from Vancouver." As Pia put coffee and croissants on the table, Jack described his fine arts studies in Canada, the United States, and Europe, prompting Margaret to ask about May Gatway and her policies relating to Nazi-confiscated art.

"The thing is," Jack said, "museum directors in North America pledged almost a decade ago to search their collections for works taken illegally during the Nazi era, but nothing much came of it. In fact, none of the searches produced any results, and it didn't look like much would change. But a year or two ago, one of the British museums came up with a list of

350 paintings with gaps in wartime provenance and that set the cat among the pigeons."

"What happened then?" asked Pia.

"People on this side of the pond started asking why rich institutions in North America hadn't found anything with problematic histories in their collections. That was when May Gatway took an interest. She started musing out loud about requiring all organizations that got money from the government to take a serious look at what they owned, to check for gaps in provenance. And she really stirred things up when it became clear she planned to bring in new legislation that would have eased the burden of proof. That would have made it easier for families with claims to get back pieces of art that are now owned by private collectors. The big question now, I guess, is whether the government still intends to go ahead with her plan."

"You think there is a lot of this stolen art in private collections?"

"For sure. Some of it we'll never know about because the collectors don't even have them on display in their homes. And they never loan to museums. It's like pornography – something that can only be enjoyed in private. Stolen art is big business. Not too long ago I saw one estimate suggesting that close to one thousand works by artists like Picasso, Miró, Chagall, and Salvador Dali have been reported stolen in recent years. The number stuck in my mind. The stolen goods are out there somewhere, we just don't know where."

"But if you were the descendants of a family that had art

taken from you during wartime, how would you even know where to start looking?" Margaret queried.

"It's a problem. Many collectors today bought their artworks in good faith and have no reason to think there is anything questionable about their ownership. They acquired the paintings or sculptures in an above-board way and have no idea the stuff has a murky past. Since they don't know they have anything to worry about, they often display pieces in their homes or loan them to museums where they are publicly presented and cataloged," Jack told them. "Descendants of the victimized families might hear about the piece by seeing it in one of those catalogs or exhibits, Then they make a claim and the trouble starts because often the descendants don't have much paperwork to support their case. Maybe they just remember it hanging on the walls of their grandparents' home. Or maybe the original family did sell it, but for a pittance because they were forced to give it up. Like I said, in many cases the current owners legitimately bought the piece without giving much thought to the gaps in its ownership history. But you can bet a whole lot of them have been going back over their records since the minister started talking publicly about all this."

"I wonder if any of Wilson Scott's art collection was in danger?" Pia mused. "I suppose if he risked losing something of great value, it could have been another reason he wanted May Gatway dead."

"You're having trouble letting that story go, aren't you?" Jack said, smiling indulgently. "Nothing like a murder-suicide among politicians to whet a reporter's appetite."

"You are in the company of two women who consider being called snoopy a great compliment," Pia retorted. "And yes, I am having trouble letting go of the story. I'm actually thinking of doing a book on it, so for me, at least, the investigation continues."

"Aah, so you've had enough of made-up murder and now want to write about the real thing." He looked slightly abashed. "I've read all the Leone books. I think they're great."

A few minutes later he rose to go.

"It's been a pleasure, ladies," he said, taking Margaret's hand and raising it to his lips. Smiling at Pia, he suggested they get together for another run sometime soon.

"Nice guy, don't you think?" Pia asked after he left.

"He *is* interesting, if you like those arty types," Margaret said. "And he certainly seems interested," she added meaningfully.

"Margaret, if you were looking under rocks you'd be keeping an eye out for a suitable guy for me. You are incorrigible."

"True," Margaret admitted cheerfully. "But enough about him, charming though he is. What's this book idea?"

"I'm thinking about trying my hand at nonfiction. I'm pretty well equipped to write it. I saw the murder scenes and I knew both Gatway and Scott."

"You've also got that young man as a resource when you go to write about Gatway's art policy. Even if nothing else comes of it, he might be turn out to be a good source."

"There's somebody else too," Pia said. She told her aunt about her date with Martin Geneve.

"Now him I've heard of – in fact, I've met him a number of times at charity dinners and that sort of thing," Margaret said. "You are certainly hobnobbing with some eligible ones these days. If you keep this up you might actually find yourself falling for one or the other of them."

"It won't be Martin Geneve. I didn't inherit my mother's genetic weakness for playboy types."

"So why are you going out with him?"

"Research for the book."

"So going on a date with him is all in the line of duty? Such sacrifices you make!"

Pia glared at her aunt. "For your information, he's a big-time art collector and I'm trying to find out if he might be the kind who owns a painting or something that was illegally seized during the Nazi era. Now wouldn't that be a story?"

"Yes, dear," Margaret said, rising to leave, "it would be. But remember, there's more to life than work. Maybe you should give him a chance instead of writing him off beforehand as a lying, cheating polecat with a penchant for stolen art."

"Thank you, Auntie. Now don't you have to go home and drink champagne with Sergei or something?" Margaret and Sergei had been dating for nearly five years, but it had only been a month since they'd moved in together. Sergei considered that progress, although he still couldn't understand why his marriage proposals came to naught.

"Your Auntie Margaret, she knows how to break a man's heart," he confided sadly to Pia recently after being rebuffed yet again. "She says she's a modern woman who doesn't need a wedding ring. But me, I'm an old-fashioned man who is being forced to live in sin."

Neither Pia nor Margaret took the broken-hearted routine too seriously. Margaret had confided to Pia that Sergei, still had too many secrets to qualify as husband material. Just last week she'd discovered a handgun locked in the back of the safe that Sergei had insisted upon installing in her apartment when he moved in.

"He says he has a license for the thing and that it's all above board, but I wonder," Margaret said skeptically. Then there was Sergei's business, which he described in vague terms as something to do with providing security for rich people. It took him out of the country for weeks at a time.

"People who are too rich for their own good come to me for advice so that they can feel secure and enjoy peace of mind," Sergei would say when pressed to elaborate. While he insisted to Margaret that he was too old to play the role of bodyguard himself, apparently his services as a consultant were still much in demand.

Sergei at that moment was about to board a plane to fly home from a job in Ukraine, and was thus unavailable for a champagne-sipping session. But Margaret knew how to take a hint. She picked up her purse, kissed her niece on the cheek, gave Winston a parting hug, and left.

Pia spent most of the next day writing. While she was trying to solve the murder of a child that dated back ten years, Leone was being courted by a professional pianist she'd met on the case. Pia sent her protagonist's daughter to summer camp for a few weeks and concocted a passionate scene between Leone and the piano player. If only I could orchestrate my own life as easily, she thought later as she stepped out of a hot bubble bath. She pulled on tight black jeans and an off-the-the-shoulder black shirt that showed the tanned skin of her neck and arms to great advantage. She added heavy teardrop-shaped gold earrings and a matching bracelet and slipped her feet into a pair of high-heeled black sandals that consisted of little more than two straps and a sole.

The doorbell rang on cue, and when Pia opened it she found Martin Geneve holding a bouquet of lavender, white daisies, and yellow roses.

"I'm glad you didn't stand me up," he said, smiling as he handed her the flowers. Flustered, Pia thanked him and offered a before-dinner drink in the garden.

"That would be great. We're in no rush and the restaurant will hold our table," Martin said, following Pia into the kitchen and watching as she put the flowers in a vase. "This place is great. And I see that you have a serious guard cat to keep the premises secure."

Pia looked over toward the garden. Winston was curled up sleeping on the mat in front of the door, but he raised his head and yawned as Martin walked over. The cat began purring appreciatively as soon as his newest admirer crouched down and began scratching him behind the ears. Then he rolled over in anticipation of having his tummy rubbed by a complete stranger.

"In theory, he should be good at guarding this place against mice, but I actually do a better job than he does," Pia said, showing Martin the mouse-kill score sheet on the refrigerator. "He's really a poor excuse for a cat."

Pia poured herself a glass of white wine and served Martin the beer he'd requested. As they settled into chairs in the garden, he told Pia he had a malamute named Freddie.

"They are huge dogs originally bred in Alaska for hauling heavy sleds and he's true to the breed," Martin said. "I got him as a pup and thought he would never stop growing. People think he looks like a wolf – he's gray and white – but he's got the personality of one of those goofy, love-you-to-death, yellow Labs. Unless of course, you are a cat," he added, looking meaningfully over at Winston, who was lounging on the deck in a spot of warm evening sun. "In Freddie's mind, the only good cat is a cat in a tree."

"Winston has similar opinions about dogs."

Pia, realizing she had been nervous, began to relax and even enjoy herself as Martin regaled her with stories of Freddie's clumsy and invariably unsuccessful attempts to hunt down unsuspecting felines.

"He has yet to learn that there's no way he can fit under a car when he's got a cat on the run no matter how fast he charges into the space. And I really do wonder what he'd do if he ever caught one. My housekeeper was once looking after a kitten for her sister, and by the end of the weekend Freddie was letting the little thing crawl all over him. I think he might just like the thrill of the chase," Martin said as they left the house for the College Street bistro he'd chosen for dinner.

A half-hour later, a pudgy woman with lively, dark eyes and masses of upswept hair welcomed them as they entered a small restaurant that stretched back from the street but was only wide enough for one table on either side of a central aisle.

Martin introduced the woman as Diana, after she'd kissed him on both cheeks and followed up with a hug. Diana smiled warmly at Pia, kissed her too, and then led them through the restaurant to a tree-canopied terrace at the back.

"This place is magical – why didn't I know about it?" Pia exclaimed as she sat down at the candlelit table.

"The Italians keep it a closely guarded secret so that they can always get a reservation," Martin joked. "I only know about it because I grew up on the same street as the Benedettis. Joe Benedetti was my best buddy and his big sister, Diana, who runs this place now, was forever getting us out of trouble."

"Is Joe involved in the restaurant?"

The light went out in Martin's eyes. "He died," he said abruptly. There was silence for a moment and then Martin resumed. "We both joined the military when we were eighteen. Joey didn't have to – his family would have found him a job or helped him with the cost of university. But my parents split up when I was twelve. My dad disappeared, and my mom and I were pretty strapped for money after that. I figured out that the military was a good place to get a paycheck and a university education at the same time. Joey decided he wanted the same sort of adventure and eventually we ended up in the special forces unit."

"The commando types who do those secret missions?"

"That would have been us," Martin said. "Unfortunately, Joey never came back from one of those assignments. That was almost twenty years ago and his family still mourns him. Such a waste of a life. I put in my time in uniform because you have to serve a certain number of years in return for the education, but I got out as soon as I could."

Pia wanted to ask how the shadowy life of a special forces officer prepared him for the business world, but was interrupted by the arrival of two heaping plates of puttanesca. The pasta dish, created with an olive oil and anchovy base, took its name from the prostitutes of old who would assemble it for clients using whatever they had on hand in the kitchen. Pia closed her eyes rapturously after the first taste.

"I see you appreciate the finer things in life," Martin observed smiling, his eyes taking in the way her hair shone in the candlelight.

"I love food," Pia said, slowly opening her eyes. "I gather art does it for you. It's not something I would have immediately associated with soldiering."

"My parents were both artistic types. My father played the

sax in jazz-bands around town. At least he did until he got involved with a local singer and ran off with her. We didn't hear from him for ten years after he left. When we finally did get word, it was through the police. He died of heart failure in New Orleans right after playing a gig. He'd been living down there, apparently.

"My mother loved to paint and she was the one who taught me to love art. She couldn't afford to buy anything, of course, but we were art gallery regulars. She was still alive when I started making some real money, and so she was a big influence when I began building my collection. But she died a few years ago. Since then, I've had to trust my own judgment. I'll take you around to my place so you can see some of the collection if you are interested. We can have coffee there." A while later, Martin pulled into a circular driveway in Toronto's tony Rosedale neighborhood and stopped in front a house that was uncompromising in its modernity.

"It's a little big for one man and a dog but I need room for the art," Martin said as he unlocked the front door and admitted them both to a huge foyer. "Marco and Julieta have their own suite at the back. They take care of me and Freddie and the place in general." He was interrupted by what sounded like the thundering approach of an elephant.

"Prepare to meet my backup security system." The words were scarcely out of Martin's mouth when a huge dog appeared at the top of the black marble staircase. Freddie's tail wagged furiously as he flew down and slid to a halt in front of them.

"Sit!" Martin commanded in a firm voice that drew an instant response from the malamute. "Freddie, meet Pia. You can pet him, but I'm warning you, if you do, you will have a friend for life. He'll assume you are yet another human put on earth to ply him with love and attention," Pia hesitantly reached out a hand to rub the big dog's head and was delighted when he closed his eyes blissfully.

"Some guard dog you have here," she joked as Freddie tried to wiggle closer and lean against her legs.

She followed Martin into the sort of kitchen that makes professional cooks swoon and amateurs like Pia wide-eyed with envy. Martin poured them each a glass of wine, put the coffee on, and then took her on a tour of the main rooms, stopping to explain certain paintings and sculptures as they went along. Pia did her best to file what she was seeing away in her memory so that she could report it all to Jasmine, but she eventually gave up. If Martin Geneve's collection held any artworks of questionable provenance, she wasn't going to find out this way. There was just too much stuff and she knew too little. With Freddie in tow, they eventually wandered into the back garden where a swimming pool cantilevered out over the edge of the Rosedale ravine.

"This is heavenly," Pia sighed, taking in the moonlight reflected on the water's surface and luxuriating in the warm, soft embrace of the evening air. She felt Martin stir at her side and then started as he removed her wineglass from her hand.

"You are heavenly, Pia," he said, gently grasping her shoulders and turning her toward him. Before she could say a word, his mouth gently nuzzled hers and one of his hands slid up the back of her neck into her thick hair. Her lips clung to his and her body, of its own accord, pressed against him.

"I've wanted to do this since the moment I met you," he murmured. "So smart, so beautiful."

It was just a kiss, but Pia knew where it would lead if she didn't put a stop to it. Did she want him to stop? If she didn't, was it because she liked him or was it really about trying to defy the baby-making odds? She could just take a chance and worry about it later. She pulled away abruptly, uncomfortable with where her thoughts were taking her.

"I'm not sure this is a good idea," she muttered, her voice shaky as she recognized that her words were true on so many levels. Pia took a few steps back, pushed her hair out of her face with a trembling hand, and looked down at the ground. In a bid to regain her equilibrium, she switched into work mode.

"Look, you promised you would help me with information about the Gatway case," she said briskly. "I'm working on this book on the whole thing and I have a few questions. When we met at the charity lunch, why didn't you tell me you were at the legislature the night May Gatway was murdered? Why did you try and point me in the direction of her husband as the killer?"

Martin looked taken aback at the sudden change of mood and subject. "What the hell does May Gatway have to do with what's happening here?" he asked incredulously.

Pia was stubbornly silent, her questions hanging in the air.

"Okay, damn it. First, I didn't bother mentioning I was at the reception because the information was in your own paper. I thought you knew. There was a picture of me on the society pages. As for the husband, I told you about his problems because at that point Gatway's murder hadn't been solved, remember? He seemed a likely suspect and if Wilson Scott hadn't killed her, I firmly believe her dearly beloved would have done the job. He's back on drugs and apparently there was an insurance policy. The idiot has been boasting about it all over town. Says it was his dear wife's parting gift to him. Next question."

"If May Gatway had gone ahead with changes making it easier for the owners of art looted in the Second World War to lay claim to their property, would anything in your collection have been up for grabs?"

"Forgive me for being a bit confused," Martin said, stepping back and drawing his hand through his hair. "What's this all about? Just two minutes ago, weren't you kissing me with quite a bit of enthusiasm?"

Pia turned away, her long, heavy hair sweeping forward to hide her face before he could see the admission written on it. This was business, she reminded herself. In more ways than one. And he hadn't answered her question.

"Okay, okay. Let's make peace," he said, the frustration fading from his voice.

"Martin, it's so late, what I want right now is to go home," Pia said, a wave of tiredness overwhelming her. He started to protest, thought better of it and instead picked up his car keys.

It was a short, quiet ride to Pia's house. He saw her to the door where he stole a soft, gentle kiss.

"I'll be in touch."

Pia walked into her house, shut the door, and fell back against it for support, her eyes closed. The evening hadn't gone exactly as planned. Then again, what exactly was the plan?

Chapter Nine

PIA ARRIVED IN THE NEWSROOM Monday morning to find James Nowt at his desk with his head in his hands. "It's a bit early in the week for despair, isn't it?" she asked her second-in-command.

"You'll understand when you check your messages," he moaned. "No, let me deliver the news personally. Apparently the wretched creature we sent to review *Little Shop of Horrors* made a big impression on the theater group."

"What do you mean? "

"I just got off the phone with Mrs. Whiticker, the president of the Little Theater Association. She informs me that our reviewer arrived at the theater with a member of the opposite sex and spent more time canoodling and playing kissy-kissy, as she put it, with this fellow than watching the killer plant at work."

"You're joking."

"Oh, how I wish I was. And to make matters worse, the review she wrote is unprintable. I've got it here for you to take a look at but, trust me, it barely makes sense."

"So she was too busy 'canoodling and playing kissy-kissy' to appreciate the play's finer points? Some people might consider that a sign of good judgment," Pia said, smiling in spite of herself.

"You can laugh, but we've still got to publish a review of this damn play. You should also know that I've checked and it turns out that our canoodler really is the daughter of Perry Alton's wife's cousin. It should be great fun telling our esteemed publisher the difficulties we've run into in dealing with his relative. Then for light entertainment you can explain to the misguided creature herself that canoodling and theater reviewing don't mix."

"Point taken. Let me look at the review. If it really can't be used we'll have to send somebody else to see the play tonight. Let me know when this girl shows up so I can speak to her."

This was exactly what she hated about being a manager, Pia thought, feeling sorry for herself as she plowed through what Shawna Regent had written. An hour later, the tearful girl walked out of her office with a copy of a book on the art of the theater review under one arm.

"How did it go?" James asked.

"Well, I explained how the canoodling had got all of us into trouble. She started to cry. Then I told her the review was too awful to publish and she started to sob. Then I gave her a copy of a book on reviewing that might help her and told her to take another crack at producing something that's printable by three o'clock today. If she can't do it, we'll have to find another reviewer for tonight." Pia paused. "Are you free by any chance?"

"Pia, you know I'd do almost anything for you but this is asking too much," James said, horror written all over his face. "Apart from my aversion to singing plants, I'd probably write a negative review and then all of those theater mavens will put *me* at the top of their most-hated list. And really, I don't want to displace you. So the answer is I'm not free. But I'll find somebody to go if Shawna can't clean up her piece."

In the early afternoon, Pia received a new version of the review and heaved a sigh of relief. The girl apparently could string words together in logical sequence when she wasn't distracted. Pia edited the review and let James know the crisis had been averted.

Then she looked up an address for Alex Juarez. Mohammed and Tariq's late-night peeping meant that everything and everybody associated with the May Gatway and Wilson Scott murders had to be revisited. Alex Juarez didn't strike her as the kind of fellow who would chase, slash, and kill a woman. But maybe he'd had enough of Gatway's sexual demands and just cracked that evening in the attic.

Pia remembered Alex's comments about recently buying a condo as she pulled her car into a parking spot in the city's thriving downtown entertainment district. Richmond Street had been transformed in recent years by a string of popular clubs and an explosion of condo construction. What used to be a gloomy stretch of old industrial warehouses on the western edge of the downtown core now came alive every night with thousands of young people in search of good times.

Chris answered when Pia rang from the lobby. She sounded less than thrilled to hear who had come calling, but she opened the building's security doors and let her unexpected visitor in.

"Alex isn't home – what's all this about?" she asked as she led Pia into a compact loft. In a bid to feed young Torontonians' insatiable appetite for affordable downtown living, the city's condo developers had cut back on the size of units so they could squeeze more of them into each building. Alex's place was small, probably not much bigger than one of the living rooms in a suburban monster home, but it did have high loft ceilings and the requisite exposed-brick wall. It was sparsely furnished with what looked like thrift shop bargains dressed with colorful fabric throws. Pia concluded these additions came from Chris because the young woman obviously eschewed black, the mainstay of Toronto fashionistas. She wore a pair of tight, bright green capri pants with hot pink sandals that matched a linen top. With her blond hair and delicate features, the whole effect was like cotton candy on steroids.

"I'm sorry I missed him. I just needed to check something with you two," she said. "He told me you both went out for dinner with friends the night May Gatway was killed. Can you tell me what time that was and who you went out with?"

"Why are you dredging all this stuff up again? She's dead, buried, gone, and I don't want to think about her anymore."

"I'm working on a book about the Gatway and Scott murders."

A look of panic passed over Chris's face. "You aren't going to name Alex in it, are you? He'll just die if people found out what was going on with May."

Pia wasn't going to make any promises she might not be able to keep.

"I don't know right now if I will need to name Alex or not. The fact that May was sexually exploiting an employee is pretty central to the story. I say that because I think Wilson Scott found out about Alex and confronted May. Maybe he thought he could force her to quit so he could have her job. Anyway, I think she retaliated by somehow getting a photograph of Wilson in a bar with a young guy and then threatening to make it public.

"Please, Chris, all I really want from you are the names of the people you two had dinner with the night she was killed. I just need them to tell me you were all together that night. Were they friends, colleagues?"

"You aren't going to tell them about Alex and May?"

"No, no, I'll just say I'm doing research for my book, trying to trace the whereabouts on the night she died of everyone who knew her. And I'm not even sure I'll call them. It will only happen if I need additional details to make it all more real."

Chris hesitated a moment longer, then reached for a piece of paper on the nearby table and scribbled down three names and numbers. "I'm trusting you to protect Alex," she said as she pushed the paper toward Pia.

"You're crazy about him, aren't you?"

"He's the best thing that ever happened to me. We met when we were both in May's office. He was doing policy work for her and I was in charge of correspondence – a lot of the job involved dealing with people from the riding where she was elected. We started dating, but kept it very hush-hush at the start because neither of us knew where it was going. Then we had to keep it hush-hush because that crazy woman started hitting on Alex, inviting him for lunch and dinner and insisting that he work late. She practically drooled over him in front of all of us. It was disgusting. Then they traveled together on a business trip and she came to his hotel room and wouldn't leave, and that was the start of the sex. I sensed there was something new going on between them as soon as they got back from that trip, and I just blew up. I told him I didn't want to see him anymore.

"It was pretty tense in the office between the two of us and May noticed. I think she finally figured out that we had been dating – somebody might even have told her. So all of a sudden she started finding problems with my work and the next thing I knew, I was out of a job. The good thing about it was that when Alex came to me begging forgiveness a few months later, I was working somewhere else. He swore that everything with her had ended so we got back together."

"But the sex thing didn't end."

"I suppose I suspected it all along, but I wanted to believe

I had him all to myself. And I knew he didn't love her. So when he said he was working late, I just chose to accept it and beat down my doubts. Love is humiliating, don't you think?"

"You must have hated her."

"Hate isn't a strong enough word."

Pia acted on a hunch. "Chris, somebody told Eric Paivanen in Wilson Scott's office about Gatway and Alex – somebody who wanted to bring her down. Was it you?"

The young woman was sitting opposite Pia on a stool pulled up to the granite-clad island that provided the only real counter space in the condo's diminutive kitchen. Her hands, which had been busy shredding a paper napkin, stopped moving. She rose abruptly, swept up the paper shreds and turned to put them in the garbage. After standing a moment or two with her back to Pia, she sighed deeply and turned.

"I hated May Gatway more than I've ever hated anyone in my life," she said, her eyes locking with Pia's. "And for a while after Alex and I broke up, I hated him too. So yes, I told Eric Paivanen. I regretted it immediately and then when Alex and I got back together, I regretted it even more. He – Alex – doesn't know what I did and I'm not sure he'd forgive me if he ever finds out I told Eric.

"The worst of it is that it didn't do me or Alex any good. I think Wilson Scott confronted her and accused her of sexually harassing an employee, and after that she did leave Alex alone for a while. But then I guess she decided to fight back. I never really understood how she did it. Maybe it was with this photograph you're telling me about. She must have thought she was home-free once she had that so she sunk her claws back into Alex. God, I'm glad she's dead."

The words hung in the air until Pia rose and broke the silence.

"Thanks for this," she said as she slipped the list of names Chris had left on the counter into her purse and turned toward the door. "Let's stay in touch."

In her car, Pia scribbled down some notes based on the conversation. Then she pulled out her cellphone, called Jasmine, and suggested they meet for dinner, drinks, and some brainstorming.

An hour later they were sitting in a Thai restaurant on Queen Street West and Pia was describing her conversation with Tariq and Mohammed.

"Wow, this is just like in one of your books. What would Leone do?" Jasmine said as she began demolishing a heaping plate of pad Thai.

"This is the real thing, Jasmine. It's not a joking matter."

"Well, if you really think there's a murderer – or murderers – still out there running around, maybe you should be going to the police."

"I've been struggling with this," Pia said. "But it's not clear those boys will repeat what they told me to the police. They're afraid of what their parents will say if they find out they were spying on the neighbors. I guess there's also the chance that they made the whole story up for my benefit, though I don't really believe that. I'm going to dig further. In the meantime, I'm keen to do a book about the case. But I might need a little help."

"Why do I get the feeling I'm about to get dragged into this?"

"Because you're the only person I know who has real links to the criminal world," Pia said, only half joking. "If Wilson Scott didn't kill himself, then the whole case is blown wide open. May Gatway's husband, for instance, is once again a potential suspect in her death. I need to find out what I can about him and his finances and his cocaine habit. Could we get in touch with Raj to see if he knows anything?"

Jasmine liked to joke that whenever her traditional Muslim parents despaired of their daughter because of her secular, liberal, westernized ways, she would defend herself by reminding them of her cousin Raj. "I may be a disappointment to Allah," she would point out, " but at least I'm not a convicted criminal."

Raj and Jasmine's fathers were brothers who came to Toronto together from Pakistan in the 1970s and settled in the same tough neighborhood. The Jane–Finch area, in the city's northwest quadrant, had always been rough-and-tumble, but in recent years the gangs had come into their own and the gun was now their preferred method of settling disputes. Raj, seven years older than Jasmine, had deep roots in the neighborhood's murky criminal world, roots that he continued to nurture. While he was a source of great shame to his immediate and extended family, he had used his notoriety and his fists to protect his little cousin from the worst of the neighborhood during the years they spent growing up there.

"You go to school, sweet cousin. And you paint and you study art and you get out of this place," Raj would say to Jasmine on the many days he made a point of walking her home after school. "Don't you start up with any of these guys around here. I know them all and none of them are good enough for you. Anybody bothers you, you tell me and I'll take care of it." He was as good as his word. Jasmine was never hassled by the young toughs at school or in the neighborhood. Raj, she always said, was the reason she didn't go out on her first date until she was nineteen and had moved away from Jane and Finch. No guy from the 'hood thought a date with Jasmine Assad was worth dying for.

The bond formed between the two cousins all those years ago had survived. Jasmine was one of the few family members to maintain ties with Raj. During his several sojourns in jail, she was his only visitor. These sojourns weren't as common as they used to be because Raj's criminal IQ improved with time, as did his financial wherewithal to hire top-notch lawyers.

"I'll call him right now and see what he's up to," Jasmine said, swallowing the last bite of her dinner and reaching into her handbag for her cellphone. "It's after ten o'clock. His work day should just be getting underway."

An hour later, Pia followed Jasmine into one of the huge downtown clubs not far from where Chris and Alex lived. The bar's shiny metallic counter glowed eerily in the subdued lighting, and the city's young and beautiful writhed to pounding music on the crowded dance floor.

"Over this way," Jasmine said, leading Pia to a table in the far corner where there was less noise. They no sooner ordered drinks than Raj materialized out of the gloom. Pia had always found him a little bit frightening. He wasn't much taller than she was and he was slight. But his face belied the immaculately tailored tan summer jacket, black T-shirt, and matching pants that made him look like one of Bay Street's young financial wizzes. A long scar ran down one cheek, jagged and white against his brown skin. Jasmine said he got it in a street fight back at Jane and Finch and that he purposely didn't get plastic surgery to make it go away. The mark apparently served as a reminder of what happened to his enemies: the guy who scarred Raj disappeared not long after the fight and was never heard from again. The two cousins had large, dark eyes in common. But while Jasmine's eyes were pools of mystery that drew you in and enveloped you in their warmth, Raj's eyes were hard, wary, and unforgiving. They smiled only for Jasmine.

"Sweet cousin, so good to see you," Raj said, bending down to give her a kiss on the cheek before folding himself into the remaining chair at their table. "And you have brought the lovely and intelligent Ms. Keyne. I know you need something from me, ladies. But before we get to that, Jasmine, you have to tell me – what the hell happened to your hair?"

He reached over and rubbed his hand on Jasmine's brush

cut. "Your beautiful hair – it's gone. You look like a U.S. Marine. How could you? Your mother must be beside herself."

"You might say that," Jasmine agreed, smiling. "But I take comfort in knowing that whatever I do pales to insignificance compared to your record for pissing off the family. So, here's the thing. After all these years, your life of crime is finally going to be put to good use. We need you to find somebody for us and we need that somebody to give us information."

The three of them leaned forward over the table. Raj heard them out, nodded thoughtfully, and then disappeared to make a call. A few minutes later he was back.

"Okay, I've got the guy you need to talk to if you want to know about the dead chick's husband. He's one of mine. He'll be here in a while," he said. Pia groaned inwardly, thinking she'd be lucky to get four hours sleep at this rate. "Let's have another round, ladies. The night is young."

But Raj's contact didn't keep them waiting long. "This is Jason," he said, introducing the young man who approached their table about a half-hour later. "He's going to tell you whatever you want to know about this Paul Stark guy, right, Jason?"

Pia guessed the new arrival was in his early twenties. Five gold studs lined the curve of each ear, drawing attention to short blond hair that was shaved in a brush cut similar to Jasmine's.

"Do you two share the same barber?" Raj asked, momentarily distracted by the twin haircuts. "Whoever it is, the guy doesn't have much imagination." Jasmine laughed, but Pia noticed that Jason swallowed hard and managed barely a smile. He's scared, she realized. The young man jumped nervously when Raj ordered him to pull up a chair.

"So ask your questions," Jason directed in a voice barely audible above the pounding the music.

"Is Paul Stark one of your, er, clients?" Pia asked.

Jason had been staring down at the table but now he looked to his boss for direction. "I told you, tell them everything they want to know," Raj hissed.

"Yeah, he scores off me all the time. He's one of my better customers. These rich business guys, you know, they don't like making their buys on street corners at night. Too afraid of being caught. So I do office deliveries during business hours."

"Did you deliver anything to him the day his wife was murdered?"

"Oh, yeah, I remember that day. I went to his office in the afternoon – hadn't been around in a while so he was real happy to see me. I mean he was real happy to see the bag of coke I had with me. Just the kind of customer we like – the kind who really needs to see you and pays cash. These days he's in for a lot on each delivery – it's creeping up very nicely over time. Like I said, the guy is a good customer. That's what made me freak when I heard about his wife on the news the next day. I was afraid he'd done something stupid and that business was going to take a hit."

"What do you mean?"

Jason's eyes were back on the tabletop in front of him but he had relaxed slightly as he described his business dealings with Stark. Pia's question prompted him to look up at her directly for the first time. He remained silent. Raj leaned over and said something quietly so that the two women wouldn't hear. Jason's eyes widened, he swallowed hard and began to talk.

"Okay, okay, I'm telling everything I know. I was interested to hear Stark's wife turned up dead because a couple weeks before, another time when I was delivering to his office, he'd sat me down and kind of hinted he was looking for somebody to put her out of her misery. We're not in that business, but I said I'd ask around. I wasn't really going to do it, but I said I would because I like to keep the customer happy. So you can imagine I pay attention when I hear she's dead. I figured he'd found somebody to get the job done or that he did it himself."

"What do you mean he kind of hinted he was looking for somebody to put her out of her misery?" Pia asked.

"Well, we were just finishing our business – I was check-ing the cash – when he said he might have to start cutting costs because his wife was wondering where all the money was going. Then he asks if I know anybody who specializes in getting rid of bitch wives. I've just finished counting and I think he's joking until I look up and I see he's dead serious. He says he's got the money to pay for the job if I can come up with somebody to do it. I told him I'd get back to him."

"That's more than a hint," Pia observed dryly. "Did he ever mention it again?"

"I didn't see him again until earlier on that day she was killed. I didn't have any information for him so I didn't raise the subject and besides, he was really antsy – I could tell he wanted me out of the office so he could sample the product right away. Like I said, I don't know who killed the wife, but you gotta believe me when I say I was really relieved to find out it wasn't him – that somebody else had done the deed." He fell silent. Pia nodded when Raj asked if she'd finished with her questions.

"Get back to work," he growled at Jason, who finally smiled, albeit in relief, and nearly knocked his chair over in his haste to depart.

"If you got what you need, you two better get home to bed so you can do an honest day's work tomorrow," Raj said, brushing off Pia's thanks and smiling at Jasmine. "You need your rest, sweet cousin, if you want that hair to grow back."

Chapter Ten

PIA WAS IN HER OFFICE the next day editing a story on fashion dos and don'ts for Hollywood starlets when her phone rang in the early afternoon. Richard Bellington, a young *Gazette* reporter who had been covering the legislature for the last six months, chatted briefly with her about a recent government decision to close down a number of hospitals, and then got to the point.

"Pia, there's a rumor going around that you are working on a book about Gatway and Scott and how they came to their sorry end. If it's true, I want to do a short piece about it for tomorrow's paper. It will look bad if the competition has it before we do."

"News travels fast," Pia said, mentally running through the growing list of people who knew about the book idea. "So for the record, it's true. I'm hoping to pull something together. I'm guessing you also need a quote?"

"You betcha."

"Okay, how about this? I think I may already have information that will shock a lot of people and raise questions about the accepted version of events, but it all requires a lot more checking."

"Well, now I'm intrigued. Is there anything I should know about?"

"Not yet, my friend. I really mean it when I say I'm still trying to pull all the bits and pieces together. It's slow work since I have my obligations to the entertainment world to fulfill in the meantime."

Pia smiled after hanging up the phone. A bit of publicity wouldn't be a bad thing – once word was out that she was continuing to work on the Gatway–Scott story, there was no telling who might approach her, eager to get their version of the events into print. In the meantime, she would continue to follow up on what she already had.

With that in mind, Pia dialed Paul Stark's number and was immediately put through to his office.

"What do you want?" he said, sounding less than pleased to hear from her.

"I want to come and talk to you about May. I don't know if you've heard, but I'm writing a book about what happened to her and Wilson Scott. I'm hoping you will help me with some of the details."

"There's nothing in it for me and I don't see how a book by some reporter would be at all to my advantage. So, Ms. Keyne, I suggest you fuck off and leave me alone." Stark clearly intended to hang up for maximum effect but before he got a chance, Pia rushed in.

"Trying to take out a contract on your wife and sniffing a fortune up your nose are the sorts of thing that can get a guy into big trouble. Especially when that wife turns up dead and there's a big insurance payout. I think you do want to talk to me, Mr. Stark, it's just taking you some time to realize it."

She heard his sharp intake of breath and then a long pause. Pia could almost hear the gears in his cocaine-addled head trying to turn. "Be here at my office tomorrow morning at ten-thirty," Stark said in a strangled voice. Then he hung up on her.

Pia shrugged, looked at the clock, and realized she had just fifteen minutes to get from the newsroom to her appointment with Dr. Garcia. She'd been going to the psychologist for nearly three years at the same time every week, yet she still managed to forget about some appointments and be late for others. The doctor, on more than one occasion, suggested her tardiness might reflect her desire to avoid confronting "the tough issues."

"Personally, I think of it as self-defense," Pia grumbled once she became more comfortable with Garcia and the process. "You always pick away at the nasty stuff. Nobody in their right mind would come in here and pay for that month after month. So I must be crazy."

"You're not crazy. You're just a little confused and have made a habit of packing away what you call the nasty stuff so that you don't have to deal with it," Dr. Garcia said. "Your decision to come and talk to me suggests you're ready to start unpacking. The fact that you can't get here on time? Well, it's true what they say. Old habits are hard to break."

Pia was ten minutes late when she rushed into the reception area of Dr. Garcia's office in one of downtown Toronto's medical arts buildings. "I guess this means I'm not cured yet," she thought unrepentantly as the receptionist waved her through to the inner sanctum. Still, she had to admit that walking into Dr. Garcia's office was less traumatic now than it used to be.

As with so much else in her life, that she was there at all was largely due to Margaret.

"You know I'm not the type to say you should chart a traditional path in life," her aunt had said one day as they lingered over a coffee in Margaret's kitchen. "God knows settling down permanently with someone has never really been my thing either. But I worry that you will never to have the sort of relationship that brings you comfort and joy. And yes, before you say it, I may be getting mushy in my old age. I've fallen for this rascal Sergei, but God's truth, Pia, he makes me feel adored and loved. I want you to know that kind of happiness."

"I hope you're not suggesting I fall in love with Sergei too," Pia joked.

"He's not tall enough for you. Actually, he's not tall enough for me either but it's too late – I love the guy. Now seriously, I've been doing a lot of thinking about you and maybe part of the problem is that you've never sorted through what happened between you and Patrice and Max. They were killed before there was time to force it out into the open to deal with it."

"This conversation is making me nervous," Pia said apprehensively.

"Relax. You don't have to do anything you don't want to. But I have been asking around and there's a therapist who might be of some help. Her name is Gabriella Garcia and she specializes in dealing with women who have been abused. Why don't you go and see her and see how it goes?"

"Ugh. I can't think of anything I'd rather do less."

"Please, Pia, do it for me. I'm asking you to go as a favor. This was something I should have insisted on years ago, right after you told me what happened. At first I was so angry with Patrice and Max I couldn't think straight. And then they died and I didn't know what to feel. You seemed to have put it all behind you, and never want to talk about it. In the end, though, I think it really has affected your ability to have intimate relationships with men."

"Aunt Margaret, I have dated all sorts of men. "

"My point exactly. You have dated them. You have slept with them. But have you really loved any of them – had anything that resembles intimacy? You keep them around until they seriously start falling for you and then you find a reason to send them packing. Maybe you don't want to hear this from me, but I'm just telling you what I see."

"Maybe I just haven't met the right guy," Pia said stubbornly. "You know that old saying about kissing a lot of frogs before the prince comes along."

"It's possible. But I'm not so sure anybody will qualify as a prince for you in your current frame of mind. Please, please go and see her."

Gabriella Garcia was a petite woman in her early sixties. She had the big, dark brown eyes of a Latin beauty, gray-streaked black hair drawn back in an elegant chignon, and impeccable taste. Pia had observed more than once over the years that the doctor's designer shoes probably cost more than the average sales clerk made in two weeks. But she didn't hold it against her. Good shoes made life more bearable.

The psychologist's office was a reflection of its occupant – understated and elegant yet comfortable and warm. A lush Persian carpet in deep browns, golds, and burgundy was underfoot, an imposing oak desk sat off to one side off the room, and heavy oak bookshelves covered the walls. The corner office on the twenty-fourth floor had a spectacular view of Lake Ontario's moody waters. On clear summer days, the lake nestled against the city like lapis lazuli, all glowing blue and sun-kissed gold. On cloudy, wintry days, the water was steely, uncompromising, and deadly to anyone who dared challenge its cold depths.

Pia had arrived twenty-five minutes late for her first appointment with Dr. Garcia. She apologized for her tardiness and, once she was settled in a dark brown leather chair, acknowledged that she was there at Margaret's behest.

"But you did come," Dr. Garcia observed.

"I'm forty years old and I've never come close to thinking I'm in love. Does that mean I'm damaged goods? I don't know.

If you can help me sort out whether it's normal or not, I suppose that might be useful."

During subsequent meetings, Pia talked about Max's abuse and her mother's betrayal and realized that she was still furious with both of them. With a little prodding from Dr. Garcia, she was also forced to acknowledge that the whole ugly experience had made it difficult for her to trust any man.

"I never thought seriously about it in those terms, but I guess it shouldn't come as a big surprise," Pia conceded during one session. "I mean, look where my mother's trusting nature got the two of us."

Over time, the dread she felt at the thought of walking into the soft-spoken psychologist's office had eased.

"You must be getting to like me. You're almost on time," Dr. Garcia joked when Pia arrived for her latest appointment.

"That's because I've got lots to talk about. I've met a man – no, I've met two men. But don't start thinking your voodoo is working and that I've turned into one of those women who falls head over heels for every guy who spares her a second glance. I'm know this sounds awful, but what if I just slept with them to find out if the doctors are right when they say I can't get pregnant? Oh, now I've shocked you," Pia said, noting Dr. Garcia's raised eyebrows. "I thought people in your position weren't supposed to be judgmental?"

"Well, you have to admit, Pia, there are some real ethical and moral – not to mention legal – questions here," the therapist said. "I hope you are going to take some time to think through the consequences, just in case you conceive. I'd also like to point out," she continued, "that there is another option. It sounds like it's early days in both of these relationships. Why not just give them both some time and see where things go? Maybe you'll end up having a real relationship. I think you are better equipped emotionally now to fall in love and to be loved."

"But what if I actually fall for one or the other and he turns out to be a cad?" Pia said quietly.

"Pia, you aren't fifteen any more and you aren't your mother. You have to learn to trust in your ability to judge people. And you have to accept that falling in love is, when it comes right down to it, a risky business. There are no guarantees. At some point, you just have to try it. But only when you are ready. Don't attempt to talk yourself into something that doesn't feel right. If you think there might be something there, admit it to yourself and give yourself permission to enjoy it, to explore it."

Anything was possible, Pia thought later as she drove home. When she came to a red light, she punched Jack Cleary's number into her cellphone and caught him just as he was leaving the office.

"Want to go for a run and then have dinner at my place?"

A few hours later, he was sitting in her kitchen sipping gin and tonic and watching as Pia assembled a salad. The day's heat had lingered so that after running for nearly an hour, they came back to the house soaked with sweat. Pia gave Jack a towel and sent him to the shower in the guest bedroom. He emerged fifteen minutes later looking fresh in a white T-shirt and khaki shorts.

"It's going to be your job to barbecue these," she said, gesturing toward a bowl of giant prawns marinating in olive oil and garlic.

"No problem," Jack said. "I'm going to prove to you that I'm not just another wonderfully good-looking guy. A man should be useful, not just handsome."

Pia laughed out loud, thinking that he was much too thin and gangly to be considered handsome. But she like the way he looked at her through those funky black glasses of his. He'll be kissing me before this evening is over, she thought. I don't think I'm going to mind one bit. And to hell with you, Gabriella Garcia, I'm not going to examine my motives too closely.

They ate in the garden, drinking white wine and laughing at Winston as he prowled around the table, begging for a prawn or twenty of his own.

"He's shameless when it comes to food," Pia warned when Jack finally weakened and tossed a morsel to the cat. "Indulging him is only going to make him beg even more."

"Well, I hardly think he's learning all his bad manners this evening. Seems somebody must have fed him a thing or two from the table in the past," Jack said, glancing meaningfully at Pia as Winston gobbled down the offering and looked up for seconds.

"My guests are the problem. They are pushovers where he's concerned," Pia said, watching as the cat jumped onto one of the unoccupied chairs and surveyed their empty plates. She swept him into her arms when he suddenly hooked his two front feet over the edge of the table.

"Winston, you are a bad, bad boy and should be severely punished," she joked as she rubbed her face against his head and patted his substantial stomach. "There, now he'll never do that again," she said, laughing as the cat slid from her grasp.

"I see the discipline is tough around here," Jack replied, grinning. "Now beat it, pussycat. She's already crazy about you. It's my turn to ingratiate myself by offering invaluable assistance."

Jack walked over to the leather briefcase he'd brought with him and pulled out some documents. "I've brought you some background on art theft, just in case you need it for your book. I came across these articles in a magazine the other day and thought of you right away. I'll leave them with you so you can look them over when you have time. You can keep all of this. How's the book going anyway?"

"I'm chasing down some angles that might just turn the whole story on its head. I'm still working on it so I don't have much to tell at this point. But thanks for this," Pia said, flipping quickly through the pages he'd handed her. "I'll read through all this and probably call you with questions. I hope you won't feel used if I take advantage of your expertise."

Jack leaned across the small table, raised her hand, and caressed it with his lips. When he looked up at Pia his face was serious. "I've got an idea about how you can make up to me, if you're willing," he answered quietly. He stood up slowly, pulling Pia to her feet and toward him. His eyes never left her face as he bent his head and brushed her lips with his. Her hands were on Jack's shoulders, exploring the muscle and sinew, enjoying the sensation as his lips settled on hers more firmly.

To hell with it, Pia thought to herself. I'm forty-three, I can deal with consequences if there are any. She took Jack's hand and led him into the house, up to her bedroom. His hands gently explored her body as he took off her clothes. She pulled his shirt over his head and undid the buckle on his belt. It felt right.

Pia was alone when she woke up the next morning. She was taken aback until she saw the note on the pillow beside her. "Had to run because I have a breakfast meeting at 7:30 and I need to go home first to change. Had a great time last night. Didn't want to disturb your beauty sleep. Will call you. Jack."

Pia shrugged. She felt vaguely offended that he hadn't woken her up to say goodbye. Dr. Garcia's advice had been to take her time and explore the possibilities. I don't know if this would qualify as taking my time, but I'm well on the path toward exploring the possibilities, Pia thought wryly. There was zero chance she could get back to sleep so she got up, made coffee, and went to her study, where she began updating her files on the Gatway–Scott murders. Meticulously, she outlined the information obtained from Chris and Paul Stark's drug dealer and added it to the notes about Mohammed and Tariq.

An hour later, she smiled contentedly as she opened the *Gazette* and read the story outlining her plans for the book. Apparently the paper's editors considered it news fit for the political pages. She scanned the story and wondered who else might be reading it. Speculation, however, would get her nowhere. Going to see Paul Stark, now that might yield results.

She called James in the newsroom to say she would arrive late and went directly to Stark's office. Walking across the room toward him, she saw that he looked decidedly worse than the last time she'd seen him. His eyes were even redder around the rims, his hair was limp, and his skin looked nearly alabaster. He was immaculately dressed though. Her first clue that he was furious was when he didn't bother to get up from his desk to greet her and instead silently pointed to the chair opposite. Then he opened his mouth and confirmed her suspicions.

"Look, lady, I don't know what you're up to but I had nothing to do with May's death," he said, firing the first salvo.

"Like I said on the phone, Mr. Stark, I'm writing a book on what happened to May and Wilson Scott. But as I dig around, I'm finding out stuff that makes me wonder about the neat and tidy explanation we've been given for their deaths. And some of that stuff makes you look bad. For instance, why were you looking to hire somebody to kill May?"

Stark's pale face suffused with sudden color but his voice was quiet, controlled and, she thought, a little bit scared. "You don't know anything," he said, rising suddenly from his chair. "You're bluffing."

Pia felt a thrill of fear but the moment passed when Stark, instead of coming toward her, turned and went to stare out of one of the office's big windows. As she watched, he rolled his shoulders, flexed them, and then suddenly let them slump. When he turned to face her, his voice was flat and lifeless. "I did ask about hiring somebody to kill May but it never came to anything. You have to believe me. The truth is, Wilson Scott got to her before I had the chance to make the biggest mistake of my life."

"Why did you want her dead?"

"She was on my back again about my habit – my bad habit."

"Your coke habit?"

"Yeah. I was supposed to be clean after my brush with the law. But about a year ago I started having cash-flow problems here at work and I was feeling stressed. I didn't want to have to ask May for more money to bail me out. She never let you forget stuff like that. I just needed a little comfort, you know, so I tried a line or two and then before I knew it, I was back into it big-time.

"That stuff I told you before about May wanting to have a baby, it was something I dreamt up. I needed to protect myself during those days before Wilson Scott confessed he'd killed her. The truth was she wanted a divorce. My habit doesn't come cheap, so I was panicking at the thought of her walking away with all that money her old man left her. I would have been shit out of luck – there's no way this place generates the kind of cash I'm needing these days. And May would not have been generous if we had parted ways."

"Mr. Stark, what if I told you I have some information that suggests Wilson Scott didn't kill May – that it might have been somebody else? If this information is reliable, it means you are back in the picture as a potential suspect. You could easily have followed May up into the attic the night she was killed. And you had reasons to want her dead."

"That fag confessed that he killed her – there was a note to prove it and the police closed the case."

"Did you go straight home from the reception on the night May died, like you said?" Pia persisted. "You can tell me or you can tell the police when they come sniffing around again after I publish what I've got."

"Christ," Stark said in a shaky voice. Then to Pia's astonishment, his eyes filled with tears. "Okay, okay – I'll tell you. I did go home that night, but I made a stop first, just for an hour or so to see somebody. A girl. I picked her up off the street down by Sherbourne and Dundas and drove to one of the back lanes in the area. She directed me. We were alone there for a bit while she gave me what I needed – what I wanted. I paid her and she got out of the car and then I came home. The whole thing didn't take very long. I was home when the cops showed up to tell me about May."

"So you had sex with a prostitute on your way home after leaving the reception?" Pia said, keeping her voice neutral.

"Yes, yes I did," he said, dropping his hands into trembling hands. "I think her name was Joline. Like I said, she was working down at Sherbourne and Dundas."

"Even if you can find this girl again and she says the two of you were together, you know you've still got a problem, right? You could have hired somebody to do your dirty work for you."

At her words, Stark nodded wretchedly and crumpled into his chair. Then he put his arms on his desk and began sobbing. Pathetic, Pia thought as she walked out. May Gatway's taste in husbands left a lot to be desired.

Chapter Eleven

PIA SPENT THE REST of the afternoon working with James Nowt on plans for covering next month's Toronto International Film Festival. The event was now a major date for the film world's glitterati and all their hangers on. It was Pia's first festival in her new job and she looked in dismay at the pile of party invitations on her desk.

"You need to put those in a locked drawer," James said, just before they began discussing how many photographers they would need to cover the red carpet line-up. "Some of them will be priceless when the festival gets going and there are folks around here who are so desperate to hobnob with the stars they won't think twice about helping themselves to your invite."

"I'm really looking forward to sipping cocktails at a party in a jewelry store filled with cases of stuff I can't afford," grumbled Pia. "We definitely need to do a story in advance about how all these high-end retailers are offering their stores for swank parties in return for the publicity. Put that idea on the list, will you?"

James smiled pityingly. "Publicity is what the festival is all about. Selling stars, selling movies, selling the stuff that goes with them. The good news is that every once in a while a great movie gets thrown into the mix. Many readers are obsessed with finding out who is in town and where they can catch a glimpse of the big-name stars. But a lot of other people look forward to the festival because it's a chance to watch movies morning, noon, and night. I have friends who take a week off to see as many as they can."

"Well, let's try to give everybody a taste of what they want," Pia said, settling in to look over the long list of movies the paper's senior film critic planned to review.

It was just after six o'clock when she left the newsroom and walked into a wall of heat outside. Weather reports had been warning that the city was in for some hot days and for once the forecasters got it right. The heat and humidity were oppressive. To make matters worse, the absence of anything remotely resembling a breeze meant heavy smog generated by cars, power plants, and industry on both sides of the Canadian–American border hung in the air. Where there should have been a clear, sparkling horizon out over Lake Ontario, there was a malevolent yellow haze that shrouded the islands just offshore in an Impressionistic fog.

Pia wasn't in her car long enough for the air conditioning to really make a difference, but she did hear the minister of energy on the radio saying that the widespread use of air conditioners had pushed demand for electricity to record highs. The provincial power system, he warned, was stretched to the limit and rotating blackouts would be necessary if consumers didn't cut back on electricity use.

By the time she unlocked the door to the house she felt hot, tired, grumpy, and contrary. She stripped off her work clothes, walked over to the thermostat, and cranked down the temperature, smiling defiantly as she heard the air conditioning system kick in. The house was cooler than the outside air temperature, but that wasn't saying much. The heat was so oppressive that Winston hadn't bothered to eat his breakfast. She didn't add anything to his dish, and for once he didn't bother asking. Instead, he sprawled on the floor near one of the vents now pumping cool air into the house. Pia pulled on a long T-shirt, went to the kitchen, and pulled out vanilla ice cream for dinner. Some days, you just took your comfort where you could find it, she thought as she scooped three huge spoonfuls into a bowl.

It was late evening when she finally stopped working on *Too Young to Die*. Events earlier in the day nagged at her, making progress difficult. If Stark, reptile though he was, spent the hour immediately after the reception with a hooker, then he could not have been in the attic going after his wife with a box cutter, because she was killed in that hour right after the party. But had he really spent time with a hooker? There was no way around it. She needed to find the girl.

Pia tapped into the *Gazette*'s photography data bank on her computer, found several pictures of Stark in the company of his wife, and printed them. Then she threw on some clothes and went out to her car.

Torontonians and tourists were out in force despite the hour as she drove along the strip of Bloor Street that was home to some of the country's most expensive shopping. Designer labels, six-dollar coffees, and exquisitely coiffed sales clerks were what it was all about in this part of the city. The streetscape got shabbier and shabbier after she turned south on Sherbourne, leaving behind the glittering jewelry stores and minimalist chic of the high-end boutiques. On one side, she passed a cluster of massive apartment towers glowing in the night sky. Older reporters had regaled Pia with stories of how the complex once was the hip place to live and party back in the 1960s and early 1970s when the development was hailed as the cutting edge of urban design. These days, new immigrants and the city's poor occupied most of the apartments, struggling to the pay the rent and to keep their children out of local gangs. Further down Sherbourne, the green space that was Allan Gardens opened up on the other side of the street. The city-operated greenhouse on the far side of the park gleamed like a giant crystal in the night. Inside, tropical plants thrived. Outside, the city's homeless and hopeless prowled through the surrounding park, seeking a bench to sleep on or a quiet corner where they could administer a fix. The next morning city workers cleaning the park would find used needles and discarded condoms mingled with the other detritus of wasted lives.

The corner of Dundas and Sherbourne, where Stark had shopped for the girl, was within walking distance of Bloor's unapologetic opulence. But it might as well have been on another planet. A church sat on one corner of the intersection. The others were home to a gritty accumulation of apartment blocks, shabby fast-food joints, and anonymous doorways adorned with signs offering rooms for rent. The real business took place on the sidewalk where young girls, wearing as little as possible, stood either chatting in groups or standing apart, trying to catch the eye of each passing driver. Pia slowed her car down to a crawl, ignoring the scowls and occasional curses directed her way. She pulled into a parking spot, got out, and approached a heavy-set white woman who had staked out space just north of the intersection. The woman wore a wig made of blond hair that fell down below her buttocks and a tight, ultra-short black dress. Pia noted with relief that she didn't look particularly hostile.

"I'm looking for a girl called Joline – could you send me her way?" Pia asked, doing her best to hide her surprise now that she could see the woman up close. Her face, under heavy layers of makeup, was that of a fifty-year-old. And what at first glance appeared to be the elbow-length lace sleeves of her black dress were in fact dense tattoos of intertwined serpents.

"Why do you want a girl when you can have a woman, darlin'?"

"Sorry, I'm not shopping. I just need to talk to Joline." The older woman shrugged and pointed across the street to a tall, mocha-colored girl in a band of stretchy red material that barely qualified as a skirt. The red set off the girl's smooth brown skin, while the clinging material emphasized a voluptuous, round bottom that she wiggled suggestively as she strolled back and forth on the sidewalk. She wore a black string-bikini top that revealed more of her bouncing breasts than it covered and black stiletto sandals. Pia took it all in as she crossed the street.

"Are you Joline?"

"Who's asking?"

"I'm a reporter and my name is Pia Keyne. If you are Joline, I'd like to buy you a coffee."

The girl looked at her watch, pointedly. "Look, lady, my time is worth more than the price of a cup of coffee. You want to talk, you pay. That's the way it works out here."

"Okay, okay. I'll pay. But first you have to tell me if you know this guy," Pia said, pulling one of Stark's photos out of her bag.

"Yeah, I know him. He your husband or something?" Joline said, sounding more cautious than before.

"God, no. Look, I've got fifty dollars here if you have time to tell me how you know him." Joline took a moment to consider, then nodded in agreement. She walked with Pia over to the car and got in, oblivious to the hoots and hollers of the other women who had been watching their conversation with interest.

"Okay, Pia the reporter," Joline said as the car pulled into the line of traffic, "we need to make this fast. It's hot out and that's good for business. I'm passing up real money while I'm gabbing with you for a lousy fifty bucks."

Pia drove for a block or two and then parked in front of a forlorn-looking coffee shop. Eight stools were lined up in front of a counter with a cracked surface. Four booths lined the walls. Pia was relieved to find the air conditioning working and only two other customers in the place, both of them old men huddled at the counter over cups of coffee. One had a plastic bag stuffed with clothes at his feet. The other wore mismatched running shoes, one black, one red. They were either homeless or too poor for air-conditioned apartments.

"Evening, ladies. What can I do for you tonight?" The question, delivered in a weary voice, came from a middle-aged man sitting on a stool behind the cash register at the entrance. His glance slid over Pia. It lingered much longer on Joline as she sashayed over to the first booth.

"Two coffees," Pia ordered on her way past him.

"No, I want a chocolate milkshake," Joline said over her shoulder. When she got to the booth she made a show of pulling down her tiny skirt before sliding in.

Pia sat down on the other side of the table and studied her companion. Under the dim street lighting, it had been impossible to gauge Joline's age. But here, under the harsh glare of fluorescent bulbs, the skin on her arms gleamed with the silken sheen of youth. Her hair, long, black, and straight, fell like curtains on either side of a pert round face dominated by a rosebud mouth and the rounded cheeks of innocent youth.

"So you're going to pay, right? I just want to be clear."

Pia nodded.

"Okay then, what do you want to know about Paulie?"

"Paulie? Does that mean you know him well?"

"I'd sure like to. The dude's loaded. I did him twice in a row not so long ago – in fact it was just before I got busted this last time. Fucking cops. Anyway, the first time it was a blow job in his car. A sports car. It was kind of small in the front, but we managed, though it took him forever to come because he was so high. I remember him because he came back the very next night in a mood to really celebrate. Said he wanted a party because he was a man newly freed from his wife."

"So you had a party with him? "

"Yeah, me and Starlet did. She's a white girl. He said he wanted chocolate and vanilla pussy at the same time so we went to one of the rooms around here. I remember the night real well because he was a return customer and I like that, and because he had lots and lots of coke and we got to do as much as we wanted during the party."

They stopped talking for a moment to take delivery of the milkshake and coffee. The server, the same guy who had greeted them when they came in, took his time, staring hotly at Joline's breasts in their minuscule wrapping.

"Fuck off, man," she said mildly, glancing up at him. "Come up with the cash and you can have whatever you want. In the meantime, just leave the shake." His face turned red and he scuttled off. Pia watched Joline take long sips through a straw for a minute or two.

"So the first night, what time did he come by?"

"I don't think it was too late. I'd just got out on the street so it was probably around eight. It was a bit early for most customers, but like I said, he was pretty high and that makes guys less cautious."

"Did he say anything about his wife that night?"

"Nah, he was just talking dirty to me and paying me to suck him off. It was pretty much business as usual." They sat in silence for a few more minutes until Joline reached the end of her milkshake. She continued to draw on the straw, producing a loud gurgling sound as she tried retrieve every last drop. It was annoying, childish behavior at odds with the harshness of her words. And it got to Pia.

"Joline, how old are you?" she asked abruptly.

"Eighteen, of course," the girl said warily. "Hey, you aren't a cop are you?"

"No, no. Listen, like I said, I'm a reporter at the *Gazette*. I'm working on a book and your Paulie is one of the people I'm writing about. Here's your money. And here's my card with my phone numbers. If you want to get out of this business you're in, give me a call because I know some people who can help you." The words were no sooner out of Pia's mouth than anger replaced the wariness in Joline's dark eyes.

"Fucking great. So you're a social worker pretending to be a reporter writing a book. Just what I don't need. Lady, I don't really know who you are or what you want from me but I do know I don't want you messing around in my life. Let me guess. You think maybe I should go back to my family, don't you?

"Well, my family is why I'm here in the first place. My father, may he die a long, painful, horrible death, liked young girls even if they were his daughters. My sister and I were both about ten when he started with us. 'Special training' he called it. My mother didn't know anything about it or at least she pretended she didn't know. My older sister, she escaped for good. Hung herself in the garage one night. Naked. So he'd find her like that when he went out to work in the morning. Me, I just left. I've been using that special training he gave me for a few years now. It's come in real handy. And that's all I got to say to you because your time is up. The truth is, you don't get much for fifty bucks any more. You want me to stay and talk, put some more money on the table."

The child in Joline's face had disappeared. In its place was an angry, hard mask. She slid out of the booth, adjusted her skirt, and looked speculatively at the man behind the cash register. He'd been watching her as she got up but his gaze fell to the counter under her bold stare. Joline snorted in disgust and walked out.

Pia took her time paying the bill and driving home. So Stark had an alibi of sorts for the night his wife was murdered. But he could have hired somebody else to kill May and that meant he had to remain on the list of suspects.

The inside of Pia's house was cool, comfortable, and a welcome change from the heavy night air. She ran a bath and soaked in it, but still couldn't relax. The coffee this late at night had been a big mistake. But that wasn't the only reason for her agitation. Pia realized she was upset because the girl's fate reminded her of what could have been. Patrice had chosen to stay with Max, but she had sent Pia to Margaret. I was betrayed but not completely abandoned, she thought ruefully. Joline and her sister hadn't been so lucky.

It was well after midnight before she finally drifted into an uneasy sleep. Pia woke abruptly some time later, feeling uncomfortably hot. But when she reached up to turn on the lamp beside her bed, nothing happened. Then she noticed that the house was in complete darkness. Usually the far corner of her room was indirectly illuminated by a street light but tonight even that was absent. There would be hell to pay, Pia thought, if the province was in the midst of another major power failure. When the lights went out and stayed out for three days during one sweltering summer a few years earlier, voters had shown their displeasure during the subsequent election by defeating the government.

Pia wondered how long the power had been off and what Winston was up to. Even on the warmest summer nights, he liked to curl up at the foot of her bed, but he wasn't there now. A moment later, she heard a sound from downstairs. What was he doing, she wondered? Wide awake once again, Pia decided she needed a drink of juice. It would also be a chance to get the flashlight she kept in the kitchen drawer. She pulled on her robe and made her way gingerly through the hallway and down the stairs, marveling at how dark the house was when light from the city wasn't stealing in.

She was at the bottom of the staircase when she heard the sound of movement coming from behind the half-closed door of her study. The damn cat was in there again playing with something he wasn't supposed to touch. It could be pens she'd forgotten on her desk. Or one of the crumpled up pieces of paper she'd thrown around the room for him to chase. Or the plant in front of the garden doors that he delighted in torturing.

Pia pushed open the door and stepped in just as she heard Winton's meow from the top of the stairs. She had enough time to feel gut-twisting fear. She felt the cat run past her into the study and heard someone stumbling over him in the dark. Then there was the sickening thud of something, probably a boot, connecting viciously with soft flesh. Winston's agonized shriek tore through the air.

"No, no," Pia screamed. But before she could say another word she sensed the intruder's nearness, heard another human being breathing. Something hard and unyielding connected with the back of her head. There was pain. And a whole new kind of darkness.

Chapter Twelve

PIA'S EYES FLEW OPEN and the fear returned. He had hit her. Was he still here? Would he hit her again? She stayed frozen in place on the floor, listening, willing herself to keep her eyes open. The house was silent but Pia suddenly realized she could hear the air conditioner pumping cool air. And the street lights were working: she could see shadows in her study and shards of watery light on the hardwood floor. The electricity must be back on. As her panic subsided, she heard an odd mewling sound coming from the other side of the room. It was Winston and he didn't sound good. She pushed herself up into a sitting position and then wished she had taken her time, as dizziness and nausea engulfed her. While waiting for the feeling to pass, she noticed a dark shadow on the floor where her head had been. Raising one hand, she explored the back of her skull, starting in surprise when her fingers came back bloody. Okay, she thought, no more dithering. First she needed to check Winston. Then she needed to call the police. Before she could get to her feet, however, she saw the cat coming toward her. He staggered, meowed pathetically, and then collapsed beside her on the floor, breathing rapidly. When Pia reached out and gently touched his side, his meow turned to a pained growl.

"Okay, buddy, I'm sorry," Pia muttered. "Just stay where you are and I'll get you looked after." Slowly she pulled herself to her feet, leaving the cat where he'd collapsed on the floor, and moved cautiously to her desk, where she picked up the phone and dialed 911.

The house soon exploded with activity. Firefighters, as usual the first to respond to an emergency call, arrived, sirens blaring, in one of their huge pumper trucks. A police car pulled up minutes later, followed by an ambulance. Pia opened the door and the emergency workers poured in.

"You're going to need some stitches, love, and you might have a concussion," the medic said, after ordering Pia into a kitchen chair and parting her hair to look at the gash on the back of her head. He was a big, black man with gentle hands and reassuring eyes. "We'll take you in and they'll fix you up. Do you hurt anywhere else?"

There were more questions of a medical nature and then a young police officer came to the kitchen door and summoned Pia back to the study.

"Does that belong to you?" he asked, pointing to a chunk of purple amethyst. The rock, about twice the size of a softball, usually sat on Pia's bookshelf gathering dust, but now it was lying on the floor near where she had been struck. No wonder her head hurt, she thought dully, as she acknowledged ownership.

"He must have grabbed it when he heard you coming and then he came at you from behind," the officer said. "There are some marks on these garden doors around the latch, which makes me think he came and went the same way. We'll check with the neighbors in case they saw something, though if this happened when the power was out as you say, I'm not sure what we'll get." Pia nodded and followed the officer over to her desk.

"It looks like he was about to walk off with your computer when he got interrupted," he said. The cords to her laptop were disconnected and the screen was folded down. It had been pushed to one side of her desk, displacing two piles of paper that were now scattered all over the floor. "I know you need to get to the hospital, but can you tell if anything is missing?" the officer asked.

"There was nothing much worth stealing in here except the laptop and some CDs," she said. "And it doesn't look like he had time for either of them." Her voice trailed off as she heard Aunt Margaret and Sergei arrive. She'd called them after dialing 911.

"Oh, my poor darling," Margaret cried when Pia came into the kitchen with her bandaged head. She allowed herself to be drawn into her aunt's arms. "What did he do to you?"

"I need stitches and they think I might have a concussion. I'm supposed to be going to the hospital right now. But, Auntie, Winston got hurt," Pia said, pulling back from Margaret's embrace. "I think the guy kicked him. Could you take him to the emergency vet?"

"I'll do no such thing. I'm going with you. Sergei will take him," Margaret said, glancing at the stern-looking man at her side. "Won't you, dear?"

"I will, of course I will," Sergei said impatiently. "But then my job will be to put some real security in this place. Pia, you could have been hurt a lot worse. People like you think they are safe in this city but nobody is safe if they don't take the right precautions."

"That's enough, Sergei. The poor girl just needs to know Winston will be looked after. You can deal with the security later," Margaret cut in. Moments later, Pia was in the ambulance, her aunt and the medic at her side.

The emergency physician stitched shut the cut on Pia's head and admitted her overnight for observation. Margaret was there to pick her up when she was released from hospital the following afternoon.

"I've had your cleaning lady come in because they were looking for fingerprints in your study and left the place a mess," Margaret said. "It's all cleaned up now and Sergei has gone to get Winston. The vet said he has bruised ribs but should be okay as long as nobody kicks him again. In the meantime, he's going to be on painkillers for the next few days. Apparently the medication might put him off his food, though I find that hard to imagine.

"Oh, and your friend, that fellow Jack, called this morning. He'd been planning to invite you out somewhere. I told him what had happened and he was horrified. He said he would get in touch in a day or so. After we spoke, he sent some beautiful flowers to the house with a get well card."

They arrived home to find the cat napping on the living room sofa and Sergei making plans to turn the house into the security equivalent of Fort Knox.

"You might as well have put up a welcome sign for all the bad guys," he told Pia, who sat in the kitchen while Margaret made coffee "I'm going to fix this place up good. But maybe you want to get a dog? Or how about a gun? Maybe that's not a good idea. You'd probably shoot the fat bastard – I mean the cat – or yourself or Margaret. Or me. Okay, no gun."

Men with tools came, worked, and went for the remainder of the day under Sergei's supervision. "We can't finish everything until tomorrow morning so Margaret and I will stay the night just to be on the safe side," he announced as he fitted an extra lock on the garden doors. "Once this system is running, nobody will get in here."

Pia didn't have the energy to protest and, really, she didn't want to. Her head ached, she had an assortment of dark bruises all along one side of her body, she'd been forced to book off work, and her cat was on painkillers. The truth was she owed Sergei. She never, ever wanted to find an intruder in her house again.

They all went to bed early. By noon the next day, Sergei's work was finished and Margaret, noting that the color had returned to Pia's face, ceased fussing. Pia sighed with relief when they left for home. Winston was acting more like his old self, begging for some of the tuna fish sandwich she'd prepared for lunch, but he still was moving stiffly. She decided to have a rest and then do some writing. The cleaners had restored order in her study and even her computer was back in place. Pia worked for the rest of the afternoon, had an early night, and settled back at her desk the next morning.

It was early afternoon when she finally looked out the window again. Dark, ominous clouds filled the sky and the high winds of the morning had disappeared. Nature was on pause, waiting for the sky to explode and empty its contents.

The sound of the doorbell startled her. Following Sergei's orders to the letter, she looked out the side window first to determine who was on her doorstep, and to her astonishment she saw Martin Geneve with a huge bouquet of flowers in his arms. It took two tries, but Pia eventually punched in the proper code to disarm her new alarm system and opened the door.

"I've brought some things that might bring comfort to a victim of crime."

"How on earth did you find out?" she said, standing back to let him in.

"I ran into your boss at an event last night and he told me the whole story. He also told me you were off work and at home healing so I thought I'd bring along some treats to help the process along," Martin said, handing Pia a shopping bag and following her into the kitchen. Pia opened the bag and drew out a box of handmade chocolate truffles, a carton of pralines and cream ice cream, a bottle of champagne, and two books. She thanked him and, after putting the ice cream and champagne in the refrigerator, picked up one of the books.

"I bought that one because it's new and I thought maybe you still wouldn't have it," Martin said as Pia examined the new short story collection by Alice Munro. "The other one is a mystery, a first novel by some British guy. Thought maybe you would like to check out the competition." He searched Pia's face for a long moment and then he reached out a hand to gently touch her cheek. "You're going to be okay?"

She nodded mutely, mesmerized by his eyes, acutely conscious of the hand that moved to push a tendril of hair back from her face. She realized she wanted him to hold her, to make her feel safe. On impulse, Pia reached one hand up behind his head and gently pulled him down so that his mouth touched hers. Outside, as if on cue, a blast of thunder rolled across the city and rain began to fall, hard and relentless. Inside the house, Martin pulled Pia close, slid one of his hands down her back to mold her body against his. When she groaned with the pleasure of feeling his hard, warm body, he suddenly released her, looking concerned.

"I didn't hurt you, did I?"

"No, you are doing great things for my recovery," Pia said in a low, warm voice. "Come with me." She took his hand and led him up the stairs, willing herself to think of nothing but the moment. In her bedroom, she walked to the row of windows along one wall and opened each of them so that sound of heavy rain and waves of thunder pulsed through the room.

"I love summer storms," she murmured as he came up behind her and began to unzip the cotton shift she was wearing.

"I love touching you," he said as the dress slipped to the floor, leaving Pia clad only in a tiny pair of pale blue lace panties. Still standing behind her, his hands explored silken skin and curves. He buried his face in her thick, sweet-smelling hair and dragged his lips along the side of her neck. One hand came to rest on a full, firm breast while the other reached down inside her panties. When Pia began rubbing herself against him, he gasped and explored further until his fingers encountered her hot, wet core. There they lingered until Pia twisted to face him, pulling first at his tie and then trying to undo the buttons of his shirt with shaking fingers. Impatient, he took over, rapidly shedding his clothes and then reaching for her. They fell onto the bed and her legs immediately reached up and around him, opening herself to him.

For a moment Martin lifted his lips from hers and looked into Pia's eyes. She returned his gaze with an unwavering one of her own.

"Please, please, I want this now. I need this now. Please," she heard herself gasp. He made a sound somewhere between a groan and growl and drove himself into her, hard and fierce and demanding. She matched every move, begging for more, begging him not to stop until the last vestiges of her control vanished in spasms of pleasure. His heavy, irregular breathing turned into ragged gasps and his body shuddered as he emptied into her.

When she opened her eyes a few minutes later, the rain outside had subsided into a gentle drizzle and Martin was by her side, looking at her with a bemused smile. "Now this is the way a guy should spend every rainy afternoon – comforting grateful invalids," he said softly.

"It was the ice cream that did it. A guy who brings me ice cream always gets lucky."

"Now that's something to remember. Any particular flavor?"

"I'm partial to vanilla, but butterscotch or pralines and cream will also do the trick," Pia heard herself say. She willed herself to close her eyes, to relax, to not think about what had just happened. An hour or so later, he gently shook her awake.

"Pia, I'm sorry but I have to go. I have out-of-town business to attend to and I'm scheduled to fly out in a couple of hours. I'm booked up this weekend but will you save next Saturday evening for me?" He smiled, pleased when she nodded her assent.

The heat and humidity were gone and instead, a gentle breeze played with the curtains of the bedroom window. Pia watched as Martin pulled on his clothes. She had no idea what she was doing or why she might be doing it. So she admired his long, muscular legs, wide shoulders, and easy grace.

"Do I pass muster?" he asked as he finished with his tie.

"You'll do," she said, smiling as he leaned over to kiss her.

Pia lay back in bed, listening as he left the house. After rousing herself to go downstairs to lock the front door, she wandered into the kitchen and caught a glimpse of her reflection in the glass doors to the garden. What she saw was a disheveled, copper-haired woman who looked as if she'd just spent the afternoon in bed with a man. At some point she was going to have to have to examine her motives.

"The sex was great and no, I'm not sorry I did it," she said aloud to Winston, who was staring at her intently from his perch on one of the kitchen chairs. She walked over and gathered the cat in her arms. "At least I think I'm not sorry."

When Jasmine called later to see how Pia was feeling and to propose seeing a movie, she begged off, saying she was tired and had to get to bed early. That was all true, but Pia also found herself thinking about the feel of Martin's hands on her body. Maybe getting hit in the head with a rock damaged my common sense, she berated herself.

The longest post-coital bliss of her life lasted through the weekend. It came to an abrupt end Monday morning, however, when Pia saw the front page of the *Gazette*. At first, she thought it was just another heinous crime. "One boy dead, second badly injured in attack," the headline screamed.

Then she started reading the story. Two twelve-year-olds who were staying at the Highway Inn in the city's east end had for some reason gone out into a nearby park after dark. It was a place that most of the neighborhood tended to avoid because it had a reputation as a haven for gang members and drug dealers. The pair had been in one of the darkest, most isolated areas of the park when they were set upon by a man with a baseball bat. Both boys were on the ground and the man was brutally beating them when a young man out walking his pit bull came by. When he realized what was happening, he started shouting and running toward the scene. The attacker fled into the night when he saw man and dog approaching. One of the boys was pronounced dead upon arrival in hospital. The second was in a coma. The children, both Somali, were staying with their families at the Highway Inn while their refugee claims were being examined. The dead boy's name was Mohammed Farah. The second child, Tariq Samatar, suffered major head injuries and was fighting for his life in the Hospital for Sick Children.

Pia's hands shook as she finished reading the story. Her breaths came in shallow gasps. Sick with dread she ran from the kitchen, down the hall into her study and began shuffling through the papers that Margaret and the cleaners had picked up from the floor. Just as she'd feared, the printout of her interview with the boys in the pizza parlor was gone. The document contained their names, addresses, phone numbers, and a full account of the burka-clad visitor and everything else they saw the night of Wilson Scott's murder. She took a few deep breaths, tried to calm down, and searched again, to no avail.

So this was what came of the *Gazette* story about her book project, Pia thought. Her late-night visitor had come hoping

to discover what she knew and he'd found what he was looking for. She had signed death warrants for those two innocent
children. For the second time in less than a week, Pia felt sick
with pain and fear. Only this time it was mixed with searing
guilt, something that could not be cured with a few stitches at
the local hospital.

Chapter Thirteen

IT WAS JUST AFTER EIGHT in the morning when Pia arrived at the Highway Inn to find its crumbling parking lot crowded with people. Police officers and gawkers were everywhere along with little clusters of anxious-looking people she assumed were hotel residents. Young children played everywhere, though never far from their parents' anxious eyes. Pia walked down toward the park, drawn by the huddle of cruisers and unmarked police cars lining the road.

As she approached, she noticed that the park wound around and behind an elementary school. She left the sidewalk and followed a gravel path that took her past an area enclosed by a low, black fence. The space inside was empty and forlorn. The school board had recently ordered the destruction of all older playground equipment following publication of a report suggesting the outdated structures presented a danger to children.

There would be no new equipment until somebody somewhere found the money to replace it. In the meantime, vacant playgrounds throughout the city sat in silent reproach.

The park was L-shaped, and as soon as Pia followed the path around a sharp turn she saw a stand of trees and still more police cars in the distance. Wide yellow tape of the sort made famous on television cop shows cordoned off a large area.

She spotted Nancy Morton almost immediately. The detective looked unusually drawn, pale, and discouraged in the morning light. Morton was pacing back and forth near the tape on one edge of the secured area and only stopped when she felt Pia's light touch on her arm. She turned and ran a hand tiredly through her cropped hair.

"There will be a statement in an hour or two, you'll have to wait for that," she said, her voice gruff with tension and anger. "Not that there will be much to say. Some bastard puts on a hood, lurks in the trees, and then tries to beat two little boys to death with a baseball bat. How can anyone explain that?"

"Nancy, I might have some information about why this happened. I need to talk to you," Pia said urgently, aware that the rest of the journalistic pack had caught sight of them talking and was beginning to stampede over, hungry for any tidbit to feed their hourly newscasts. Morton glanced at her sharply but then noticed the crowd.

"I'm just here to provide backup – I'm not in charge so I should be free in a couple of hours. I'll give you a call later," she said before turning and stalking away. Her departure provoked outraged cries from the reporters who had just arrived, microphones outstretched. Pia left them and made her way back to the motel to look up her old buddy Reg Wizinski. He was where she had last seen him, behind the counter in the motel reception, puffing on a cigarette and sweating despite the cool, pleasant morning.

"Oh, the big shot reporter is here again, eh?" he grunted as soon as he saw Pia. "I already talked to somebody from the *Gazette* – the crime reporter or something."

"Humor me, please," she said, smiling grimly. "You've seen a lot of cops around here lately I guess, what with Wilson Scott and now this."

"You got that right. But it would be better if the doughnut-eaters spent more time around here during the quiet times. Then maybe those kids would have been safe."

"Why do you say that?"

"Fuckin' skinheads. I'm not crazy about the government paying to put all these illegals up in a motel while honest, hard-working Canadians have to hold down jobs to pay their rent. But these skinhead creeps go too far, scaring people and killing kids with baseball bats."

"So there have been other problems?"

"I just know what I see. Take a look outside on the back wall. You'll get the idea. We been repainting it every couple of weeks now but every time we do, they're at it again." Motioning for Pia to follow him, Wizinski led her around the building that housed the reception to the wall on one end of the motel. The white stucco was stained with red and black hate: "Stinky ragheads go home." "Niggas must die." "Bloodsuckers live here." Pia pulled a notebook from her purse and scribbled it all down.

"This started about three months ago and it just keeps happening no matter how many times we clean it up," Wizinski offered.

"Has anybody been attacked before now?" Pia asked, her eyes fixed on the wall.

"I dunno. I haven't heard anything, but then I don't understand much from these guys in the motel because most of 'em, their English is terrible. You should ask 'em yourself," he said, gesturing toward the crowd in the barren parking lot. "The one thing I can tell you is that a guy called here around ten-thirty last night and asked for the room that one of the kids, Tariq, lived in with his parents. I'm thinking that whoever called must have said something that convinced those kids to go to the park. I told the cops all this last night. Maybe they can figure out where the call came from."

"Reg, if it wasn't skinheads was there any other reason these two kids might have been attacked?"

He paused, stared hard at Pia for a moment, and then reached up to pull the package of cigarettes from the sleeve of his T-shirt. Taking his time, he removed one, lit it and drew in deeply.

"I been thinking about that too. I caught these same two little buggers peeking into rooms one night a few weeks ago. Their parents work at night, you know, so they kinda run wild after dark. I saw what they were up to and then had to chase them down across the parking lot. This attracted some attention because I gave them royal hell when I got my hands on them. Maybe somebody else in the place figured out what they were up to. I mean, who knows what those kids seen going on in these rooms. Maybe their little game pissed off somebody so much that he decided to teach 'em a lesson."

Pia thanked him, walked over to three women standing in the parking lot and introduced herself. All three wore long, flowing tunics and light scarves that covered their heads. Only one spoke English well enough to carry on a conversation. She said her name was Ana and she agreed to translate when Pia asked for her help.

"We don't want trouble," she offered even before Pia could ask a question. It turned out that Ana, a tall, statuesque woman with an orange scarf tightly wound around her face and neck to hide her hair, had spent years in a Kenyan refugee camp after leaving Somalia. She said she picked up some English while working with a group of teachers sent in by a British aid organization.

"We all are here in Canada because we want more peaceful lives, no more killing and violence and death. But what do we find? Killing and violence and death," she lamented.

"Has there been other trouble?" Pia asked.

Ana looked at her suspiciously and turned to the other women. A brief conversation ensued.

"We don't want trouble so we don't say anything," Ana said

when she turned back to Pia. "But now, now we have no choice. We mothers have to speak out. There are some gangs here and they chase our children home from school. They call us names, they tell us to go back where we came from. Last week there was a fight in the park – the same park where this poor child was killed. Some white boys fighting with some of our boys. So we had a meeting and agreed that nobody would go to the park alone." Ana's eyes filled with tears. "This country was supposed to be a safe place for us finally. To come here just to have our children die like this, so far from home, it makes all our suffering for nothing."

"Ana, if there were these problems, why didn't anyone go to the police?"

"Oh no, we can't go to the police. We have to stay out of trouble here because we are waiting for the government to decide about us. Are we refugees or not? That is what the government will decide some day. If the police say there is trouble to do with us, nobody will want us to stay. Do you understand? Nobody wants more troublemakers in this country."

Pia pressed for more details. On at least three separate occasions in recent weeks, the women told her, Somali boys had been walking home when they were surrounded by aggressors. "They were white kids, yes. Our boys said these bad ones are known to everybody at school and that they are always looking for trouble," Ana said. "Lucky for our boys, they are used to fighting and can run fast so they can get away from these bad kids. The younger ones, like Tariq and Mohammed, are supposed to stay around the motel where everybody can keep them safe. But they went to the park alone, and look what happened. Just look what happened." Ana's voice was low and anguished and now tears ran down her cheeks. "I have two little boys. They are six and eight. I'm so afraid for them, I'm so afraid."

"Ana, Tariq and Mohammed used to peek in the windows around here at night just for fun. Do you think somebody might have been mad at them for that?"

Ana paused and again consulted the other two women. "Nobody here would kill children for that because nobody has secrets here in this place with thin walls and small rooms," she replied. "Everybody can see what everybody is doing and hear what everybody is saying. Sometimes strangers check in here for a couple of hours. Wicked women with wicked men. We turn our children's eyes away from this and pray that we will soon be free to remove them away from a place where such sins take place. But none of us has ever talked to these wicked people. How would they know our children?"

Pia asked after Mohammed's family but was told the dead boy's relatives were all still down at the police station. Tariq, to the best of Ana's knowledge, was in the hospital in intensive care.

Pia felt nauseous with guilt as she drove to work. Maybe the attack had been racially motivated. But if Reg Wizinski was right about the phone call to Tariq's room, the two boys had been specifically targeted. Whoever took Pia's notes would have had all he needed to find those children – names, addresses, phone numbers. She'd made it easy for him, had failed to protect her sources. The boys had paid for her failure.

It was mid-morning when Pia walked into the *Gazette* newsroom, and the place was showing signs of life. Editors responsible for sorting out the day's news agenda were briskly preparing the lists of stories they would assign to reporters. These same editors would present and defend their choices to colleagues and the editor-in-chief at the morning news meeting. Some reporters were just strolling in. A few headed out the door with their assignments. Others drank coffee and either gossiped with colleagues or read the paper. Pia knew from experience that this relaxed mood would vanish by late afternoon. By about four o'clock, reporters who hadn't heard from their sources would be frantically seeking alternatives. Those who had collected all the information they needed would be focused on their computer keyboards, oblivious to the racket around them. Editors haunted by the prospect of blank spaces on broadsheet pages would hover anxiously, monitoring what stories they'd actually have in hand by the end of the day. Everybody worth their salary would be trying to figure out what the competition might have and how best to remain one step ahead.

James Nowt was sitting at his desk but he rose to his feet the moment he saw Pia. "How are you feeling? Should you be back at work so soon?" he said, taking in her paleness and attributing it to her injury. "You look like hell."

"I've been better," Pia said, realizing that everybody would want an account of the break-in on her first day back. She gave

James the short version of events at her house and then moved on to the day's business, praying that the work would keep her distracted while she waited for Nancy Morton's call.

James brought her up to date on the arts and entertainment section. Then he brightened considerably. "And then of course you've heard about the mushroom mess?"

Encouraged by her incredulous look, he told her that the newspaper's food editor had laid out a story on picking and preparing wild mushrooms for the Monday food section. "Unfortunately, there was a problem with the page last night and at the last minute they needed an extra picture to fill some space after dropping an ad. So one of the part-time editors – someone who obviously knows nothing about fungi – went into the photo library and pulled a picture of a mushroom growing next to a tree and plopped it into the paper. Well, guess what? The phones have been ringing off the hook all morning. Mushroom experts from far and wide are calling to tell us we've got a picture of a deadly poisonous mushroom on the food page."

Pia groaned, momentarily diverted. "Surely there hasn't been enough time for some idiot to pick the mushroom, eat it and die?"

"Thank God, no. But the powers that be around here are rushing to put out radio advertisements warning readers. And there's a big correction in the works. The publisher, as you might imagine, is furious. The good news is he's not mad at us this time. I'm betting Mushroomgate will make him forget that kerfuffle over *Little Shop of Horrors*."

"James, it's bad policy to gloat," Pia said, thinking she would have to find the food editor later in the day to commiserate. John O'Ryan loved food, was a great cook, and was certainly an improvement over many of his eccentric predecessors. Margaret once told Pia that during her early days at the newspaper the food section had been ruled by an elderly woman who hated garlic. Her distaste for it was such that she automatically eliminated it from every recipe she ever published, thus earning herself a place in *Gazette* lore as doyenne of the "bland era."

Poor O'Ryan had no such aversions and much more integrity. He'd published thousands of recipes and food tips without incident. But the way newspapers worked, Pia knew, he'd be best remembered for the incident of the killer mushroom.

She spent the rest of the morning editing a feature on Hollywood divorces but found it difficult to concentrate. When the lunch hour finally arrived, the thought of food made her feel ill. She found the *Gazette*'s crime reporter and he told her there had been no change in Tariq's condition. The boy was still in a coma with major trauma to the head. If he ever did wake up, there were questions as to what he would remember about the attack and, more seriously, whether he would be capable of remembering anything ever again.

When Morton finally called late in the afternoon, they arranged to meet at a local pub after Pia finished work. The detective wore the same crumpled clothes and looked even wearier than she had in the morning.

"This better be good because I'm operating on two hours

sleep and that makes me mean," Morton said after two pints were delivered to their table.

"It isn't good, Nancy. I think those two kids were attacked because they talked to me. I met them a while ago and they told me they saw a man who arrived disguised in a burka in Wilson Scott's room the night he died. Okay, maybe it was bullshit, I haven't been able to confirm it one way or the other. But then there was this break-in at my house last week. At first it looked like a simple break and enter and that I interrupted the guy before he could take anything. But when I saw the story about the kids in this morning's paper, I had this bad feeling. I checked and it turns out the notes on my interview with the boys are missing. Their names, addresses, and phone numbers were all there."

"Whoa," said Morton, looking suddenly alert. "Start over and give me all the details."

Pia went over it all again while the detective took notes. "Nancy, I might have led the attacker to those kids," she concluded. "Somebody invades my home and steals information that leads them to my sources – two little boys. This must mean there's somebody out there who is worried about my digging around for more information on how May Gatway and Wilson Scott died. Somebody who maybe is the real murderer. The police should be pursuing this."

"I agree there might be something here but, Pia, I'm not the one who decides when closed cases need to be reopened. First of all, the baseball bat attack is not my baby. I was only called in as backup because they needed a female detective to deal with the Muslim women. Their husbands don't like them being alone with strange men for questioning, even if the strange men are cops. I'm going to tell the guys in charge about this, but I'm not sure how it will play out. The detective on today's case is chasing down the hate crime angle and I can't blame him. It turns out there was a lot of hate going on in that neighborhood."

"But you will push to get the Gatway and Scott investigations reopened?"

"Give me until tomorrow. Like I said, it's not just my call."

"There's one more thing."

"Why am I not surprised?" Morton sighed. "Okay, spill."

"I didn't show it to you before because the case seemed to solve itself. But now that we know somebody came to see Scott at the Highway Inn, maybe this matters. Take a look." Pia dug in her purse to retrieve a copy of the photo Stark gave her the first time they met.

Morton whistled softly as she took in the image of Wilson Scott with his hands all over the young man in a bar. She looked up. "I guess we should find out who the boytoy is and whether he owns a burka. Can I keep this for a while?"

"It's a copy, go ahead." They finished their beers and arranged to meet for lunch the next day. Pia felt exhausted when she finally got home and found a telephone message from Martin Geneve.

"Hi there. I'm in New York and just wanted to talk to you about Saturday night. I forgot that I'm committed to going to the Fine Arts Ball. It's a fundraiser and I have two tickets. Will you be my date?"

Why not? At least it would take her mind off what had happened to the boys. Pia left a message on Martin's cellphone accepting the invitation and then picked up Winston. But he wanted a playmate, not hugs. He leapt from her arms, chased his tail for a couple of turns, and then darted up the stairs. Pia gave up on him for company and instead went to her study, where she downloaded all the material she had related to the Gatway–Scott deaths onto a computer disk. Working methodically, she collected all printouts of her transcribed notes and then killed all the files on the computer. The disk and the documents went upstairs with her to the ensuite bathroom off her bedroom. Pia opened the cupboard door under the sink, took out a box of tampons, emptied it, and dropped the disk and folded notes into the bottom. The tampons fit neatly on top and the whole box went back into the cupboard.

Never let it be said, Pia thought grimly as the cupboard door slammed shut, that she didn't learn from her mistakes.

Chapter Fourteen

NANCY MORTON HAD LITTLE PATIENCE for overbearing, insecure men, but unfortunately they were as common as sewer rats in her line of work. The day had started badly – at just after two in the morning – when a call from the station summoned her to the Highway Inn to help interview the parents of Mohammed Farah and Tariq Samatar. It got worse when she found out the principal investigator on the case was Marcus Schmidt. Schmidt, who had at least ten years on her in age and experience, was so full of himself she sometimes prayed he would burst. Worse, he considered himself to be a real ladies' man. He'd spotted Morton when she was a young recruit on the force, and been attracted by her blond, outdoorsy look. He asked her out a number of times until she finally told him she preferred women's company and women's bodies. She wasn't hostile about it, it was just a fact designed to clear up any misunderstanding. But Schmidt took it as a personal affront, one he never got over. In the intervening years, she'd overheard him calling her the Toronto force's "token fucking lesbo," but early on she'd learned to pick her battles. You had to wait for your moment with guys like Schmidt, kick them hard in the balls and make sure they went down for good. Besides, she knew it drove him nuts every time she received another promotion. What he didn't know was that earning those promotions had cost her Rebecca. The erratic hours and emotional toll exacted by human carnage in all its forms did not discriminate when it came to wrecking straight or gay relationships. But she had earned her detective rank in record time. Schmidt had made a point of not congratulating her when she walked into her new section on the first day.

The fact of the matter was it would have suited them both if their paths never crossed. Unfortunately, Schmidt was still her senior, and now that she was a detective that meant she answered to him when they couldn't avoid working the same case.

After her conversation with Pia, Morton went to the station, where she found Schmidt in his office staring at his computer screen. He wasn't improving with age, she thought, observing with satisfaction how his heavy features seemed to be collapsing into jowls at the same time as his wispy hair receded.

"I need to talk to you," she said after knocking perfunctorily. Schmidt grunted permission for her to enter and then turned back to the screen even as she started speaking. "There's a lead we should look at related to the attack on the kids. It could also mean reopening the Gatway and Scott cases." Schmidt looked up at last so Morton outlined what Pia told her. "I think it's worth trying to follow up," she concluded. "I have a few ideas. We could – " She stopped because Schmidt had raised his hand. He was smiling but his eyes had narrowed to vicious slits.

"Let me get this straight, Detective Morton. Some reporter spins you a story about what these kids might have seen related to a case you closed some time ago. One of the kids is now dead and we don't know if the other will recover to talk about what he might have seen, which might be connected to a break-in at your reporter girlfriend's house, which might have led to the attack on these kids. Have I got it all right?"

Morton nodded, but an angry red flush began spreading across her cheeks. Schmidt took this in and continued.

"So you want us to set aside the leads that we have linking the attack on these two kids to local skinheads and instead pursue an angle that might help you correct errors you made when you closed an earlier case. That was your case, wasn't it? I seem to remember you basking in the glory when it all came together so neatly."

"I just think it is worth checking out," Morton said stubbornly, trying to control her fury. Of course he was going to make it personal. He couldn't resist.

"Well, I think this team has better things to do than trying to clean up your mistakes. In the meantime, why don't you go see the chief and tell him that you fucked up the investigation into the deaths of two prominent politicians and that you want to reopen the cases and try again. Actually, I'll pay to watch you deliver that news. Now if you don't have anything substantial to contribute to the murder we are currently trying to solve, I suggest you get out of my office. I have work to do."

What Morton wanted to do was to leap across his desk to strangle him. But she reminded herself it just wasn't worth it. Not trusting herself to say another word, she absorbed the pure antipathy on Schmidt's face, got up, and left the room. Fine with me, buddy, she thought. The feeling is mutual.

Back in her office, Morton filled out a form requesting all the evidence taken from Wilson Scott's motel room the night he died. Then she went home to get some sleep.

Pia's phone rang just before noon the next day. It was Morton suggesting they meet at a fish and chips joint near the *Gazette*. Pia arrived first, looking fresh and cool in a pale green, sleeveless linen dress, and chose a table by the window.

"How do you do it?" Morton asked, sliding into the other chair a few minutes later.

"Do what?"

"Look like you just stepped out of a fashion magazine when it's like a steam bath outside. I'm sweating like a pig and all I did was park the car and cross the street. It's hard to believe, I know, but I really did iron this blouse this morning," Morton said, tweaking her collar. "The day's only half gone and already I look like a dishrag."

"Actually I took a cab – I know, I know, I should be ashamed, it's only six blocks. But it's way, way too hot. If I'd walked, I'd look even worse than you do – and that's saying something."

Morton grimaced. "Well, at least I know now that you're not some sort of sweat-free freak." She paused, looking uncomfortable.

"Are they going to look into the connection between what happened to the kids and Gatway and Scott?"

Morton shook her head. "It's Schmidt's call because he's the lead investigator. He doesn't buy what you told me about the boys despite my best efforts to convince him it's worth checking."

Pia's groan was a mixture of disgust and disappointment, but before she could come up with something more articulate Morton leaned forward. "Look, Schmidt is an asshole. I think there might be something to what you say – in other words I'll make a few inquiries. Wait just a minute," Morton said when Pia tried to interrupt. "Before you say anything, you should know that I'm putting my career on the line if I do this. Schmidt will go berserk if he ever finds out. And the higher-ups frown on members of the force who start freelancing on other people's cases. So some discretion is going to be required. Is discretion in your bag of tricks?"

"Nancy, discretion is my business, at least up until it's time to put the story in the paper. Here's where I'm coming from. I've been asking questions about what happened to Gatway and Scott for a while now. So if you come up with something big, I don't want it shared with the competition. I'll give you what

I know about the kids and I want an exclusive if there's one to be had. I also reserve the right to use any and all material in a book."

"It's a deal. I just hope to hell the scoop isn't about a rogue detective getting her ass fired for conducting an unauthorized investigation," Morton said, the apprehension in her eyes giving away to appreciation as she contemplated the huge plate of fish and chips the waiter deposited in front of her. She took a few minutes to start her first meal of the day and then looked up at Pia.

"Okay, listen to this. Now that we know Wilson Scott might have had a visitor the night he died, I ordered up all the evidence seized from his room and took another look at everything this morning. I also reread the autopsy report. What struck me as interesting is that both the report and the empty bottle of Scotch taken from his room suggest that the drug that killed him was dissolved in the booze. Now doesn't it strike you as odd that a guy who sets out to kill himself takes the time to dissolve the pills that will kill him in a bottle of single malt? If it was me, I'd just swallow the pills and then wash it down with the good stuff so that my last taste of life is a good one."

"Maybe his visitor in the burka brought the bottle with the drug already in it and then left the pill bottle and the note beside the bed."

"That's what I'm thinking too," Morton said, returning to her lunch. "I've also been thinking you should improve the security around your house. If this guy has been into your place once, he might come for a second visit. I don't want to hear you've ended up on the wrong end of a baseball bat."

"The house is already taken care of," Pia said. She was describing the invasion of Sergei's high-tech helpers when Morton's cellphone rang. The detective took the call and scribbled something on her notepad.

"The coroner has finished with Mohammed Farah. No surprises – he died from major trauma to the head delivered by a blunt object that fits the pattern of a baseball bat. That's what the witness described and we've got the bat from the scene. His body is being released this afternoon and the funeral will be tomorrow. Muslims bury their dead quickly and this has already taken way too long as far as the family is concerned."

Morton was silent for a while but then started telling Pia about her interview the day before with the boys' parents. Some of it Pia knew already. Mohammed's father was trained as a chemist and Tariq's father had gone to medical school. They both worked, but their scant grasp of English and lack of Canadian experience meant they were stuck in menial jobs.

"I had to use a translator and that always makes stories more difficult to follow," Morton said. "But it seems the two families were in and out of refugee camps in Kenya for years. They didn't know each other until they came to Canada and met at the motel. I did some research this morning and it turns out these folks are the stragglers. Most Somali refugee claimants came here in the early 1990s. The country fell apart because of a war between insurgent groups and the local dictator, and since then nobody has been able to put it back together again. Anyway, I gather that most families with a bit of money gave up hope of returning home years ago and moved on to settle in other countries. The parents told me they lingered in the region because they still had relatives in Somalia and they were hoping to reunite before moving on. The fucking tragedy is that Mohammed was a baby staying with his grandmother in the country when some of the most serious fighting broke out. His parents ended up in a refugee camp and spent the next four years trying to find him and get him safely out of the war zone. When they finally did it, the whole family came here. And now the kid is dead anyway. Those poor, poor people."

Pia took a moment to absorb this. "I should have come to you as soon as the boys told me what they'd seen. Then maybe this wouldn't have happened."

"You are being too hard on yourself," Morton responded gently. "We have one dead kid on our hands and another in intensive care. Even with that I haven't been able to get anybody to consider linking what happened to these boys and what happened to Gatway and Scott. If you'd come to me a week ago and told me I needed to reopen the investigation into the deaths of two politicians because of what two little kids told you, it would have been a hard sell. I'm not even sure I would have taken you seriously."

"But you are taking my story seriously now."

"Well, I hate to think I screwed up and that some twisted freak is getting away with murder."

In the newsroom after lunch, Pia worked with James on the next day's pages and made plans for the Saturday section front. By sheer chance, one of her options was a feature story on the Somali-Canadian hip-hop star K'naan. He had fled Mogadishu with his mother and brother when the country descended into chaos. After some time in Harlem, the three of them came to Canada and settled in Toronto's tough Rexdale neighborhood. K'naan combined rap, rock, and reggae in his music. His lyrics attacked war lords in Somalia and the tough-guy attitudes of wannabe gangsters in his adopted hometown. She decided to buy his most recent recording when she had a moment. The story also made her think of the little boy who didn't survive to grow and prosper. Just before leaving work she made a few inquiries and found out where Mohammed's funeral would be held the next day.

Pia got up early the next morning, dressed in a black suit, and found a dark scarf to cover her hair. An hour later she was looking for a place to park near the mosque where Mohammed's funeral would be held. Members of Toronto's Somali community had turned out en masse to mourn the child they never had a chance to know. Parked vehicles lined the residential streets around the east end mosque so that when she finally found a place to leave her car, it was eight blocks away. She stepped out of the air conditioning into the heat of the day. The city was already wilting. As she walked along the sidewalk in front of the older homes that lined the street, the air hummed with racket from air conditioners. Their numbers had proliferated as average annual temperatures soared.

The mosque was in a large house that had been converted and expanded. When Jasmine's grandmother died a few years earlier, Pia had attended the funeral, so she had some idea of what to expect as she quietly entered the women's section and stood near the back. Mohammed's body would have been washed by close relatives in a specially designated room at the mosque, then wrapped in a white shroud. He would have been placed on his right side in a simple casket, and taken into the mosque where the imam would lead prayers while those in attendance stood and listened. The casket would then be escorted by mourners to the cemetery for burial. In twenty-first-century, multicultural Toronto, most cemeteries had special sections for Muslims, with the graves deliberately laid out on a north–south grid. This meant that when he was buried, Mohammed, like all good Muslims, would face Mecca in the east.

What Pia was unprepared for – what was impossible to prepare for – was the weight of grief that comes with the sudden, pointless, violent death of a child. Looking around the room, she realized she was surrounded by the tear-stained faces of women who had already suffered too much in life. The imam's prayers were supposed to be a source of comfort for those left behind. Mired as she was in regret, guilt, and anger, Pia heard only rebuke.

Chapter Fifteen

PIA SLIPPED AWAY FROM the service as it concluded and went to work. In her office, she threw herself into editing a series of celebrity interviews to run in the entertainment section when the film festival got underway. Concentrating on the stars' feelings about fame and fortune and their latest movie projects was difficult after the grief and suffering that had colored her morning, so she welcomed an e-mail from Jack Cleary asking if she was feeling better and inviting her to his place for an early dinner. He was suggesting they attend the opening of an art exhibition later in the evening. She'd been thinking about Jack and the night they spent together. But she'd also been thinking about Martin Geneve. Things could get complicated. Actually, things were complicated. Gabriella Garcia would have a field day.

Pia shrugged. Jack hadn't phoned to invite her to jump into

bed. He'd phoned to invite her for dinner and to an art show. She wrote back accepting the invitation.

Arriving home at the end of the day, Pia shed the black funeral suit and jumped into the shower. It would be a relief to spend an evening thinking of something other than the web of murder that seemed to have taken over her life.

Pia pulled on a slim-fitting, short, green skirt and added a matching sleeveless blouse. She slipped on a pair of black slides, dug out a black evening purse, and went downstairs to feed Winston the last of his painkillers. He was stretched out, sleeping on the sofa but rolled over onto his back when he heard her coming. He didn't protest when she gently patted his stomach. In a further sign that he'd made a full recovery, he refused to cooperate when she tried to pull his mouth open to deliver the final dose of medication. Exasperated, Pia gave up when he spit the pill out for the third time. She took it into the kitchen, crushed it into a powder, retrieved the half-empty can of tuna she'd left in the fridge the day before when she'd encountered the same problem, and mixed what was left with the medication. The cat, who had followed her into the kitchen, gulped everything down the moment she put the dish on the floor.

"Let me see, who is the idiot here?" she said as she watched Winston lick the last of the fish oil from the bowl. "You behave badly. You refuse to cooperate. You get tuna. I might have to rethink this strategy."

Pia parked in front of Jack Cleary's place about twenty minutes later. The house, in the city's trendy Danforth area, was a typical Toronto two-story brick building with a front porch ideal for people-watching.

"I'm renting this place from a university professor who is working in France," Jack told her a few minutes later as he poured wine into two glasses. "The university over there has provided him with a furnished apartment so he left almost all his furniture and other stuff here. I just moved in."

Barbecued lamb chops and grilled vegetables were on the menu. Jack was preparing a Greek salad when he realized he'd forgotten to buy feta cheese. Pia said she could live without it, but he insisted on walking down to the store at the end of his street.

"This is Greektown – there's feta everywhere so I'll only be a few minutes. In the meantime, just make yourself at home. When I get back I want to hear all about the break-in. Your aunt gave me the abbreviated version when I called your place the day after it happened. You have to tell me the whole story. Then I'll tell you about the artist we're going to see tonight."

Pia shrugged and settled down to wait in one of the black leather sofas in the living room. After browsing through an art magazine, she went in search of the washroom. There didn't seem to be a powder room on the first floor so she climbed the stairs to the second, opened the first door she came to, and gasped. The room was full of soft evening light that shone in through a huge skylight and a wall of windows along one side. It was filled with paintings in various stages of completion.

Canvases two and three deep lined the floor, leaning against the walls. Country scenes, abstracts, the occasional still life – they all jumped out at her in a riot of color. Pia stepped into the room to take a closer look when she heard a sound behind her.

"So you've discovered my hobby," Jack said, leaning against the doorway and smiling.

"I'm so sorry, I was looking for the washroom and found this instead. I shouldn't have snooped but it's so amazing I couldn't help myself. You are really talented."

"Sadly, I'm not quite talented enough. That's why it's just a hobby. But look, I'm just about to put the lamb on the barbecue. Will you come and keep me company?"

Pia nodded reluctantly, and after one last glance around followed him out of the room. Over dinner, she told Jack about the intruder in her house, but didn't mention that the only thing stolen was her transcript of the interview with the boys. She wasn't about to put anybody else at risk.

"If you are afraid being home alone you could always spend the night here," Jack said with a mock leer as he cleared the table and set a bowl of strawberries in front of his guest.

"Thanks for the offer, but with all the security I've got at my place now the main thing I'm worried about is setting off the alarm and ending up with the whole police department at the door."

Pia drove to the gallery on Queen Street West. The area around one of the country's main mental health treatment hospitals used to be a shabby stretch of storefronts frequented by outpatients, the homeless, and the neighborhood's poor residents. A few years earlier, however, gallery owners seeking an alternative to the high rents charged for property closer to the downtown started moving in. Cappuccino joints and Asian fusion restaurants quickly followed.

"This artist we're going to see is starting to make a big name for herself internationally," Jack told Pia on the way over. "Her name is Gina Petrus and I think her work is interesting. I saw one piece a few years ago where she made a series of life-sized figures of a woman at different stages of life. So there she was as a child, as a teenager, as a young woman, as a middle-aged woman, and as an old woman in a rocking chair. The bodies were made from cloth so they were kind of like rag dolls. She painted their faces onto the textile and dressed them in everyday clothes so they looked pretty realistic. What caused a stir at the time was that at every stage of life there were little hints that the woman was being abused – suggestions of bruises here and there or a ripped stocking or a bandage. That show was called 'Life Cycle.' Tonight's is a collection of some of her past work as well as some new material so I'm not sure what we'll see."

"If I hang around with you for a while, I may learn enough to earn some credibility at work," Pia joked.

The gallery owners had made no effort to conceal their business's antecedents. A faded sign declaring that the building had at one time been home to Mel's Meats still hung out front. Instead of trays of meat, however, the display window announced the opening of the Gina Petrus show. The space inside was surprisingly large and filled with serious-looking artsy types who chatted quietly in small groups or wandered about looking thoughtful. Jack went in search of drinks while Pia studied a painting called *X Meets Y*. Judging by the shapes, it was an egg meeting a sperm.

"Come with me and meet the artist," Jack said after handing her a glass. He led Pia around a corner to another room where a naked young woman, the right side of her slim body painted white and the left side painted black, stood motionless in front of a set of mirrors staring at her reflection. Or rather her reflections. As Pia moved closer she realized the mirrors were set up so that the woman's body was reflected over and over again into infinity.

"That's Gina Petrus herself," Jack said grinning. "The piece is called *Everlasting Beauty Is in the Eyes of the Beholder*." Pia laughed and they moved on through the rest of the show, debating the fine line that separated art from gimmickry.

When Pia dropped Jack off later, he invited her in but she begged off, saying it was all she could do to keep her eyes open. It was true. But Pia also felt the need to keep him at arm's length. He seemed like a sensitive guy. She hoped he wouldn't press her for an explanation because she wasn't sure she had one.

"No problem. But I would like to see you again," he said, turning to face her. Pia smiled uncertainly, leaned over and kissed him gently on the lips.

The next day she met Jasmine for lunch in the *Gazette*'s cafeteria and Pia recounted what she had seen at the Gina Petrus show.

"I didn't know you had taken to gallery crawling. Did you get lost on Queen West and wander in there by mistake?" Jasmine teased.

"I went with Jack, the curator. I think I told you about him. He's a nice guy, knows a lot about art obviously. And yes, he's attractive in a skinny, artistic sort of way and yes, I've noticed and yes, I did succumb to his charms and it was pleasant."

Before Jasmine started badgering her for details, Pia changed the subject.

"By the way, I'm going to the Fine Arts Ball Saturday night."

"Oh, great. Maybe we can sit together. I'm going to go with Seamus." Seamus dated back to Jasmine's days at Jane and Finch, where they attended the same schools. He'd been such a small, scrawny kid that her cousin Raj hadn't considered him worth warning off, so the two youngsters had become fast friends. They'd both escaped the neighborhood, but while Jasmine chose art and writing and journalism, Seamus emerged from university as a serious-minded young lawyer who was making a name for himself as a defender of the down, out, and dispossessed.

"So we'll get to meet this guy Jack?"

"Actually I'm going with Martin Geneve."

"Him again? Boy, your dance card is full these days. I hope

you aren't going to try telling me that old story about how you are only interested in his art collection."

"Truth is I've managed to see more than his art collection." Pia paused. "I slept with him the last time I saw him. He came by the house with presents after I got hit on the head. I think the blow affected my judgment."

Jasmine was momentarily speechless, then she said, "You've got two guys on the go at once?"

"Sort of. I'm not sure how it happened. I mean I know how it happened but I'm confused about it. I like one of them, but I'm not sure I like him enough and I like the other one maybe too much, but I also think I dislike him. Do you remember how the doctor told me a while ago that it was very unlikely I could have a baby? I think these latest bad decisions on my part have something to do with that."

"You mean you're tempting fate. Pia, this is not good. What about love, etcetera – isn't that important?"

Something about Jasmine's turn of phrase, combined with the look on her face, struck Pia as odd. "Have I missed something – are you engaging in love, etcetera and not telling me?"

"Maybe. Well, yes, sort of. It's Seamus. I think he's making a play for me after all these years. And I think I like the idea."

"You've been keeping this all to yourself?"

"Well, it's not like I'm the only one with secrets these days," Jasmine said a bit defensively. "I wasn't sure at first. But I'm getting more sure. Seamus got the tickets for the ball and invited me, like on a real date. Usually we just go out with friends or get together at the last minute if neither of us has anything better to do."

"Well, at least you know what you are getting."

"Yeah. An overly ambitious, nerdy guy without a romantic bone in his body. Oh yes, and he likes to hike and to camp. I mean camping as in sleeping in a tent. Can you imagine? He's been trying to get me to go with him for years, but I'm just not interested in being eaten by mosquitoes and bears."

"I don't think the bears in Ontario eat people, do they? I think they like berries. Maybe he just wants to get you nice and close in a little tent to make a move."

"Well, if it's wilderness he wants, he can take me to a country inn and get nice and close in 300-thread-count bed sheets."

The prospect of Jasmine and Seamus getting together after so many years would make the ball even more interesting, Pia thought on Saturday evening as she started to get ready. She did her nails, pulled her hair into an up-do, and retrieved her dress from the closet. It was a pale green chiffon concoction, vintage Yves Saint Laurent. Margaret told her she'd purchased it when she was in her late thirties and going through a midlife crisis. "Men buy sports cars. I bought Yves Saint Laurent. And I never, ever regretted it," her aunt said the day she turned the dress over to Pia. "May you have as much fun in it as I did."

Pia ran her hand over the material, enjoying its delicacy and softness. She'd tried the dress on when Margaret delivered it about a year ago, but this would be its first outing. She pulled it on with something bordering on reverence and then turned to look in the mirror. The dress had a V neckline cut just low enough to hint at cleavage. The back made no pretense at modesty. It plunged to her waist, exposing a wide swath of skin that was framed along the sides and bottom by an elegant drape of material. The skirt, which fell softly from her waist in tiny pleats, was slit to just above the knee in the front.

She hesitated for a moment, trying to decide what jewelry to wear. Then she went to her closet and reached up for a wooden box pushed off into a far corner of the top shelf. Pia placed the box on her bed, took a deep breath, and lifted the lid. Patrice had stored the best of her jewelry in the box, itself a work of art. Shaped like a miniature treasure chest, its gleaming surface was inlaid with an intricate design of gold, black, and brown wood. Margaret had bought it for Patrice many years ago, during a trip to the Middle East.

Pia had refused to take the box and its contents after her mother and Max were killed on the highway all those years ago. Faced with her angry intransigence, Margaret quietly packed it away and bided her time until Pia's thirtieth birthday. "You were too young to know what you really wanted when I last tried to get you to take this, so I'm going to try again now," her aunt had said after depositing it on Pia's kitchen table. "Only this time I'm not taking it back, so you will have to decide what you want to do with it."

After Margaret left, Pia had rubbed her hand across the smooth, glossy surface of the box, recalling how as a child she'd thought it was the most beautiful object in the world. She was thirty years old, but she had cried like a heartbroken child when she opened the box and saw her mother's prized possessions neatly lined up, just the way Patrice left them the day she and Max had walked out of the house to their deaths. In addition to a few good pieces of jewelry inherited from her own mother, Patrice had added to her collection even during the lean years before Max. Pia remembered being about six years old when her mother came home from Birks with one of the jeweler's signature blue boxes. Inside was a wide, elaborately carved silver bangle. It was thick, heavy, and dramatic, and Pia had been allowed to try it on.

"Someday you'll be grown up and I'll let you borrow it," Patrice had assured her daughter. "You'll be able to wear it to a party."

The day Margaret had left the box with her, Pia had picked up each and every piece of her mother's jewelry, touching and remembering. Then she'd put the box up in the closet, out of sight.

Now, all these years later, it was open in front of her once more. Even after all this time, she thought she could still smell the scent of Patrice's favorite perfume when she raised the lid. Pia lifted the top layer out of the box and found the silver bracelet inside a soft cloth bag in the cavity underneath. Next to it in another bag was a matching silver choker and earrings, pieces her mother must have had specially commissioned to match. Pia put on the jewelry. The gleam of the heavy silver set off her pale-honey skin and the cool color of the dress. She checked her makeup, dabbed on some extra pink lipstick, slid her feet into a pair of strappy silver sandals, and decided she would do.

Martin was at her door not long afterwards, looking devastatingly handsome and at ease in his tuxedo. She could tell from his face that he liked what he saw.

"You are stunning and you will be the belle of the ball," he said quietly after his lips had brushed against hers. "I want more than this little kiss but it would be a crime to mess with perfection."

They met Jasmine and Seamus at the entrance to the hotel where the benefit was being held. Jasmine wore a gown the color of old brushed gold with a high neckline, cutaway shoulders, and a narrow skirt that traced her curves as it fell to the floor. The color highlighted the drama of her face with its big, dark eyes and generous mouth. She glowed like a small, perfect flame beside Seamus, towering above her. The gangly child had grown into an imposing, fit man with a mop of curly blond hair and blue eyes that observed the world with lively curiosity. Pia, who often joined Jasmine and Seamus for a movie or impromptu dinner, liked him immensely.

After the introductions, the foursome arrived at the pre-dinner reception, where they sipped champagne and began bidding in the silent auction that formed part of the evening's entertainment. Dozens of Toronto artists, ranging from the unknown to the famous, had donated their work to the event, which each year raised thousands of dollars to help offset the cost of dance, art, and music classes for children growing up in the city's low-income families. Martin made offers on several pieces that captured his fancy. When Pia stopped to admire a drawing by none other than Gina Petrus, he placed a bid on it as well.

"I went to the opening of her latest show with a friend and I didn't see anything at all like this," Pia said, studying the unframed piece. Entitled *Multiculturalism*, it was a pen-and-ink drawing of three elderly women sitting on what she immediately recognized as a typical Toronto front porch. The headscarf and clothing worn by one woman clearly identified her as a Muslim. Next to her sat a wrinkled, diminutive Asian woman. The third woman could easily have been Maria, Pia's Italian neighbor.

Dinner came next. The salad and a main course were both works of art in the tradition of piling minimal amounts of food into towering structures on otherwise empty dinner plates. Pia ate it all, plus whatever bread she could get her hands on. Her stomach was still growling with hunger as she attacked dessert, which was a sliver of dark chocolate cake with raspberry coulis drizzled over it in a flower pattern.

The band playing afterwards offered a mixture of Latin, Motown, and rock and roll, and the music took her mind off her hunger for a while. Pia was in Martin's arms swaying to something romantic when he put his mouth to her ear just before midnight.

"I don't know about you, but if I don't get some real food, I'm going to collapse."

"I'm with you," Pia agreed. She glanced over at Seamus and Jasmine. They were dancing nearby, their bodies glued together in a way that discouraged interruption. "What do you have in mind?"

They settled on smoked meat on rye. Martin stopped to pick up the sandwiches at an all-night deli he knew and then drove down to the western beach. Moonbeams glanced off the lake's surface as the two of them made their way to a park bench near the water. The sound of waves lapping the shore intermittently drowned out the dull hiss of traffic on the nearby Gardiner Expressway, creating the illusion that the city had receded, and that they were alone with the moon and the lake. As Pia unwrapped her food, Martin opened a plastic bag he had carried from the car and pulled out two bottles of beer.

"I convinced the bartender to sell them to me before we left the party. I figured we could use the calories," he joked as he twisted off the lids. They ate in silence, watching the water and enjoying the gentle night breeze. When they finished, Martin took Pia's hand and they strolled along the boardwalk. He asked if she would go home with him. She said yes.

In his bedroom, he pulled her into his arms and kissed her deeply. With slow deliberation, they began the ritual of undressing one another. Martin had just lifted her dress over her head when Pia heard a sound. It was the malamute. He strolled into the room, sat down beside the bed, and stared, watching their every move. Pia opened her mouth to protest, but before she could say anything Martin put his finger to her lips.

"Freddie," he said, not even turning to look at the beast, "go lie down." There was a pause and then the sound of four big feet on the move. Just outside the room, Freddie turned his back on them, sighed forlornly, and settled down to sleep in the doorway. The two people he left behind were too preoccupied to notice.

Chapter Sixteen

PIA WOKE UP THE NEXT MORNING to the tantalizing smell of coffee drifting into Martin's bedroom. She was alone, tangled in smooth, white sheets that caressed her skin each time she moved. The room was a tribute to simplicity, albeit the kind of simplicity achieved through the expenditure of huge amounts of cash – white walls, pale, honey-colored wood floor, sparse furnishings. Narrow bureaus made of wood that matched the floor sat on either side of the bed, running the length of the wall. Two chairs in soft brown leather faced a fireplace with a sleek copper front. Opposite the bed, a semi-transparent screen filtered the light flooding in through a wall of windows that looked out over treetops. The view, while striking, had plenty of visual competition, Pia realized as she rolled out of bed. A huge painting hung over each of the bedside bureaus, while two small drawings had pride of place on a wall near the doorway.

Pia wound a sheet around herself and went to examine them more closely. The first was of a woman wearing black tights and a sleeveless green blouse. She was sitting on the floor, her hair piled carelessly on top of her head. The second work might have been of the same woman – the hair was the same – but in this case she was posed with her back to the artist wearing only white bloomers and a chemise with its straps falling from her shoulders.

The sound of Martin's voice startled Pia as he came into the room bearing two mugs. "Do you like them?" he asked as he handed Pia a steaming latte. "Back when my mother was alive and I finally had enough money to begin a serious collection, these were among the first pieces I bought on her advice. The artist is Egon Schiele. Not a very admirable human being from what I know about his personal life. Today, he is considered one of Austria's greatest artists, though many of his drawings were sold as pornography back when he was working in the late nineteenth and early twentieth centuries."

Pia murmured her admiration and sipped coffee as Martin guided her around the room telling her about the other paintings. "You really love collecting these things, don't you?" she observed when he paused at one point.

"Love it? I suppose I do. A shrink would probably say the fact that I can now afford to buy this kind of art is my way of erasing my impoverished past. Or that collecting is my way of paying tribute to my mother. Or all of the above. I admit there's the thrill of the chase when you're bidding to get something you really want at an auction. But the thing about art is that it is also a window on history and politics and the creative process. It's all so different from what I do every day – the dollars-and-cents decisions, the negotiations, legal contracts. The collection is about ideas and beauty and challenges to the status quo – the status quo that I'm now a part of. Not that I'm complaining," he said hastily.

They spent the rest of the morning in bed making love. When Pia finally got up for the lunch Martin promised her, she was so relaxed that her limbs felt only loosely attached to her body. They showered and then he led her onto a shaded back terrace overlooking the swimming pool. The sleek modernity of the house and pool was softened by gardens bursting with mauve and white flowers.

"That's Marco's handiwork," Martin said. "He takes care of the gardens and maintenance around here. We met back when we were both in the military. I was a young punk coming in and he was an old hand who knew everything. When he retired he came to work for me and discovered he had a green thumb.

"And this is Julieta," he added, as a tidy, compact older woman with closely cropped salt-and-pepper hair bustled onto the terrace. Pia had forgotten that anyone else lived on the premises, and she blushed deeply and stammered a greeting as the woman smiled and placed a heavenly smelling frittata on the table before going back into the house.

"I'm glad we dressed for lunch," Pia said, her faced still tinged with pink, "although it's difficult to imagine feeling more embarrassed than I do now."

"Marco and Julieta are the most discreet people I know. Don't even think about it. Now eat. I'm convinced Julieta makes the best frittata in the city."

It was afternoon when Pia finally got home. She napped for a while and then forced herself to work. Louise Lutkin, her agent, wanted to see a first draft of the manuscript by the end of the month.

It was just before midnight when Pia abandoned Cleo Leone, who was dressing to go to a swanky ball with a man who wanted to rescue her and her child from a life of crime investigation. Amazing how fiction imitated life. As she got up from her desk, Pia saw the collection of articles that Jack had left for her lying forgotten on a filing cabinet. She took them to bed and immersed herself in historical overviews describing Hitler's cultural plundering and details of subsequent disputes over the ownership of prized artworks. As she was reading, two small photographs accompanied by a short article at the bottom of one page caught her attention. The reproductions of the drawings were small and grainy because Jack had photocopied the pages, but Pia recognized them immediately because she'd seen them before. Recently. Like earlier in the day.

Incredulous, she read the story. The two drawings by Egon Schiele, it said, were the subject of a dispute between Canadian entrepreneur and art collector Martin Geneve and Rose Arnberg, age eighty-two. Miss Arnberg, who now lived in Paris, was the niece and last living relative of Daniel Arnberg, a Jewish industrialist in Berlin whose art collection had been confiscated by the

Nazis in 1938. Her uncle, who had no children, and her parents had perished in the Nazi camps, but they'd managed to get Rose to England before being shipped to their deaths. According to French legal documents, Miss Arnberg claimed to remember the drawings from her uncle's home in Berlin. Martin Geneve, according to the same court files, claimed to have purchased the drawings ten years ago from a reputable British gallery. The dispute, the article said, came at a time when Canadian authorities were considering new laws that would ease the rules of evidence, making it easier for people to lay claim to art stolen from their families during the war. Neither Arnberg nor Geneve would comment on the matter.

Wide awake again, Pia threw back the bedcovers and jumped to her feet, ignoring the growl of protest from Winston, curled up beside her. Throwing on a robe, she went downstairs, turned on her computer, and starting searching. First, she needed to know what was at stake. A lot, as it turned out. German and Austrian Abstract Expressionist art was in vogue. A landscape painting by Schiele sold not long ago for $2.1 million. More recently, another Schiele, described as an erotic picture of a headless woman, fetched nearly $1 million. Experts noted that in the 1960s similar works were selling for less than five thousand dollars. While there was lots of information on Schiele, who lived a short, eventful life before dying in the influenza epidemic of 1918, Pia found no more information about the fight over the two drawings she was certain she'd just seen in Martin's bedroom.

She searched and read for another two hours until her nervous energy ran out. She turned the computer off and closed her eyes. He hadn't said anything about the dispute when they discussed the drawings. She'd had sex with the guy. Enthusiastic sex. She couldn't bring herself to contemplate the implications. At least not yet.

After tossing and turning through the few hours that were left in the night, Pia went to work exhausted on Monday morning, the dark circles under her eyes highlighting her pallor. Jasmine, usually so perceptive, didn't notice right away.

"After all these years Seamus and I are an item," she announced as they sat down at a table in the *Gazette* cafeteria. "He spent the whole weekend at my place. And I've agreed to go camping with him."

Tired and dispirited as she was, this was news so amazing that it immediately took Pia's mind off her own troubles. The Jasmine she knew considered walking in a city park a waste of time that could be better used watching a film or going to a gallery. "You can't mean it. You mean like in a tent with sleeping bags and stuff?"

"Yup, we're going to drive up to Algonquin Park next weekend and canoe and camp for three days in the real wilderness."

"Jasmine, if you want this thing with Seamus to continue maybe you should rethink this. He might end up hating you after listening to three days of your whining about bugs and lousy food. What if it rains? You'll be miserable. And you'll make him miserable."

Pia spoke from experience. A few years ago, she had decided Jasmine would love nature if she gave it a chance. They rented a cottage for a week. The place was relatively civilized, with indoor plumbing and a screened porch, but Jasmine was out of sorts from day one about the lack of daily newspaper delivery, the absence of a television, and the fact that the nearest restaurant was a forty-five-minute drive away. With two days to go, she finally convinced Pia to abandon the cottage for an all-inclusive spa conveniently located on the route back to the city.

"Love conquers all," Jasmine said flippantly when Pia reminded her of the cottage debacle. "I warned him that I might be a pain in the ass and he still wants to go with me." She paused and then looked horrified. "Do you think this might be some sort of test, you know, to see if we can make it?"

"Well, if it is you'd better start studying. I think they offer canoeing lessons down on the harbor. And you'd better get some rain gear and some practical boots. Nothing you own will cut it in the wild," Pia said, looking pointedly at Jasmine's barely-there red sandals. They perfectly matched the polish on her toenails but weren't made for walking anything more than the distance between a taxi and a restaurant.

They nursed their coffees while Jasmine enthusiastically attacked a bagel with cream cheese.

"You're not eating? What's wrong?" Jasmine asked, suddenly taking in her friend's wan face.

"Just about everything." Pia began by telling Jasmine about the notes stolen from her house and the attack on the boys.

Then she filled her in on the paintings in Martin Geneve's bedroom.

"I haven't been keeping you up to date because I'm worried that whoever I confide in might somehow be put at risk. I mean somebody has already killed a little boy over this. And now I'm wondering if the somebody might be Martin. When I think about it, he had the opportunity to kill May Gatway. He was at the reception the night she died. From the start he was pointing a finger of suspicion at Gatway's husband. And now I find out that he has his own reasons – two very valuable reasons – for wanting the minister out of the way. The changes May Gatway was talking about would have made it easier for Rose Arnberg to get those paintings back."

Talking reactivated the toxic mix of suspicion and fear that had eaten away at Pia through the night. Had he been sticking close to her just to keep tabs on her research for the book?

Jasmine listened attentively, her eyes growing wider with each revelation. "Oh, boy. So first you thought he might be a good sperm donor and now you're worried he might be a killer. He didn't strike me as the murdering type," she said tentatively. "But people who have passions do crazy things. And it sounds like he's pretty passionate about his art collection."

"These two drawings were some of his first purchases. His mother – she's dead now – suggested he buy them, so they are perhaps more important to him than other stuff he has."

"What are you going to do?"

"I wish I knew."

Pia muddled through the rest of the morning, editing copy, laying out pages, and discussing story ideas with James. When noon finally came, she shut the door to her office, went to her desk and called Nancy Morton.

"Would you do me a favor and check out a guy named Martin Geneve?" Pia asked, getting right to the point.

"Isn't that the rich guy you went to that chi-chi party with on the weekend – that *was* you in the society pages with him, wasn't it? If you're going to ask me to check out every guy you date, that's abusing our friendship."

"Nancy, just see what you can find out about him and I'll fill you in later. Please."

"Okay, okay. In the meantime, I've got something to show you."

"What is it?"

"Let me see, what was it you just said? I'll fill you in later? Yes, that was it. I'll fill you in later. But it's not something we can discuss at the station. And I'll need access to a video player."

Morton agreed to come by for dinner after work. When she arrived, Pia put a rack of ribs on the barbecue and they sat down, beers in hand, at the nearby table,.

"Nancy, is Tariq doing any better?"

"He's still in intensive care in a coma. The doctors say he could wake up in a few hours, a few days, a few months. Or never. The hospital is being great with his parents. There's a room where they can sleep in shifts so one of them can be with him all the time. Truth is, though, I don't think either of them has slept or eaten for days.

"In the meantime, the esteemed Detective Schmidt is going nowhere fast on the investigation. The hate-crime angle doesn't seem to have much traction. So I've been checking on the personal life of our boy Wilson Scott to see if maybe his late-night visitor was a spurned lover."

Morton stopped talking when Pia, a look of panic on her face, jumped up from the table and ran to the grill where she threw the lid open and frantically began waving away smoke and struggling to turn the ribs. Sighing, the detective went over to join her.

"Christ, you are such a girly-girl. Give me those tongs. Where did you learn to barbecue?"

"I didn't, actually. You know I'm a good cook, but I'm better in the kitchen than with the barbecue. It seems like such a mindless task that I underestimate how much attention it requires. To be totally frank, I rarely use the thing when I'm on my own because I always end up with dinner that is burnt on the outside and uncooked on the inside. That takes talent."

"Well, this is your lucky day because you have a guest who knows what she's doing," Morton said as she expertly flipped the ribs. "It's just one of my many talents that straight women like you fail to appreciate."

"Sorry. You're still not my type," Pia said as she headed into the kitchen to get the rice and salad. A few minutes later they were piling their plates high with food.

"So as I was saying before I had to rescue our dinner," Morton said, "I've been checking on that young guy Scott was groping in the picture you gave me. It turns out his name is

Peter Willett. He claims to be an actor, but for now he's pretending to be a waiter down on Queen Street West. I say pretending because he works at one of those joints where the waiters are so cool you practically have to beg them to take your order. Then you really do have to beg them to bring the food.

"Anyway, I talked to this guy – he's twenty-four years old but looks about sixteen. He said he and Scott got together a few times but that Scott wasn't looking for commitment. In other words he wanted to be free to get it on with everything that took his fancy. Then a while ago, Scott disappeared from the scene. Willett heard that he'd met somebody and was in a serious relationship. There was also speculation that Scott's new squeeze was still in the closet because nobody ever saw them out together. So the obvious question is, who was this new guy?"

"Let me think about that," Pia said. "Maybe I can come up with something."

"Okay, now here's the other thing. We've got the baseball bat used on the kids. When the witness with the dog came along and started shouting, the suspect ran like hell and dumped the thing in some woods at the end of the park. The search team found it almost right away, but so far forensics has only found the kids' blood on it so we think he must have been wearing gloves. So that's been a dead end. But do you remember the school that's near the park entrance? You know how schools are so safety conscious these days? Well, I went to talk to the principal and it turns out they have security cameras monitoring the front door and the front yard. It also turns out one of these cameras is positioned so that just by pure chance it picks up a part of the street."

Morton retrieved a videotape from her briefcase in the hall and followed Pia into the study.

"Luckily for us, they only erase these every three months so they still had the one for the night the kids were attacked," the detective said as a black-and-white image of the walkway leading to the school's front door popped up on the television screen. "Pay attention to the upper-right corner."

The camera angle captured a small stretch of the main sidewalk, just enough to provide fleeting glimpses of anyone walking by. As Pia watched, three young men appeared on the screen illuminated by the street light. They came and went in just a few seconds so Morton reversed the tape, played it again, and froze the image so Pia could get a better look at them. The youths, who looked to be about eighteen, wore the standard baggy pants and loose shirts that identified them as gang toughs.

"These guys went by at about 10:45 p.m., fifteen minutes after the call to the motel," Morton said. "Now look at this." She fast-forwarded the tape again until the timer read 11:02 p.m. and let it run.

"Oh my God," Pia gasped a few seconds later.

"Yeah, I thought this one might bother you," Morton said as she reached down to pause the tape. Frozen on the screen was a figure in a dark burka.

"The attack on the kids occurred about a half hour later. The thing is, by that point the guy swinging the baseball bat was wearing dark pants, a dark shirt, and what the witness thought was a balaclava. So if this is the killer, he must have shed the outfit somewhere in the vicinity. Maybe he was worried about it getting in the way if he had to make a run for it."

"He was probably planning to put it on again when he finished," Pia said slowly. "But since he was interrupted by the guy with the dog, would he have had time to collect it?"

"Schmidt's guys haven't found anything other than the baseball bat, but that's not to say it isn't there. Our attacker – if it is our attacker – probably made an effort to hide it. It's too dark now, but how about we go for a walk in the area tomorrow evening."

Over coffee a while later Morton changed the subject. "I checked on your friend Martin Geneve," she said as she settled on a stool next to the kitchen counter.

"And?"

"He had a record as a young offender. Got busted for a couple of break and enters – from what I can tell, it was his mother who turned him in when she found stolen goods stashed in his bedroom. Cameras mostly, from a store he and another guy burgled. They got off easy with suspended sentences. Their lawyer spun the judge some bullshit about how they had turned over a new leaf and were going to join the military. There was nothing after that, although everybody knows he grew up to be a rich bigwig around town. Now, do you want to tell me why you are asking?"

Pia hesitated and then thought, what the hell? If Martin Geneve really was implicated then Morton should know. She outlined her suspicions, glossing over the details of her relationship with Martin and hoping that Morton wouldn't notice. No such luck.

"So you've been banging this guy and now you think he might be a killer," the detective said in a voice that mixed concern with exasperation. "Great. This is just great. You don't happen to know if his bedroom closet is full of burkas?"

"Nancy, I just don't know what to think. Could he have killed May Gatway, Wilson Scott, and gone after the kids?"

"Did he perform in the sack like a guy who plays both ways? I mean could he be Wilson Scott's lover in the closet?"

"He performed just fine, thank you very much. But you have a point. I'll try to find out if he and Wilson Scott knew each other and if so, how well. In the meantime, I take it you think that he has to be on our list of suspects?"

"I do. In the meantime, stay away from the guy until we can figure out what's going on. Agreed?"

"Agreed."

Chapter Seventeen

PIA WAS EDITING COPY the next morning when Jasmine came into her office weighed down with shopping bags. "You have to see what I just bought," she said, dropping the load in the middle of the floor. "I'm going to be the sexiest, best-dressed camper ever."

"Wouldn't it make more sense to aim for comfort, dryness, and practicality?" Pia asked, looking doubtfully at the mishmash of designer outlet bags. The sight of Jasmine's crestfallen face prompted her to move on. "Okay, okay, what do I know? The only camping trip I ever went on was in grade eight and it was miserable. The tents leaked. The food was wretched. And when we weren't getting soaked by rain, we were being devoured by bugs."

"You can be a real spoilsport sometimes," Jasmine pouted as she opened a box that contained pale blue leather hiking

"Aren't these the cutest thing? And what about this outfit?" she asked, pulling out a pair of pastel blue walking shorts and a long-sleeved, white-and-blue striped cotton shirt. "I bought another sleeveless top that also goes with these shorts in case it is really hot and a pair of black jeans for cold weather."

At least she had gone to a sporting goods store to buy a jacket; Pia wondered though, about Jasmine's choice of color – pale blue again with white embroidery around the hood and sleeves. It was the sort of thing she suspected would get dirty in about thirty-five seconds on a real canoe trip. Be fair, she chided herself. At least the tag says that it's waterproof.

"We put Seamus's canoe in the Humber River and paddled around last night," Jasmine said as she admired her purchases. "He says I'm a natural."

"He's a liar," Pia retorted. "Smitten men will say anything."

"Speaking of smitten, what's happening with Martin?"

"I told Nancy Morton the whole sorry tale. We've got a few leads to pursue. Which reminds me, pursuing a lead is what I should be doing right now. Is the fashion show over?"

Pia left Jasmine repacking her camping wardrobe and made her way over to the legislative library. She'd phoned earlier in the day and arranged to see the boxes of personal documents taken from Wilson Scott's office.

"The Scott family donated them to the library, but I'm not supposed to let anyone go through this material before it's been cataloged for the archives," Heidi Johnston said as she led Pia through to a room piled with boxes. "But I like to return favors."

Pia smiled her thanks. A few years earlier, Heidi's father had been forced to leave his home because of ill health. Her mother had already been in a nursing home for about six months after falling and breaking a hip. Heidi's father wanted to be with his wife in the same facility, but the authorities insisted they could only accommodate him in an institution on the other side of town. Pia's column about the two old people forced apart at the end of their lives provoked an uproar, a change in provincial policy, and the sudden realization by authorities that there was indeed space for Heidi's father in the same nursing home as his wife.

The dozen file boxes from Scott's office were daunting, but she soon discovered that some conscientious public servant had listed the contents on the side of each container. The first three boxes she examined contained general files of little interest, but just flipping through them took more than an hour. She would go through one more that looked promising before admitting defeat and coming back another day. The note on the outside said it contained agendas, notes, and files taken from Wilson Scott's desk. She heaved it onto the battered table. There were briefing notes on agricultural prices, a collection of letters from various farmers' groups, a file with information about art shows taking place in and around the city. Finally she came to a daybook that contained Scott's appointments over a two-year period.

It outlined a dismal life if you weren't the kind of person who liked giving speeches, attending fall fairs, consulting with hog farmers, and meetings – endless meetings. Pia checked every entry for the first six months. Then she decided that if Wilson Scott was seeing someone, it would likely be over lunch, in the evenings, or on weekends, so she narrowed her search to those times. Ten minutes later, she found the first promising entry. The note, made about fourteen months before the politician's death, said only "JJ – dinner." Thereafter the same unadorned entry – no additional details were ever provided – began turning up in the daybook about once a week, usually in the evenings, occasionally on the weekend. Her heart pounding, Pia flipped through the pages to the day Wilson Scott died. JJ was penciled in for eight-thirty in the evening.

With silent apologies to librarians everywhere, Pia slipped the daybook into her bag. She needed to talk to Eric Paivanen again.

"Pia, he kept his personal life personal," Scott's former aide told her later in the day when she finally reached him working in the office of another minister. "We didn't socialize after hours, so I just don't know who JJ could be."

Of course, Pia thought. Nothing was ever easy. She scrambled to get through everything that needed to be done for the next day's paper and then rushed home to change into jeans and a T-shirt. An hour later, after fighting the traffic all the way over to the park near the Highway Inn, she found Morton waiting for her.

Pia told her about the entries in Wilson Scott's daybook.

"I'll ask around in the gay community to see if anybody has heard of a JJ," Morton said. "In the meantime, let's get to work here. We've only got a couple of hours before it gets dark. We'll go through the park first and then expand into the neighborhood. I'm not sure Schmidt's boys did much of a search, because they found the murder weapon almost from the start. For sure they weren't looking for a burka. If you find anything at all that looks promising, don't touch. Just yell or call me on my cell."

Morton opened her packsack and pulled out a pair of gloves for each of them. The detective said she would search the park's large open area. Pia volunteered to go through the woods. She tried to think like a criminal. The murderer's prime concern would have been to protect his identity, so he needed a place where he could shed the burka and immediately put on the balaclava to hide his face. Since a man changing out of a burka and then pulling on a black face covering was the sort of thing that witnesses would remember, he needed a secluded spot. He also needed quick access to his disguise so that he could put it back on once he finished dealing with the boys.

And so the tedium began. Most city parks are too small to be home to anything resembling a forest. But this park tried valiantly to offer residents a little bit of the wild. Pia estimated the wooded area was about twice the size of a hockey rink. She decided to walk back and forth through it in a grid pattern. An hour later, when Morton found her, she had leaves stuck in her hair, burrs attached to her socks, gloves that looked like a health threat, and a disgusted look on her face.

"Nothing so far, I see," Morton said dryly, taking in Pia's bedraggled appearance. "It looks like a raccoon took a round out of you."

"I've been digging around in mounds of leaves just in case. I found plenty of used condoms, a dead squirrel, and a plastic bag full of shit dumped by some pathetic excuse of a dog owner. But no burka. And, I might add, no raccoon. I gather you weren't any more successful," Pia said resentfully, taking in Morton's tidy appearance and empty hands.

"Nothing. Maybe what we saw on the tape was a real woman in a real burka and not our guy."

"I've got one last idea," Pia said, motioning for Morton to follow her. They walked to the back edge of the woods and came to a stand of bushes. Through the leaves, Pia pointed out a low stone wall separating the park from the cemetary next door.

They found a place where the bushes thinned out, clambered over the wall, and a few minutes later stood amid gravestones, most of them darkened with the passage of time and dating back to the early twentieth century.

"Nobody has been to see these folks in ages" Morton said as she began to walk slowly along a row of graves. The plots were neatly tended but there were no fresh flowers or other signs of recent visitors.

"I think people come for the first little while, but then it's back to the business of living. We're all destined for obscurity,"

Morton continued morbidly. "I've always thought gravestones should do more to keep a person's memory alive. It would make these places a lot more interesting. Mine could say I was the first openly lesbian cop on the Toronto force and that I loved women and hated doughnuts, dogs, and dope pushers. What would you want yours to say?"

When she didn't get a reply, Morton glanced up and saw that Pia had stopped to study one of the more elaborate headstones. The slab of marble that marked the grave of one Hilda Lonsdone (1884–1926) was topped with a two-foot-high marble angel with its hands clasped in prayer. The angel had once been white but time and pollution had stained it dull gray.

It wasn't the angel, however, that held Pia's attention. Two heavy black urns, each about knee high, flanked the monument. She ignored the empty one, but walked around the other, which held a makeshift bouquet of dried flowers and leaves that looked as if they had been collected from the immediate vicinity.

"Doesn't it strike you as odd that somebody went to the trouble to fill the urn on the grave of a woman who died so long ago?" she asked Morton, who had hurried over.

By way of reply, Morton retreated about ten paces, dropped the packsack she carried onto the ground and began unpacking clean gloves, a large plastic bag and a camera. After taking a couple of photos, she approached the urn, reached out and carefully lifted the dried branches out. The two women peered inside the urn.

"Bingo," Morton said quietly as she reached in and grasped

a black plastic garbage bag. She pulled it open and they found themselves looking at a small swatch of black mesh sewn into an expanse of heavy, dark material.

"That's what you look through when you wear one of these things," Pia said, her voice barely audible. She reached out to touch the material only to have her hand slapped away by Morton.

"No touching. Forensics will have to go over this to see if they can find a hair or anything else to analyze for DNA. If we can get that, we've got half the story. Then we'll just have to find a murderer with matching hair."

"That should be easy, what with all the murderers coming forward to confess," Pia said skeptically.

"Fair enough. But maybe if we keep quiet about finding this burka, he'll come back to get it. There have been a lot of cops around here in the last little while, but the park reopened yesterday so the uniforms are gone. Burka Boy might come get his costume to make sure there are no loose ends. I'm thinking we should put a watch on this site and see what happens over the new few days. I have a feeling that when Schmidt sees what we've found, he's going to be more open to pursuing a connection between Wilson Scott's death, the break-in at your place, and what happened to the kids."

A humorless smile flashed across Morton's face as she flipped open her cellphone and dialed the station number. "Schmidt? Oh good you're still there. It's Morton. I'm in the cemetery behind the park where the kids were attacked. I've got something here you are going to want to take a look at." She hung up and turned to Pia.

"We'll have to take it from here. I'm going to propose that we put the flowers back in place once the investigation is through. If we can make it look like nothing has changed, we can set up surveillance and maybe catch this creep if he decides it's safe to collect the props for his show."

When Pia got home there was a message from Martin Geneve inviting her for dinner at his place Saturday evening. The intimacy in his voice made her stomach feel queasy. She really had no idea who she was dealing with. The real Martin Geneve might be the man on the phone with the voice that caressed her even as he delivered a dinner invitation. Or he might be a stranger so obsessed with his possessions that he would kill to keep them. He had motive and opportunity to kill May Gatway. But was there any sort of link between him and Wilson Scott? She pondered her options as she stepped into the hot shower and washed off the adventure in the park. Scrubbing away her agitation, however, was impossible, so Pia didn't even bother trying to go to bed after drying off. Instead she went to her study and sat down in front of her computer.

She knew from her years as a reporter that sometimes the simplest approach is the best. She started searching the Internet for anything that contained the names of both Martin Geneve and Wilson Scott. Moments later, the results popped up on her screen. The first few references were newspaper and magazine articles that identified both men as being avid art collectors.

She found what she was looking for when she opened the fourth item – a website for the Toronto Schools Art Program. The program, which supported artists' visits to local schools, was governed by a volunteer board that included the two men among its directors. She forced herself to go on. Within the hour she knew that the pair had also co-chaired a fundraising campaign for the Ontario School of Fine Arts, one of the country's top institutions in the field.

Pia stared at the computer screen while her brain kicked into full-blown reproach mode. Between her own stupid act-now-think-later attitude to baby making and Dr. Garcia's advice about exploring her romantic options, she'd really mucked things up. Her mind raced as she worked through the scenarios. Martin had a motive and the opportunity to murder May Gatway. Maybe he was Wilson Scott's mysterious friend JJ. Maybe he'd arranged to meet Scott at the Highway Inn, fed him the pills dissolved in Scotch, and then left the suicide note neatly solving the Gatway murder. Pia had told him she was working on a book – he could have broken into her home and stolen the information that led him to Tariq and Mohammed. He might be a child killer. Shakiness gave way to nausea as Pia forced herself to connect the dots. Dots that set her to wondering if the man she'd slept with was a murderous, manipulative, bisexual psychopath. What if nature had played a sick joke on her and she was pregnant?

Pia felt the same sickening mixture of clammy fear, guilt, and betrayal that she'd experienced once before in her life. And just like on that weekend when Max returned over and over again to unlock her bedroom door and rape her, her body rebelled. Winston was asleep in his usual spot on the corner of her desk. But he jumped in alarm as Pia, her legs too wobbly to carry her to the bathroom, slumped over and vomited into the garbage can.

Chapter Eighteen

PIA CLEANED UP THE MESS in the study and went to bed, but sleep was as elusive as an empty taxi during a Toronto rainstorm. After tossing and turning for hours, she finally gave up. It was just after five, and Winston, still stretched out in a deep sleep, had to be nudged off the bed so she could straighten the covers.

Downstairs, Pia made coffee and opened the front door, but it was too early for the morning papers. Daylight was a creeping into the eastern sky as she took her cup and went out on the back deck. Life always seemed more manageable at the start of the day, Pia thought as she watched the sun's first watery rays caress the garden and gently take over from the soft pearly light of the early morning. The corrosive fear and anger that had poisoned the night gradually yielded to resolve as dawn washed over the city. If Martin had anything to do with the deaths of

Gatway and Scott or the attacks on Tariq and Mohammed, she had to know.

Pia went back inside to her study, signed onto the *Gazette*'s online library, and printed out some pictures of Wilson Scott. She fed Winston, scanned the papers when they finally arrived, and then got dressed. By newspaper standards, it was still early when she walked into the newsroom just before eight. At this time of morning, the newsroom was still a lonely place except for a few news editors trying to organize for the day ahead. Most reporters are not early-morning people, in part because their days often stretch into evening as they pull together information and then write their stories. Pia also suspected that people who chased news for a living tended to be night owls.

"Are you coming in straight from a party?" Einstein deadpanned when he looked up and saw her. "Or did your alarm clock screw up?"

"Neither. I'm turning over a new leaf because I want your job," she said, making her way to her office. Once settled, she put in a call to Morton.

"Yes, Schmidt admits our angle has to be pursued," Morton growled after realizing who was calling. "Yes, we had a watch on the cemetery last night. No, Burka Boy didn't show up. That about cover your questions?"

"Wow, remind me never to call you before noon again," Pia said. "I thought you would be in a good mood after getting the big guy to admit that he should have listened to you in the first place."

"Well, now that you mention it, that does make me feel better. He looked none too happy when I pointed out that he should have listened to me in the first place. In any case, this has got his attention. We've sent off some hairs from the burka for DNA analysis. And there will be surveillance in the cemetery for a while. It's an expensive business, though, so if our guy doesn't return to the scene soon I doubt we will be there to see him.

"With these latest developments I think it might also be worthwhile reviewing the evidence from all three crime scenes. It will take a bit of time to arrange for all the stuff to be brought up again, but I can probably get you in here to have a look at it if we are discreet. You interested?"

"Just tell me when and where."

Pia hung up and began sorting through her desk. Contrary to popular belief in the newsroom, where her office was famous for its litter, she did have a system. Whenever she came across anything worth saving, she added it to a pile. Then after a month or two, she would go through the pile starting from the bottom. Inevitably the stuff that seemed important when she saved it had been overtaken by events or turned out to be irrelevant, so dumping it in the garbage was easy. She'd instituted the system after the newspaper's health and safety committee representative decreed the office a fire hazard and warned that the filing cabinet, with its top drawer wide open and heaped with paper, was poised to topple.

After about an hour of sorting, Pia glimpsed the top of her desk but the garbage can in her office was now full. If she wanted to continue avoiding the real business of the day, she would have to go in search of another one. Or she could just make the call. She sighed and dialed Martin Geneve's cellphone number. She left a message accepting his dinner invitation. Then she phoned Aunt Margaret and invited herself over for the evening.

"We'd love to see you, dear. Sergei and I have something to tell you," Margaret said, sounding relaxed and cheerful, everything that Pia was not.

She threw herself into her job for the rest of the day, issuing assignments, laying out pages, reading copy that came from around the world on what journalists still called "the wires," even in the Internet age. By the time the concierge waved her through the sleek lobby of Margaret's condominium building, she felt in desperate need of her aunt's reassuring attention. Running home to what's left of your family for comfort isn't such a bad option when life is beating you up, she thought gloomily as she knocked on the door.

Margaret, looking cool and comfortable, hugged Pia and led her into the sitting room, where Sergei was pouring champagne into three flutes.

"I'm happy you are here because this is a special occasion," he announced, handing a glass to Pia and smiling broadly as he slipped a thick arm around Margaret's slim waist. "Your auntie has finally agreed to marry me."

Pia stared at her aunt, who shrugged helplessly. "He wore me down," Margaret said, leaning over to kiss Sergei on the cheek. "When he asked me for the hundredth time, I figured he was pretty serious."

They settled back to talk marriage preparations. Sergei lobbied for a wedding at the end of the month. "I don't want her to have time to change her mind," he told Pia. Margaret said she was thinking of New Year's Eve.

"I don't want to rush into anything," she said, sending Sergei a smile that was one part apology and one part flirtation. Pia stayed out of the debate and instead admired the large square-cut diamond Margaret now wore on her left hand. Maybe she should try to find out more about Sergei's business. Neither his answers to her occasional questions nor her examination of his company's website, available in both English and Russian, provided much detail.

"Romance must be in the air," Pia said. "Jasmine is acting crazy too. Believe it or not she's accepted an invitation to go camping this weekend with Seamus. After all these years I think they've finally realized they are in love." She entertained them with an account of Jasmine's new camping wardrobe in between helping herself to the fresh white bread, unsalted butter, and caviar that had become a staple in the household since Sergei's arrival. Aware from the beginning that one way to Margaret's heart was through her stomach, he'd taken her to the immigrant-owned Russian and Ukrainian stores in the city's northern suburban fringe. Although tiny by Canadian supermarket standards, the stores were bursting with delicacies including vats of fresh caviar in a range of qualities and fine dark chocolate imported from the anachronistically named Karl Marx Chocolate Factory, among others. Pickled mushrooms for garlic-laced salads and smelly canned fish that Margaret insisted only a starving cat could love now regularly made their way into her kitchen cupboards.

While enthusiastically expanding her food repertoire, Margaret had also made it her mission to ensure that Sergei lived to a ripe old age by cleaning up his diet. Full-fat sour cream was no longer a daily staple, salami had become an occasional treat rather than a regular menu item, and the pre-dinner glasses of vodka were replaced, for the most part, with wine. He nonetheless looked like a happy man, Pia thought as they sat down at the table.

"So has the cat recovered from his injuries?" Sergei asked, his eyes twinkling. Pia reported on Winston's return to good health and then became serious.

"I think I know what the guy who broke into my house was after," she said quietly. She told them everything, beginning with the theft of her notes identifying the boys and ending with the discovery of the burka in the cemetery and her growing suspicions about Martin Geneve.

"Oh, Pia, I'm so sorry. And I encouraged you to spend time with him," Margaret said in a strangled voice. "Maybe you should come and stay with us for now – or we could come and stay with you. I don't like the idea of your being alone in the house while all this is going on. You've already had one knock on the head."

"Don't worry, Auntie. Thanks to Sergei, my house has more security than your average bank vault. Nobody can get in. But if you have any bright ideas about how to catch the bad guy in all this, make sure you let me know. I've gone from what I thought was a straightforward book project to being embroiled in a triple murder investigation with no obvious end in sight."

Margaret was still fretting an hour later as Pia was leaving. "I know you've had your share of trouble with the arts community, but I'm certain you would be a lot safer if you'd just stuck with movie reviews and the like," Margaret observed, the anxiety in her voice belying her smile.

Pia could see her aunt was worried so she didn't tease her. But the fact was that Margaret herself had never been one to err on the side of caution. As the *Gazette*'s first-ever female foreign correspondent, she'd traveled the world, drawn like a magnet to war zones, coups, and natural calamities. She'd gone on to smash through a huge number of glass ceilings to become a powerful senior editor. And in an era when women got married and settled down, she'd remained stubbornly single – until she met Sergei. And Pia wondered about Sergei. He wasn't exactly a safe, predictable choice. She said none of this. Instead she smiled reassuringly at her aunt.

"Don't worry so much. I'll stay in touch."

When the weekend finally came, Pia spent the whole of Saturday fretting about Saturday night. She tried to work on *Too Young to Die* but each word put up such a fierce resistance that she finally gave up. She went for a long run in the ravine, driving herself up and down hills, hoping the pain would clear her head. When it came time to get dressed, she pulled on a pair of jeans, a white, sleeveless blouse and slid on her flip-flops. She was desperate to get this over with.

Julieta answered the door and showed her to the back terrace where Martin and Marco appeared to be on the losing end of a battle with the barbecue.

"Just a few technical difficulties," Martin muttered as he kissed her quickly before turning to pick up a blackened metal tube from the dozen or so barbecue parts scattered on the table. "We'll have it fixed in no time."

"Either that or you two will blow up the neighborhood," Julieta harrumphed. "I advise you, Miss Pia, to go stand on the other side of the pool where you might be safe. I've got Freddie in the kitchen where he won't be exploded into one million pieces. Me, I'm going to get you a drink if you tell me what it is you would like."

Marco uttered what sounded like Italian curses as he tugged at something underneath the barbecue. Martin, armed now with a sturdy metal-bristled brush, was bent over the top, vigorously cleaning some part of the inner workings.

"If you don't mind, maybe I'll come with you and say hi to Freddie," Pia said to Julieta, beating back twinges of guilt as the other woman nodded her enthusiastic approval.

While Julieta mixed her a gin and tonic, Pia told her about Winston and patted Freddie. Then she made a show of digging around in her purse for a picture of the cat but instead came up with one of the Wilson Scott photos she had printed the night before.

"This is that politician who killed himself in the motel a while ago. Did you know him, Julieta?" Pia asked, tossing the photo on the counter with deceptive casualness.

Julieta picked it up to take a look, "Oh, him, yes he came to dinner at the house sometimes. He was the one who liked art, I think."

"Yes, he had a collection. I'm trying to write a book about his death and the murder of the other minister, the woman, May Gatway. What did you think of this guy Wilson Scott?"

Julieta suddenly frowned and looked up at Pia. "Miss Pia, I work for Martin and I shouldn't be talking about any of his guests. Especially not for a book. I don't think he would like me to be gossiping, even if it is with you."

"Sorry, Julieta. It's just that I'm trying to get a sense of the fellow. To do that I'm talking to anyone who knew him."

"Then you really should talk to Martin, my dear. I don't think I can help you very much," Julieta said, making it clear the conversation was over. It wasn't a lot to go on, Pia thought, but at least she now knew Scott had been to the house for dinner with Martin. She chatted for a few more minutes with Julieta and then wandered back out to the terrace.

The barbecue was back in one piece. Marco and the tools were gone and Martin was giving the grill a final brushing.

"I see you are a fair-weather friend," he joked when he saw

Pia. "Your type always come out when the risk of death by gas explosion has disappeared. Oh, and look at this, you have the four-legged traitor with you. Freddie, my old buddy, I thought you at least would stick with the hand that feeds you. But no, off you ran to the kitchen with Julieta just because she promised you a treat. It's enough to break a man's heart."

Pia smiled and turned to watch Julieta carrying out a tray laden with food. Martin took it from her, put two thick rib eye steaks on the grill and began describing how he had mastered the barbecue despite Julieta's misgivings.

"Admit it, Julieta, I'm now good at this, don't you think? I hardly ever screw things up anymore, not like in the beginning."

"Yes, Martin, you have made progress," the housekeeper conceded as she set the table for two. "But in the beginning there was so much waste. Food was burnt. Food was raw. Food fell on the ground. Freddie was the only one who was happy because he got to eat everything you dropped. Look at him now. He still thinks we're living in the bad old days."

The dog had installed himself next to the barbecue and was greedily eyeing the steaks. A gleaming drop of drool from the corner of his mouth undermined what passed for dignity in the canine world.

Martin laughed as Julieta left the terrace and then turned his gaze on Pia. In the moment of silence that followed, she realized that she was as tense as an overtuned piano string. One that was about to break.

"What's wrong, Pia?" Martin asked in a gentle voice. "You look like you're worried about more than my cooking."

Pia willed herself to smile while she mumbled her excuses. "Nothing, nothing at all is wrong. It's just been really busy at work and I probably haven't been getting enough exercise," she said, offering the first explanation that came into her head. "That means I also have trouble sleeping, and then I feel too tired to force myself to go for a run. It's a bit of a vicious circle, but it will pass."

Martin looked quizzical, then seemed to accept her excuse. A few seconds later the lights on the terrace flickered off and on, and they began to reminisce about what they had been doing the summer of a massive power blackout that had plunged Toronto and much of northeastern North America into darkness.

Martin's house, it turned out, had been without power for exactly ten minutes – the time it took Marco to start the backup generators on the property.

"Some guys had it made," Pia said dryly. "I worked until late the first night – we had to wait for the premier to come out and tell us everything was going to be okay even though he hadn't the faintest idea whether things were really going to be okay. I was lucky though, because my Aunt Margaret's friend Sergei is a good guy to have around in an emergency. As soon as it became clear it was something bigger than your regular local power failure, he put together enough batteries and candles and drinking water for to last a month. When I finally got home, he and Margaret came over to my place and we sat in the garden staring at stars that I don't think have been seen in Toronto in a century. I remember being amazed at how different the city sounded. It was both quieter and yet more alive. Somebody in my neighborhood was playing a guitar. You could hear people talking in their backyards. Candles were flickering everywhere."

Pia's neighborhood was one of the last in the province to have power restored three days later. "But I'll never forget how magical it was that first night," she sighed.

Martin smiled at her as he served the steaks and brought the plates to the table. "You are beautiful all the time but you are really beautiful when you get involved in telling a story. It must be the journalist in you."

Much to her irritation, Pia blushed. They moved on to other topics, everything from the latest bungling by the city's mayor to whether the province's growing problem with electricity shortages meant they were destined to freeze in the dark come winter. Everything, that is, except the questions hammering away in Pia's head. Her opportunity came just after dinner when the telephone rang inside the house and Julieta summoned Martin to take the call.

Pia followed him in from the terrace and made her way to one of the bathrooms on the main floor. She could hear Martin still speaking on the telephone when she emerged a few minutes later. Heart pounding, she ran up the stairs to his bedroom and went into the ensuite bathroom. There, she pulled open the top drawer but found only an elaborate collection of shaving-related items. Who knew there were that many types of shaving cream?

She finally found a hairbrush in the third drawer. She quickly pulled out one of the small freezer bags she had stuffed into a pocket before leaving home. She drew a tangle of hairs from the brush and put it into the bag. Then she spotted Martin's toothbrush in a holder on the counter and thought, what the hell. She picked it up and after several tries succeeded in pulling out two tiny bristles. They too went into a plastic bag and into her pocket.

Satisfied with her haul, Pia began contemplating her exit strategy. As far as she was concerned, the evening was now over. She opened the bathroom door, turned off the light, and was about the leave the bedroom when she heard his voice.

"I'm so happy you found your way up here on your own. I was trying to figure out a graceful way of delivering a proper invitation," Martin said as he unfolded himself from one of the leather chairs in front of the fireplace and walked toward her. His manner didn't appear threatening, but Pia nonetheless felt a spasm of anxiety as he approached, his gray eyes holding her startled gaze. Martin reached out and touched her shoulder, gently drawing her toward him. Stiff with anxiety, she took a step in his direction but held herself rigid as his arms folded warmly around her.

"I've been wanting to do this all evening but you seemed so preoccupied," he whispered as he lowered his face into her hair. One of his hands drifted softly up the nape of her neck and became tangled in her curls. His thumb began to guide her face up so he could claim her lips, but before he could go any further Pia abruptly turned away.

"Martin, the truth is I don't feel very well. I probably shouldn't have come over. I thought I was going to be okay, but I think the drinks or something have made my headache come back. I need to go home, take some painkillers and go to bed. By myself. It's the only way I can deal with this. I'm so sorry."

Pia's head really was aching by this point, so she was relieved when he said he understood. At home a while later, she pulled the two plastic bags from her pocket, laid them on the kitchen table, and smoothed them out. Martin Geneve, she thought gloomily, you understand nothing. Nothing at all.

Chapter Nineteen

PIA STRUGGLED THROUGH another unhappy night, haunted by a confusion of memories and anxiety. Martin's smile. The way his breath warmed her skin when he held her close. The touch of his hands. Persistent, nagging questions about whether those hands belonged to a murderer. The sun was again nudging at the night sky when exhaustion finally prevailed over agitation. Pia felt as if she had just fallen asleep when an imperious ringing dragged her back to reality. She groaned and, eyes still closed, reached out to locate the offending telephone.

"It's noon, Keyne, you should have been up and around hours ago," Nancy Morton said abruptly, not bothering to say who was calling. "But never mind. I have news."

"You caught the bad guy?" Pia croaked, opening her eyes and struggling frantically to extricate herself from tangled sheets.

"I wish. What I should have said is that I have bad news. That moron Schmidt is calling off the watch in the cemetery. It hasn't been a week, but he's decided the money would be better spent, as he put it, on some potentially more useful aspect of the ongoing investigation. Of course he hasn't said what the other potentially useful aspect might be. My suspicion is he's trying to keep costs down because that goes over well with the brass," Morton said, making no effort to hide her derision. "And really, who wants to spend a hell of a lot of money chasing down some sicko who bashed a couple of refugee kids? It's not like they were nice, white, taxpaying citizens or anything."

"You still think our guy might show up for the burka?"

"Well, what little we know about him suggests he pays attention to detail. And I can't imagine he's comfortable with this detail out there in the flowerpot. I'm going to keep watch myself for the next night or two."

"I'll come with you."

"I think not. You aren't my idea of a useful backup if there's trouble."

"But you shouldn't be out there alone. At least I'll be there to scream for help if we need it," Pia countered. "And besides, you can't really stop me from showing up – and I will show up – so we might as well be organized about this."

Morton protested a while longer before conceding defeat. "I'll pick you up just after ten and we'll head over there. Wear something practical. Have something warm with you because sitting around in the dark can be a chilly business. And bring some bug repellent in case there's a mosquito or two hanging around in all that greenery."

Pia slumped back on the bed after finalizing the arrangements. Another sleepless night awaited her but at least she would be doing something useful. She pulled the covers up and dozed. When she finally crawled out of bed it was mid afternoon. She tried two cups of coffee to banish her grogginess. When that didn't work, she went for a run. Then she got to work. She typed up her latest notes on the murder investigation, copied them to a disk, printed a copy, and tucked everything in safely with the tampons.

Darkness was settling in as Pia put the thermos of coffee in a packsack already stuffed with six apples, two mugs, a flashlight, a can of mosquito repellent, an extra sweater, a small blanket to sit on, and some Russian chocolates left over from one of Sergei's recent visits.

"You do realize we are going out for overnight, not for a week?" Morton said when she saw the bag Pia tossed into the back seat of the detective's car.

"Remind me of that when you are begging for coffee or apples or some of the chocolate I'll be gobbling down in front of you."

Morton grunted and then suddenly became all business. "I'm not going to move this car until we agree on a set of rules for tonight. First, this isn't about tackling the guy in the graveyard and bringing him in. He's dangerous, he might be armed, and we don't need to do that. If he shows up, all we need to do is follow him. I'm calling in some favors from a few uniforms I know who are patrolling tonight. Once we are on his tail, I'll call them for backup and that's when that handcuffs are going to go on this asshole. So what I'm saying that is this is no time for heroics. You got that?"

"Got it. I'm supposed to jump on him as he goes by, wrestle him to the ground, handcuff him, and then let you know when it's all over and it's safe for you to come out," Pia joked. "No, seriously, Nancy, I hear you. I just hope he shows."

The cemetery ran between two main streets, with entrances off both. They parked a few blocks away and entered through the park's wooded area, debating various strategies as they crawled over the stone wall. Pia, they decided, would settle in behind a large white mausoleum crawling with angels. From her hiding place, she could monitor the gravestone where the burka had been hidden by leaning to the left and peeking through the space that separated the body of one angel from its wing. If she leaned to the right, she could see around the corner of the mausoleum to one of the cemetery's entrances. Morton set up in some tired-looking lilac bushes so she could monitor both the entrance from the other street and Hilda Lonsdone's gravestone.

They settled down to wait. It was a beautiful night but, even so, after the first hour Pia realized she was in for an ordeal. The time crawled by. She'd read somewhere that waiting could be made less painful of you divided it into five-minute intervals and concentrated on each minute as it passed. Maybe this strategy worked in theory, but in practice, it did nothing to ease the tedium. She began mentally plotting out future developments in *Too Young to Die*. Leone's daughter was now in the clutches of a villain who was threatening to kill the child if her mother didn't provide the names of police moles in his criminal organization. Pia needed to figure out how, when, and where the child would be rescued.

Her musings were interrupted by the unhappy realization that Morton was right about the mosquitoes. Pia often marveled at how Torontonians could sit in their gardens spring, summer, and fall and only rarely have to swat away an insect. Now she knew why. They all hung out in the city's cemeteries waiting for fools to come by, camp out, and offer up their blood for the night. She got out the bug repellent, sprayed the smelly stuff through her hair, on her hands, and over her jeans and long-sleeved T-shirt, praying it would work its magic. Miserable as she was, Pia smiled when she thought about Jasmine spending a whole weekend at the mercy of the little beasts. Mind you, she and Seamus would have had a tent – and plenty of activities to distract them.

Just after midnight, Pia ate an apple with a few of Sergei's chocolates and washed it all down with a cup of coffee. The caffeine should have kept her awake but a half-hour later, the sleepiness that had eluded her for too many nights to count overcame her. Pia fought to keep her eyes open. She gobbled a few more chocolates, poured herself another cup of coffee, and tried see how many mosquitoes she could snatch out of midair in one minute. But it was no contest. The wake-sleep game began in earnest. Her eyes would close, for God only knew how long. Then she'd jerk awake. She thought of her comfortable, warm bed and moaned silently with need. Then she knocked over her coffee cup. It happened during one of those moments when her whole body started awake. Her elbow struck the empty metal cup, sending it clattering off the ledge where she'd left it and onto the marble base just below.

Pia prayed that Morton hadn't heard the racket, She didn't want to be sent home in disgrace. A second later she realized Morton's wrath was the least of her problems. A quick peek around the side of the angel told her that the sound had attracted the attention of a shadowy figure near Hilda Lonsdone's grave. He must have come into the cemetery while she was dozing, Pia realized as soon as she saw him rising quickly from the plastic bag he'd just cut open. Morton had told her the police had left the bag in the urn as a decoy, filling it with an old blanket. Under different circumstances, Pia would have enjoyed imagining the expression on his face when he found out the burka was gone. But she had other things to worry about – like the vicious-looking blade in the guy's hand.

Fully awake now, Pia took another quick look out from her hiding spot and realized the shadowy figure was coming straight toward her. He was all in black and wore a black bala-clava over his head. She positioned herself in a crouch, prepared to sprint for her life. Before she could bolt, however, Morton's voice splintered the night silence.

"Police. Halt! Freeze right where you are, buddy."

The hunter, realizing all of a sudden that he was the prey, quickly changed course. With less than thirty feet to go before he reached Pia, he veered toward the main exit. Morton, gun in hand, sprinted across the cemetery after him, but he had a significant head start and he was fast. The detective would never catch him.

Pia wasn't thinking straight or she would have realized it was an extremely bad idea to dart out from behind the angel and hit him sideways, smashing up against the arm that ended with the hand that held the knife. He grunted, surprised by the impact, and stumbled. Propelled by her momentum, Pia stumbled with him. For a moment she thought he would fall and that she would land on top of him, nice and close so that he wouldn't have to reach very far to finish her off with his weapon. Instead, he regained his footing. In desperation, Pia grabbed his arm and pushed him sideways again so that their bodies separated.

He turned on her silently, raising the knife. It arced through the air and came slashing down at Pia's face. She turned her head and shifted her body, but the glistening blade still caught the loose material of her shirt, slicing through it like butter. Pia saw him hesitate for a fraction of a second as he tried to decide whether to come at her again. But Morton was bearing down on them. He ran, disappearing through the gate in the distance seconds after the detective arrived at Pia's side.

"Did he get you?" Morton asked urgently as she radioed for help, describing the suspect and the direction of his flight.

"I don't think so."

"Okay, stay put."

Pia was trembling so much she had little choice. She stumbed her way over to a bench. Sirens wailed in the distance. She tried to remember the color of her assailant's eyes, the only part of him visible behind the face covering. But she hadn't been able to tell in the darkness. The front of her left shoulder began to sting; when she reached up to touch it, her hand came away sticky with blood. She wondered if she should be making some attempt to put pressure on the wound, but was unable to make even that decision. Shivering, she thought about the intensity of her fear. May Gatway must have felt that and more as the killer came after her, slashing, peeling open her skin so that the life would drain from her. Tariq and Mohammed would have been even more helpless and vulnerable.

A cruiser, all screaming siren and flashing red lights, careened into the cemetery and picked up Pia in its headlights. She remained on the bench, staring down at the blood on her hand, as two officers emerged from the car and came over. Nobody, she thought numbly, had arrived in time to rescue May Gatway or the boys.

An hour later, Morton joined Pia in the hospital emergency ward and told her their quarry had escaped. "He was gone by the time I came out the cemetery gates. We're trolling for witnesses but we're talking Sunday night in Toronto. World-class city or no, you just don't get that many people wandering around or even looking out their windows at three in the morning."

"Nancy, I'm sorry about what happened. I kept falling asleep and then I knocked over my coffee cup," Pia said, deciding she'd best get the discussion out of the way. "We might have him by now if I wasn't such an idiot."

Morton sighed glumly. "Yes, you are an idiot. But I'm one too for letting you get anywhere near that cemetery tonight. I'm going to have to do some fast talking to explain myself. My only hope is that Schmidt won't be interested in broadcasting it because it was his fucking stupid decision to take the surveillance out of there in the first place."

"So, okay, I'm an idiot. But I paid the price," Pia said, looking down at her shoulder. "I'm going to be scarred for life."

"Nice try. I talked to the doctor on the way in and he told me it's a scratch that doesn't even require stitches. You are one lucky cookie."

Indeed she was. The officers who found her in the cemetery insisted on calling an ambulance when they saw the blood on Pia's clothes. At the hospital, an older nurse with gentle hands helped her out of her shirt. The front of Pia's shoulder was a bloody mess but it looked far worse than it actually was. Once all the gore was washed away, she was left with a thin, shallow scratch the length of a new pencil.

"You were very, very, fortunate my dear," the nurse clucked after the doctor had come and gone and she was bandaging up the wound. "So fortunate."

Pia hitched a ride home from the hospital with Morton and slept for a few hours before heading to work in the late morning.

Jasmine materialized at her office door almost immediately and they made their morning trek to the cafeteria for coffee.

"So ask me how the camping trip went," Jasmine urged.

"How did the camping trip go, Jasmine?"

"Well, I thought it was going to be over before we even got started because Seamus made me leave my cellphone at home. He said it would spoil the ambience if I was taking calls all weekend. You know I hate being unwired. So imagine how I felt when I discovered out in the canoe at the end of the first day that he brought his phone. He said that it was different because he kept his off and only had it with him in case of emergency. Pompous ass. But I forgave him."

"That's kind of out of character – the forgiveness stuff, I mean," Pia said, thinking that she really must be sleep deprived because even the sludge they called coffee in the *Gazette*'s cafeteria tasted good.

"Yeah, well, I didn't have much choice. I owed him one after I tipped the canoe over with all our stuff in it."

"Now this sounds more typical. Did everything go to the bottom of the lake?"

"No. It was just a little accident at the very start. Seamus showed me how to put the paddle across the canoe to steady it as I got in, and I did what I was told. But this huge horse-fly – it must have been the size of a hummingbird – landed on my shoulder. When I tried to whack it before it consumed my left arm, I lost my balance and the canoe tipped and I fell in. There was only about two feet of water and Seamus had wrapped everything up in watertight bags anyway because it looked like it might rain. But it wasn't the best start, I admit. Actually, after it happened I was kind of wondering if I would need to hire a taxi to get back to the city. But you know what? He was completely sweet about it all. He said that if dumping his stuff out of the canoe is the worst thing I ever do to him, he'd be a happy man."

"How did your boots stand up? I hope you didn't get any mud on them or anything."

"Smarty-pants. They were just fine. I was wearing my flip-flops when I fell out of the canoe so the boots didn't get wet. And they were great later in the day when it rained like hell for an hour or two."

"That must have been fun."

Jasmine startled Pia by breaking into a huge grin. "You bet it was. We'd arrived at our camping spot and Seamus had already set up the tent. So when the rain started we crawled right in and did some – what is it your star theater reviewer does again? Oh right, we canoodled. Then it stopped raining and the sun came out and we had grilled shrimp and tomato and asparagus salad for dinner. Then as the sun was setting, Seamus asked me to marry him and I said yes."

"He asked you to marry him and you said yes?" Pia parroted in astonishment. "Talk about burying the lede of the story. You panic at the sight of a little fly, dump his camping stuff in the lake and the guy proposes. And you said yes?"

"That's right. Look, here's proof," Jasmine said, holding

out her left hand to show off a thick gold band embedded with three emeralds. "We're going to tell my parents tonight and after that's done, drive over to his parents' house to tell them the news."

"There must be something in the water. Aunt Margaret and Sergei just told me they are getting married. Are you sure you aren't rushing into this?"

"Pia, I've known Seamus since I was eight years old. We hung around all through high school and university and ever since then. I think I can vouch for his character. I just didn't realize until recently that there's more than friendship between us. I mean, he's hot."

"Okay, okay, I don't want too much information." Pia, who had raised her arm in a bid to make Jasmine keep the details to herself, grimaced involuntarily when the bandage on her shoulder pulled at her skin.

"What's wrong with you?" Jasmine said, noticing Pia's sudden paleness.

"Oh, I was in a cemetery last night around two in the morning and a guy – actually he's a murder suspect – tried to stab me. Lucky for me, he pretty much missed, so I ended up with just a flesh wound. The doctor says there won't even be a scar."

"I don't believe it. You're just trying to one-up my news."

Pia smiled, leaned forward, and pulled the collar of her shirt aside to reveal the bandage.

"I'd love to be pulling your leg, Jasmine dear, but unfortunately I've just told you the whole sorry truth. You made one silly mistake this weekend and ended up soaked and engaged. I made one silly mistake this weekend and ended up fighting for my life with a knife-wielding maniac. Let's have another coffee and I'll tell you all about it."

Chapter Twenty

PIA WORKED THE REST of the day on autopilot, desperate for the time to pass so she could get some sleep. Before connecting with her bed, however, she had to stop by Louise Lutkin's office to deliver the first ten chapters of *Too Young to Die*. She didn't really want to deal with Louise in person, but her luck deserted her. The agent, tall, slim, brassy-blond, and dressed as usual in black, ushered her guest into her office. Pia sat down on one of the sleek, fire-truck-red sofas and tried to stay awake while Louise produced two cups of espresso from a space-age-looking machine near her desk. Today she wore black pants and a sleeveless black blouse that set off her glossy good looks. Louise's husband was one of the city's top plastic surgeons, and she admitted unabashedly to drawing upon his expertise. It was impossible to tell how old she really was, but based on little clues, such as when she went to university and the age of her two children, Pia put her somewhere in her late fifties. She looked forty.

"It's good you are here because we need to chat about a couple of things," Louise said as she delivered the coffee in a small gold and white cup and saucer. Pia groaned inwardly. Louise could be dangerously persuasive when she wanted something, whether it was a tighter deadline or changes to the proposed title for a book. Pia wasn't all that committed to *Too Young to Die*, but she did not want to discuss a new title or any other major changes on two hours of sleep. You were certain to lose an argument with Louise if you weren't in top form and Pia wasn't in top form. Emotionally, she felt like a worn-out dishrag: limp, grubby, and fraying badly at the edges.

"What's this about you doing a book on those dead politicians and why do I have to read about it in the newspaper?"

Pia realized that this was the real reason she'd been hauled in for coffee. "I'm not keeping secrets," she said in a mild voice. "I just haven't had a chance to talk to you about it. Do you think a publisher would be interested?"

"Dead politicians, seedy motels, and suggestions of blackmail tend to pique people's interest. Will you have any sensational new revelations? That always helps," Louise said dryly.

"Oh, I think so. But I'm still working on it."

"You're being awfully mysterious. If you don't want to share the story with your agent, who over many years has given you so much good advice and helped you make enough money to renovate that dump you live in, that's your business," Louise said huffily.

Pia managed to placate the agent, assuring her she would provide an outline of the new project within the next two months. She was home in bed by seven-thirty.

It was amazing how twelve hours of sleep could make the world seem so much more manageable, Pia thought after work the next day. For the first time in what seemed like ages, she felt enthusiastic about getting some exercise. She'd gone back and forth all day on whether to call Jack Cleary about going for a run. He was good company, and he would take her mind off Martin and her troubles. But she wasn't ready to reinstate Jack as a romantic interest. After the mess with Martin, she wasn't sure anybody would ever be in that category again. She finally decided it would be nice to have a running buddy, but when she finally picked up the phone and dialed Jack's number, he begged off, saying he had work he needed to do. They arranged to meet the next night for a drink. Pia was pulling on her running clothes when the telephone rang.

"I hope you are feeling better," Martin said by way of greeting. Pia was furious with herself for grabbing the phone without first checking the display to see who was calling. Now she had to deal with him.

"Much better, thanks," she said, trying to sound as blasé as possible. Not so long ago, the sound of his voice had made her shiver with anticipation. Now it reminded her that she still hadn't given the hair samples to Morton to check against those found on the burka. "So good, in fact, that I'm heading out for a long run while there's still enough light."

"I don't suppose you'd like to grab a bite to eat when you finish?"

"Under normal circumstances I would, Martin, but I've got some work that I absolutely have to get through tonight. May I take a rain check?" The excuse sounded feeble, but it was the best she could do.

"I was starting to think you were enjoying my company, but it seems I've suffered a setback. Care to tell me what's going on?"

"Nothing is going on. Nothing at all. I've just got some deadlines to meet. And I'm desperate to get some exercise. How about if I call you later in the week?" Pia suggested lamely.

After hanging up, she did a few warmup stretches and checked her watch. She had maybe an hour of daylight left. The heat of the day had eased and a light breeze was blowing the worst of the air pollution north to the unsuspecting souls in cottage country as Pia followed the forested path down into the ravine. Rays of sun played against the trees on one side of the path. The other side was already blanketed in shadows. She ran slowly at first. The first half hour was always tough, as if her body were rebelling at the sudden surge of activity. But then her muscles resigned themselves to their fate and she relaxed into a regular rhythm. She felt as if she could run forever.

Pia passed three solitary runners, but otherwise she was on

her own with what passed for nature in the big city. Ahead of her she watched dozens of small brown and black birds settling in the branches of a huge maple to noisily discuss the day's events. Pia slowed almost to a walk to listen to them. From early spring, through to mid-fall a similar flock took up residence in the tree in front of her house. She knew winter was over when they returned from wherever they spent the cold season and began serenading her every day at dawn. After the morning concert, the birds flew off, returning at dusk to reoccupy the tree for the night. Her neighbors complained about the droppings that rained down on vehicles parked under the tree by unsuspecting drivers, but Pia loved the birdsong that drifted through the open windows twice each day.

Finally, she turned around and headed home. The sun, after lingering in the sky like an old friend who is reluctant to depart, suddenly made up its mind to rush off. Deep shadows cloaked the ravine as she retraced her steps.

Pia had covered about a quarter-mile when she thought she heard footsteps behind her. At first she felt reassured to know there was another runner in the vicinity. But there was nobody behind her when she glanced back. Eager now to regain the city streets with their reassuring lights and pedestrian traffic, Pia increased her speed. Then she heard the footsteps again. They also picked up the pace. This time when she took a quick look over her shoulder, Pia saw a figure running off to one side of the path in the deep shadows of the trees, a figure that was gaining fast on her. For the first time she felt uneasy. She checked again and this time could not suppress a tiny whimper of fear. She was almost certain he had something in his right hand. Something that glinted for a second in the scattered light that cut through the trees from the street above.

A long, straight stretch lay ahead with no help in sight. Pia pushed herself into a flat-out sprint, but her adolescent track and field experience told her the other runner was rapidly closing the distance between them. She tried without success to remember what was around the next corner. As it turned out, two older men were strolling along the path with their backs to her. One of them held the leash of a boisterous chocolate Lab. Relief, like a big, warm wave, washed over Pia. She thought the steps behind her faltered and then stopped, but she wasn't certain and she had no intention of slowing down to look.

"Wait, wait!" The plea came out more like a faint sob but the urgency in her voice galvanized the two men, who immediately turned around. One reached out to steady Pia when she stumbled to a halt. "Somebody is chasing me. I think he has knife. Please. Please wait."

"Easy," said the taller man. "We're not going anywhere."

Her breath was coming in short gasps. The shorter of her two rescuers, the one with the dog, ran back toward the corner. "No, don't go, he's dangerous," Pia warned in a strangled voice. "Don't go near him." But there was nobody to go near.

"Whoever it was, he's gone," said the man with the dog, who a few minutes later introduced himself as Gerry. "I followed the path down to the next corner but nobody was around.

The creep might be hiding somewhere back in the trees, but I think he probably ran off on one of the little trails that take you out of the ravine."

Karl, the taller of the two, wanted to call the police but Pia convinced them it wouldn't do much good. Back up on the street she started to doubt herself. Perhaps she had been mistaken and her pursuer was really just some guy out for his evening exercise. Maybe her imagination was working overtime after the incident in the cemetery. Karl and Gerry walked Pia home, confiding along the way that they were newlyweds who had recently gone to the altar under Canada's liberalized gay marriage law. She invited them in for coffee or a drink but they said they wanted to get home themselves, so she wrote down their names and address and made a mental note to send them a proper thank-you. They again urged her to file a report with the police.

"If there is some pervert down there, the cops need to nab him because he might go after somebody else and she might not be as lucky," Gerry observed. Pia nodded and said she'd think about it.

As it turned out, she was able to tell Nancy Morton the whole story within the hour. There was a message on the answering machine from the detective suggesting that Pia come down to the station to view the evidence from all the cases. Morton said she would be around throughout the evening so Pia took the time to have a shower. Before leaving, she checked all the doors to the house and did a test on the security system. The siren blared right on cue and the monitoring company called to check in, just as they were supposed to do. Thank you, Sergei, she thought as she walked to the car.

Morton was eating the last few bites of a hamburger when Pia walked into her office.

"You gotta try one of these, my friend. Eight ounces of pure beef, garlic, and onions. You'll never eat a vegetable again," Morton rhapsodized. "The place over on the corner makes them. And they deliver."

"You're going to be dead before you are fifty," Pia predicted somberly. "But that means you'll still outlive me, the way things are going."

"What's up?"

Pia told her what happened in the ravine and then dutifully listened to Morton's lecture on the dangers of running alone. "It could have been your usual run-of-the-mill freak down there," the detective said, "Or maybe our suspect is just sick of you poking your nose into things. You were the one who found the boys and got them talking about seeing him in Wilson Scott's motel room. And there you were again in the cemetery, messing with his plans. If he spent any time at all watching your house before he broke in that night, he would have known you are a runner. He probably couldn't believe his luck when he realized you were going out by yourself in the ravine. In the dark. Honestly, sometimes I think you have shit for brains."

Pia didn't know what to think. Maybe her imagination was out of control. Or maybe not.

"It wasn't dark when I started out," she offered in self-defense. "And it was really just dusk when this happened."

Pia decided to change the subject. "Do you think you could get the forensics guys to compare these with whatever they find on the burka?" she asked quietly, handing over the hair and toothbrush samples she'd taken from Martin's house. Morton looked down at the plastic bags, read the label with his name on it, and nodded.

"Did he know you were going running tonight?"

Pia felt her heart sink. "Yeah, but it wasn't a secret. I talked to somebody else before I went out so he also knew."

"Well, maybe we should check this other guy out too. His name?" Morton demanded.

A few minutes later Morton pulled Jack's photo up on the provincial government website.

"Think you can get some hair or saliva samples from him?" the detective asked. "Oh, silly me. Of course you can. Do the two guys know about each other by the way?"

"No, not really," Pia admitted, prompting Morton to roll her eyes and mutter something about the morals of an alley cat.

In the basement of the station, rows of carefully labeled evidence had been laid out on long tables. Pia did a quick survey of all the material and a few minutes later began going over everything again, this time more slowly. The baseball bat used on Tariq and Mohammed was the first item, the end stained dark with blood. When she came to the material seized from the Gatway murder scene, she realized that it too was about blood. Only a few drops were evident on some of the items. In other instances, there was so much blood Pia's imagination conjured up the macabre image of Gatway's body as a high-pressure pump spraying drops in all directions.

It was all there. The box cutter that had slashed the minister as she ran for her life. The fireplace poker. Piles of old photographs. A rolled-up canvas Pia hadn't noticed the night of Gatway's death.

"What's this about?" she asked, prompting Morton to hand her a pair of gloves so she could remove the canvas from its transparent plastic evidence bag. The answer to Pia's question became immediately apparent. The painting, about two feet wide and three feet tall, was a street scene dominated by two angular women painted in shades of black, dark blue, and green. They wore elaborate, fur-trimmed coats, hats with huge feathers, and had a lean, hard look that in Pia's opinion made them seem a bit crazed. She wasn't sure she liked the painting, but then art criticism wasn't what this exercise was about. It was about the presence of six large drops of blood on the pale blue and gray sky behind the artist's subjects.

"I wonder why this was in the attic?" Pia mused, before turning to go through the crime scene photographs from the attic.

On the night May Gatway died, Pia noticed, the painting had been unfurled on a battered desk. Two outdated editions of the *Parliamentary Guide*, the red book that records federal and provincial election results, held it down on opposite corners.

Pia made a mental note to ask Jack Cleary if he knew

anything about the painting and then moved on. Two hours later, they weren't much further ahead than when they started. No great undiscovered clues surfaced. Extensive fingerprint samples lifted from all three crime scenes had produced zilch in the way of useful leads.

"I really hope that DNA evidence from the burka turns up something," Morton said as they parted outside the station. She didn't sound particularly optimistic. "I've been bugging them every day but I still don't have anything from those wankers. They keep telling me they need two weeks, but I've been doing some reading on what's involved because I'm the suspicious type, and it turns out that as far as the science is concerned they should be able to do the analysis in thirty-six hours."

The next morning, Pia took more care than usual with her appearance. After weeks of delays, she'd finally been granted a one-on-one interview with May Gatway's replacement in the culture ministry. She had requested the interview the week after Gatway's demise, but Mario Bellini's communications aide put her off, insisting the new minister needed time to brush up on the issues.

Bellini had coasted to elected office in the previous election on the strength of name recognition. He owned a large car dealership in his home town of Windsor and for years poured money into local radio and television advertisements for Bellini Auto Sales – Where the Customer Is Always Right. How and why he rose from the obscurity of the backbenches to the culture ministry was less obvious. The only hint she picked up in her research was that Bellini, a long-time party stalwart, had a soft spot for opera and donated generously to the arts community in his home town. That, combined with the government's need for cabinet-level representation from Windsor, meant Bellini's reward for being a patient and loyal foot soldier had finally come through.

Pia had met the minister, a short, stocky man with a ready smile and dancing brown eyes, once or twice in the past, before he was important. He hadn't changed much from his days as a backbench member of Parliament, she noted as he welcomed her into May Gatway's old office just after 10 a.m.

He ushered her to the sofa and the two of them exchanged pleasantries as Pia and the minister's aide put their tape recorders on the coffee table and turned them on. She was a big believer in the value of a tape-recorded interview. It kept both sides honest. A secretary brought in coffee, and for the next forty minutes Pia asked questions, beginning with the usual ones about government funding for the arts. She noted with interest Bellini's reluctance to make a firm commitment to carrying out Gatway's policies on the restoration of looted art. She wondered if it had anything to do with who had contributed to his election campaign and she scribbled a reminder to check who his financial supporters were. Near the end of the interview, when Pia was asking about the minister's personal support for the arts, he suddenly became very animated and told her he had sung tenor in some amateur opera productions.

Before she could say anything more, he stood up, walked to the far side of the room, struck a pose, and started warbling something in Italian while Pia and his horrified aide looked on. After a few minutes he stopped abruptly.

"Do you know this music?" he asked Pia, who promptly admitted ignorance. "It's from *Tosca*. By Puccini. He was a genius, an absolute genius, don't you think?"

Perhaps he expected an answer. But Pia, although she had never before been serenaded during an interview, wasn't listening. She couldn't take her eyes off the painting on the wall behind Bellini.

"I'm sorry to interrupt, Minister, but this painting, has it always been hanging here?"

Bellini, who was outlining the plot of *Tosca* for Pia's benefit, was caught off guard. "What? That painting? Oh no, it used to be in Wilson Scott's office behind his desk. Such a sad story about him, eh? Anyway when I moved in here I had my choice of art from the legislature's collection. I know that this one is pretty famous and since it was available – I mean, poor Wilson wasn't going to be looking at it any more – I requested it, though to tell you to truth, I'm not sure I want to keep it. Those women, they are kind of scary after a while. Not beautiful to look at."

Pia got to her feet. Ignoring Bellini, she walked over to the painting and read the information tag on the wall beside it. It was the work of Stefan Tischler of Germany, born 1881, died 1940. The piece, entitled *The Ladies*, had been given to the government by an anonymous donor in 1954.

So now she knew what she was looking at on the wall in front of her. What she couldn't explain was why the identical painting had been in the legislature's attic at the time of May Gatway's death.

Chapter Twenty-One

THE COINCIDENCE OF THE identical paintings nagged at Pia until she got home from work and found Margaret on the front porch. During the years they'd lived together, Pia had witnessed her aunt's fury only on rare occasions. Margaret wasn't the type to lose control, or to scream and shout. She didn't need to. She was at her scariest when a tense stillness took over. She would look at you with narrowed eyes and speak in a voice that hinted at terrible things to come. The first time Pia saw her like this was the day she finally told Margaret about Max.

The second time was when Pia, seventeen years old by then, ignored Margaret's midnight curfew and stayed out all night partying with friends. It was only when she was crowded into a booth with her friends at a greasy spoon, watching the sun rise and the short-order cook whip up eggs, bacon, and home fries that trepidation set in. Then, as now, Margaret – still, pale, her green eyes seething – had been waiting for Pia to come home. Fearing a scene that day so many years ago, Pia started apologizing the moment she walked in the door. Margaret had listened in silence and then lit into her in a low, furious voice. She spoke of mutual respect, responsibility, and trust, and concluded with a piece of advice Pia had never forgotten.

"Don't abuse the people who love you most," Margaret warned. "A little bit of them will die every time. And so will a part of you."

One look at her aunt's face brought that long ago scene rushing back.

"We need to talk," Margaret said, abruptly vacating the rocking chair on the porch. Pia nodded silently, worried that whatever she said would make things worse. She unlocked the door, disarmed the security system, and braced herself. Margaret, now standing in the vestibule, didn't keep her in suspense.

"So I was at my yoga class this afternoon where one of my classmates is a nurse. And she tells me a fascinating story about recently seeing my one and only beloved niece in the emergency ward of her hospital having a knife wound bandaged up. A knife wound!" Despite a Herculean effort to remain calm, Margaret's words had began to tumble out more quickly and two spots of red appeared on her pale cheeks. "What the hell is going on?"

Pia was now old enough to see what hadn't been so obvious to a seventeen-year-old. Margaret was afraid – afraid for her.

"I'm sorry, Auntie. I didn't want to worry you with all this.

Come on into the kitchen so I can pour us a drink and tell you all about it." It took a while to get through the whole story, beginning with the bungled cemetery surveillance effort and ending with the knife attack. Pia took off her suit jacket and pulled aside her top to prove her injury was more of a scratch than a stab wound. She hadn't even bothered with a bandage that morning.

Then, just to be on the safe side, Pia also described what had happened in the ravine the night before. It was a defensive measure. With her luck, Margaret probably knew Karl or Gerry and would find out anyway. Then there would be real hell to pay.

Margaret's anger gradually evaporated, but she was more worried than ever by the time Pia finished. "Really, I think you should come and stay with us until all of this blows over. Or we can come and stay with you. Please."

"Let me think about it. I can't really make any decisions right now. I'm due to meet Jack for a drink in his neighborhood. I really need to talk to him."

"Maybe I should come with you."

"Does this mean you want to come on all my dates?" Pia teased. "Aren't you busy getting married or something?"

Margaret relaxed enough to laugh. "Well, yes. In three weeks, as a matter of fact. I need something to wear and was wondering if you wanted to come shopping with me later this week. I think I'll have stopped being angry with you by then."

"Three weeks? I thought you were thinking of a New Year's Eve wedding? What happened?"

"Sergei really is worried that I'll change my mind. I won't, of course. But he's spent so much time trying to get me to agree to marry him, it seems pointless to put it off now that I've said yes."

They discussed wedding plans until Pia realized it was getting late. She changed out of her work clothes into a cotton shift, and accepted Margaret's offer of a ride to the pub where she and Jack had arranged to meet.

"But you have to promise not to muscle in on my guy," she joked as they got into the car. Margaret said nothing. Pia, preoccupied with digging around in her purse for the piece of paper with the pub's address on it, didn't notice.

Jack was waiting for her on the outdoor terrace. Pia ordered a glass of white wine and couldn't resist the pub's burger special, complete with bacon, cheddar cheese, fried mushrooms, and thick-cut fries on the side.

"It's nice to see a woman who enjoys her food," Jack observed before they began trading stories about their respective days.

"I got a call from a guy who has inherited a bunch of nineteenth-century drawings and paintings from a great uncle," Jack told her. "The old man was a member of the legislature years ago. His heir is not at all interested in art, but he *is* interested in tax-deductible donations so he wants to give everything to the legislature's collection."

"Do you automatically take these donations?"

"God, no. Sometimes it is all junk and you just have to find a diplomatic way of saying it doesn't fit into the mandate of the collection. Where it gets tricky is if you want a few pieces but the rest are worthless. Then you have to figure out how badly you really want the good stuff and whether it is worth taking all the bad to get it. In this case, the collection is up in Huntsville, so at some point I'll have to go up there to take a look at everything. You just never know what you'll find."

"Well, I listened to the new culture minister sing bits of *Tosca* in his office today," Pia offered. "I think it was pretty awful, though I'm no opera expert. But I couldn't help liking the guy. There aren't enough singing politicians in the world."

"That might be a good thing. You wouldn't necessarily want the finance minister singing the blues in the middle of his budget speech even if that's how he felt."

"Or the agriculture minister breaking into country and western." It was lame, but Pia couldn't help herself. Finally, she changed the subject and asked Jack about the Tischler painting in Bellini's office.

"Oh, that's one of the more valuable pieces in the collection. For the last twenty years we've only collected art by Canadians. but before that curators accepted whatever was offered provided it had merit. That Tischler is probably worth a million dollars right now, although that's not something we broadcast. If its value were common knowledge, we could never have it hanging even in a minister's office because the security would be inadequate. We'd probably have to keep it in storage."

"The thing is, Jack, I recently saw the same painting down

at the police station. It had been seized as evidence from the attic where May Gatway was murdered."

Jack's face revealed his skepticism. "I'd be very surprised. To my knowledge – and I think I'm the guy to know – the Tischler is a one and only in our collection. Are you certain they're the same?"

"So certain I'm going to tell the police. Maybe they should be getting you or some other expert to look at both of them to see what's going on."

Pia excused herself to go to the washroom. When she came back, Jack had ordered another round of drinks.

"When will you talk to the police? I should probably do some advance research if they are going to come to me," Jack said, picking up where they left off.

"Tomorrow. I'm amazed that painting in Bellini's office is worth so much money."

"Tischler was one of the key figures in Expressionism, an art movement that emerged mostly in Germany in the early twentieth century. Maybe you've heard of some of the others. Erich Heckel, Emil Nolde, Max Pechstein? No? It doesn't matter. One of the things Tischler is best known for is a series of street scenes. The angularity in the painting you saw today reflects his interest in medieval woodcuts. Anyway, he had a nervous breakdown, as I recall, after being drafted into the German army. Then in the late 1930s the Nazis declared his work 'degenerate.' He shot himself not long after that."

Jack stopped to sip his beer. "As to the value of his work

today, if you like, we can go back to my place. I have access to some auction house websites. As a subscriber, I can look up all the recent sale prices for works by individual artists."

They took a cab back to Jack's neighborhood, getting out on the Danforth so they could take in the street life. People filled the outdoor terraces that lined the sidewalks, eating Greek specialties, basking in the warmth of the evening, seizing the moment in a city where summers were often as fleeting as a hummingbird's attention.

Pia felt relaxed for the first time in days, so relaxed she tripped over her own feet when she glanced into the window of a flower shop that featured a spectacular arrangement of dark red Asiatic lilies and birds of paradise.

"Good catch," she joked as Jack grabbed her arm to steady her. "I don't know how it happened, but I think I'm a bit drunk. I only had two glasses of wine. It used to take at least two and a half before I started falling down in public."

After they arrived at his place, Jack left Pia in the living room for a moment and returned bearing a round of drinks. "Really, Jack, I'm starting to think you're planning to take advantage of me," Pia said in protest when he handed her a wineglass.

"You got that right. I've missed you," he said mildly. "But let's not get into that just yet. Come up to my study so we can do that search." He led her upstairs to a book-lined room opposite his painting studio. While Jack sat down in front of his computer, Pia examined the shelves, discovering volume after volume of Canadian, American, and European history.

"I guess the guy you rent from teaches history?"

"What was your first clue?" Jack responded dryly, his attention on the screen in front of him. "Take a look at this."

He'd come up with a number of reports about a recent record-setting auction price for a Tischler painting. Paintings, actually, since one was a 1910 work called *Night and Day* and the other was an earlier painting called *Woman with Daisies*. The sale price was $8.6 million U.S.

Pia took in the information but wasn't processing it very well. When had she become such an easy drunk? It must be the effects of aging, she thought dully. Jack continued to search for information on other Tischler sales so she excused herself and went to the washroom, taking her glass with her. He seemed hell-bent on drinking the night away but she was not going to pour more on top of what was already making her feel out of touch with reality. She emptied the white wine in the sink and replaced it with tap water. Jack was standing in the doorway to the study when she emerged.

"I'm not feeling so good. Would you call me a cab?" Pia asked as a wave of dizziness hit her.

"Maybe it was the bad-quality wine at the pub. Mine is better. Why don't you take it easy for a bit? Maybe you'll start feeling better. In the meantime, I'll give you a guided tour of the studio. I didn't take you through it the last time you were here." Before Pia could protest, he pushed open the door across the hall and stood aside for her to enter.

"Well, okay, but after this I really need to get home to bed," she said, draining her glass and putting it on a table just inside the studio doorway. The table was cluttered with tubes of paint and jars filled with various liquids and paintbrushes, but one container in particular still caught her eye. She shivered involuntarily, and after a moment she realized why. Before her was a clear glass jar full of yellow box cutters, the same type used in the attack on May Gatway. The chilling image of the blood-spattered implement lying on the floor near May's body forced its way out of her memory as if propelled by gale-force winds. The box cutters were common enough. You could buy them in any hardware or craft shop. Still, Nancy Morton's words from the night before came rushing back. "Maybe we should check this other guy out too."

Pia sensed Jack standing behind her now, even as Morton's words bounced around in her head, tangled in a mental cobweb, unable to escape. She was being ridiculous. But before she could stop herself, the words were out of her mouth.

"What are these for?" she blurted, pointing to the box cutters.

"Tool of the trade. I use them when I need to trim a canvas or when I'm framing something," Jack said quietly.

He was so close she could feel his breath against her hair. Pia was in no mood for hanky-panky. She supposed she should follow up on Morton's suggestions and try to get hair and saliva samples from Jack. But right now she wanted to go home, nail her bed to the floor so the world would stop spinning, and get between the covers. She moved away, further into the room, and turned. Jack was watching her. There was something wrong here but she couldn't piece it all together. "So are you going to show me what you are working on?" she asked to mask her confusion.

"Go ahead, look around. If there's anything you find interesting, just ask me about it."

Pia walked over to the far side of the room. Dozens of canvases were stacked against the wall. She forced herself to flick through the closest ones. She flipped though a few and then stopped abruptly. Her mind was seething like one of those balls of mating snakes so popular on television nature shows. She needed to make sense of what she'd seen. Of what she was seeing.

Pia realized she was looking at repeated attempts to paint a winter scene, an old-fashioned tableau featuring happy skaters on a pond. She'd seen the image somewhere before. She moved to the next stack. It too contained studies, in this case of a vibrantly colored northern Ontario fall scene. Golds and reds shimmered in late autumn sunlight.

Pia recognized the Tischler – or attempts to replicate the Tischler – as soon as she came to it. Confusion and fear washed away her groggy uneasiness. Whatever was going on, she wanted to figure it out somewhere else.

"Jack, I'm sick or something. Really, I need to go home," she said, turning to look at him. He walked over to the studio's door and pushed it shut. When he turned toward her, the amiability she'd come to expect from him was gone.

"You don't get it do you, Pia?" he said in a mild voice that was at odds with his words. "*I'm* in charge. *I* decide whether you will or won't go home. And right now, I say you stay."

"Don't be ridiculous." She walked over and tried reaching around him to grab the door knob. "Let me out of here."

She saw him move, but before she could dodge he seized her arm, spun her around, and yanked it up behind her back. With his other hand, he grabbed her by the hair and viciously pulled her head back. Pia whimpered.

"You're pretty lively for somebody who has swallowed as many drugs as you have." He looked at his watch. "It's ten o'clock. I fixed up your wine at the pub and gave you some more of my special preparation just now. You really should be passed out by now."

"You drugged me?" Pia gasped as he shoved her away. It took a moment for her to regain her balance, and when she looked up he was pointing a short, stubby pistol at her. This was not good. An unbidden thought came to Pia: What would Leone do? Even with the drugs clouding her brain she knew she was being ridiculous. But she knew the answer to the question. Her heroine would keep Jack talking until she could implement an escape plan. The problem was, Pia had no escape plan. She was already afraid. Now she felt the beginnings of panic. Just keep him talking, she told herself. Maybe he would respond to reason.

"You copied the Tischler," Pia said slowly, raising her head to look at Jack as she struggled to put the pieces in place. As soon as the words were out of her mouth, she recalled where she'd seen the skating scene before. Bellini had said the Tischler had once hung in Wilson Scott's office. Pia realized she'd seen the winter scene in Scott's reception area. "And the skaters, you copied that one, too."

"None of this unpleasantness would be necessary if you had just minded your own business," Jack said. "But no. You had to keep meddling, digging around, sniffing at things you shouldn't be sniffing at."

"You were copying pieces from the collection. Are you afraid the fakes will be discovered? This all has something to do with May Gatway, doesn't it?"

Jack sighed. "She was becoming a problem. Just like you. The other night in the ravine should have been the end of it. But those two assholes with the dog turned up. If they hadn't been there, you would have been just another silly dead woman who insisted upon her right to run alone in the city after dark.

"I wasn't planning on bringing you back here tonight – one doesn't like to mess up one's own place – but you left me with little choice after all your talk about bringing in the cops. They would talk to experts and figure out fast enough that one of the paintings is a forgery. The Tischler in Bellini's office is the copy – a pretty good copy, if I do say so myself – but still a copy. Once that was discovered, there would have been questions about other forgeries in the collection. The police would have come to me with those questions because I'm the curator. And I really don't like cops asking questions." He stopped and again sighed deeply, sounding put upon and annoyed. "I should never have left the original up in the attic. I didn't think there was any reason for the cops to take it, so I was unpleasantly surprised when I went up a few weeks later to get it and it was gone. That mistake cost me money. A lot of money.

"But where was I? Right, you have forced me to improvise. I brought along a little magic powder with me to the pub tonight as a precaution only. I wasn't going to do anything with it. But you have to be dealt with now that you know about the Tischlers. Are you feeling really dopey, by the way? I hope so, because then this won't hurt a bit." Pia stared at him. Out of the corner of her eye she saw that one of the windows in the studio opened onto a fire escape. But there was no way she could get there, never mind get out, with a gun pointed at her. Just talk, she thought, desperately trying to stay focused. Otherwise, he is going to get down to the business of killing me.

"May was supposed to meet somebody else up in the attic. Instead she found you. That was no reason to kill her."

"But when she found me, she found me with the Tischler. I'd already substituted my copy for the real one in Wilson's office a few weeks earlier. Every time I make a switch, I hide the original in the attic until I find a purchaser. It's the perfect place because nobody ever goes through the stuff up there. And if somebody did come across one of the paintings, the first person they would call would be me."

"What did May say?"

"She was smarter than I thought. I had just unrolled the

painting to spend a few last minutes with it – it's not that easy to pass on such treasures – when she wandered in. She took one look at the Tischler and recognized it right away. She'd been asking to have it taken away from Wilson and moved to her office on the grounds that such a cultural treasure should not be slumming with the assistant minister of agriculture. Then she saw that I was wearing gloves – I didn't want to leave fingerprints anywhere up there – and started asking awkward questions. Like why the painting that was supposed to be down in Wilson's office was up in the dusty attic with me. She wanted to call security, but I couldn't have that, could I? Not good for my career, if you know what I mean."

"Killing her wasn't good for your career either."

"It didn't hurt. Like I said, her whining about poor little rich Jews who lost their art in the bad old days was also getting to me. All that talk of having outsiders come in to examine major art collections was making me nervous. It was quite possible one of those experts would be asked to examine the legislative collection. My copies are good – very good, in fact – but an expert would have figured out that some of the most expensive paintings under my care weren't the real McCoy. May Gatway went from being an irritant to being a serious concern. Just like you."

"The cops are going to get you, you know. They're going to have DNA results from the burka."

"That's an unpleasant possibility, I agree. But then I expect to be long gone before Toronto's finest figure anything out. I mean they haven't been able to sort out what happened to those kids, have they? It's a shame, really, about those kids. If you'd left well enough alone, they'd be fine, Wilson would have gone to his grave in peace and I'd still be accumulating funds for my early and luxurious retirement."

"Why did Wilson have to die?"

"He suffered from a failure of nerve. Oh, and he fell in love with little ol' me." Jack smiled coldly. His mild tone had given way to hard, clipped words.

Pia's stomach felt queasy but her brain was starting to function. Her only advantage was that Jack believed she'd consumed all the wine and drugs. He thought she would be getting more disoriented by the moment. In fact, she'd never felt less like keeling over in her life. But she couldn't let him know that.

"You were lovers?" she said, spitting the words out more slowly and staggering just a little for effect.

"We had sex, let's just put it that way. Are you jealous? I was happy to oblige you, too. Wouldn't mind doing it again if I didn't have to kill you. There's so little time for the finer things in life, isn't there? Anyway, where was I? Oh yeah, Wilson. He was desperate to make me happy and he loved art so it wasn't too hard to convince him to cooperate at the beginning. He would request new paintings for his office. I'd see that he got them and then I'd paint copies. I'd bring the copies in and replace the originals in his office. The beauty of having the paintings displayed so publicly was that if the fakes were ever discovered, suspicion would fall on everybody from the janitors to political staff.

"I'd sell the originals and give Wilson some of the proceeds once in a while. But what he really wanted was the art, so occasionally I'd also let him keep one of the originals. Nothing too valuable, but still, it was more than he'd be able to afford, even with that inheritance he got. Things were going very well.

"So you can imagine my dismay when that bitch's body is discovered in the attic and he starts to panic. He was afraid the cops would suspect him of killing her if they found out about her petty blackmail attempt. She had a photo of him with some kid in a bar and was threatening to post it on the Internet if he didn't stop campaigning for her job. He was also worrying that if the police started snooping around, they might find out about the big bank deposits he'd been making due to our painting exchange. And then he started talking out loud about how to keep our little secret if the police really laid on the pressure. The next thing I know, he was ranting on about how all the risks he was taking entitled him to more paintings. It was not the way a guy in love should behave. That made me mad. And I get nasty when I'm mad. So we arranged to meet at that shitty little motel to discuss all this and do those things that guys like to do in shabby motels. I brought the suicide note with me. How about that for advance planning?"

Pia's throat was so dry she couldn't speak.

"Anyway, when I got to the motel he was well into the Scotch as usual, so he didn't even notice the drug when I added it to what was left of the bottle. It was the same little treat, by the way, that you've been having with your wine this evening. In his case, I put in enough to kill a horse. Or a politician. But don't you worry, I've only given you enough to make sure you don't put up a fight. I don't like scenes, you see."

Pia glanced up quickly. She saw there would be no mercy.

Chapter Twenty-Two

AT LEAST IT WAS a nice evening, Sergei thought as he lounged on the park bench across from Jack Cleary's house. And sitting here for a few hours meant he could reassure Margaret that her niece was alive and well. Margaret had been pale with worry when she came home after seeing Pia earlier in the evening.

"First she gets hit on the head by an intruder in her own house, then she almost gets stabbed, and then somebody chases her when she's running in the ravine. Sergei, she doesn't seem to be taking the danger seriously enough," Margaret had said as she paced back and forth in the living room of the apartment, bringing him up to date. "I don't know what to do. I have to do something though."

Sergei thought he knew Margaret in all her moods: furious, sad, whimsical, anxious, happy, pensive. But today, for the first time, he was seeing her distraught. Her hands clenched and unclenched as she spoke and her huge green eyes, so like those of her niece, glistened with tears. He sighed. This is what happens when you fall in love. You do whatever you can to bring your beloved peace of mind.

"I could keep an eye on her," he offered. "She'd probably never forgive me – or you – if she found out, but she doesn't have to find out."

Margaret stopped pacing. "You mean, follow her to be sure she's okay?"

"Yes, sure."

"Oh Sergei, that would be wonderful. Would you really do that?"

"I will, if it will make you feel better."

"She's at a pub with this fellow Jack Cleary right now. I just dropped her off." Margaret gave him the address. As he turned to leave, she rested one hand on his arm, her face taut with anxiety. "Sergei?"

"Yes, my love?"

"You two are the people I love most in the world."

He smiled and kissed her. "I'll take good care of both of us. I promise."

And so he was following around a perfectly capable adult woman while she went on a routine date. He'd arrived in the pub about a half-hour before Cleary and Pia finished eating. Then he'd followed them to the house and watched them go inside. That was about an hour ago. Now he was wondering what to do next.

From the park bench, Sergei saw lights go on upstairs in the house. He rose and moving silently, entered the back garden. His new vantage point near a large lilac bush was much better. Pia and Jack Cleary were in the upstairs room right above him, their moving shadows visible behind the half-drawn blinds. He noted that one of the room's windows opened onto a fire escape that snaked its way down the exterior of the house. Margaret would have to bail him out of jail if any of the neighbors saw him on the way up and called the police, but he could live with that. He couldn't live with Margaret the way she had been just a few hours earlier.

Sergei swore to himself that he would go home as soon as he confirmed that all was well in the house. A few minutes later, he was crouched near the top of the fire escape, cursing silently as he listened to the conversation inside through the half-open window.

"You attacked those boys in the park," Pia was saying in a thick, groggy, frightened voice that Sergei hardly recognized. "You broke into my house, stole my notes, and went after them."

"Well, it started to worry me when you said you were working on a book," Cleary replied, sounding calm and relaxed. "You were so mysterious I started thinking maybe you had discovered something that the cops missed and, sure enough, right there in your notes, I found out about those two little shits. It was bad luck that you came downstairs and interrupted me. Sloppy on my part, really. I was preoccupied, with collecting your notes and disconnecting the laptop, so I didn't hear you on the stairs. But break and enter never was one of my strengths."

"Murder is?"

"Come now, don't be nasty. If you want somebody to blame for what happened to those boys, blame yourself. I doubt they would have told anyone about seeing me in Wilson's motel room if you hadn't tracked them down. But you are a busybody and so I needed to make sure they would never tell the same story to police. I'd just about guaranteed that when I was interrupted. Another dog walker. There are just too many of the beasts and their owners in this town for my taste. Not that it matters now. It seems that my time in your fine city is coming to an end anyway. Let's get you tied up, shall we?"

Sergei realized he needed to get into the house, but there was no way he could get through the window and take down Cleary at the same time. He flew down the fire escape to the garden and located the back door. It was locked, so he pulled a compact leather kit from his pocket and extracted a small tool and a tiny flashlight. He turned the flashlight on, put it between his teeth, and went to work. Less than a minute later he had the door open. He moved swiftly through the kitchen, into the living room and up the stairs. He could still hear the drone of their voices. Just keep talking, mister, he urged silently, and this will all soon be over.

Back in the studio, Jack had pulled a sturdy wooden chair away from the wall and into the center of the room. He then went to the table just inside the door, put down the gun and opened the lid of a wooden box. From inside it, he removed a paint-covered rag, a length of rope, and a knife – a vicious-looking weapon with a black handle and an eight-inch blade. Standing on the other side of the room, Pia couldn't take her eyes off the knife as he used it to cut the rope into two lengths. He turned back toward Pia, the weapon still in his hand, and gently ran his thumb along the blade. She trembled from fear, from the drugs, from the sudden, certain knowledge that he planned to use the knife on her.

"It's nice and sharp," he said. "Just for you. Sit."

"No," she said, staggering again for effect. "No, I won't."

"Of course you won't," he sighed. "Everything's a battle with you. Well, not any more." With the knife in one hand, he slowly walked toward her. He reached out, grabbed one of her arms, turned, and shoved her toward the chair. This was it, Pia realized with shocked clarity. Her one chance. She pretended to stumble past the chair toward the table where the gun lay, gleaming with promise. She reached out and heard him curse as her hand closed around the gun. In a second she twisted back to face him. He was advancing, the knife raised and ready.

"Oh come on," he said. "You aren't the type to shoot. It'll be on your conscience forever."

"Stop!" Pia ordered, hoping that her voice sounded more determined than she felt. But he didn't stop. He took another step toward her. She could see his knuckles were white as they clasped the blade; she could hear his breathing, suddenly loud and uneven. He was going to keep on coming. He thought she was his to obliterate, just like May Gatway and Wilson Scott and Tariq and poor, dead Mohammed. Fear gave way to hot, searing rage as he took another step and reached out, still full of confidence, to take the gun from her hand.

Pia pulled the trigger.

The short, sharp roar was so loud it masked the crash of the door being thrown open and Sergei hurtling into the room. Cleary fell to the floor. Pia stood frozen, the gun welded to her skin of her hands.

"It's okay, Pia, it's over," Sergei said with deliberate calm as he took in the situation. He gently guided her to the chair and one by one loosened her fingers from around the weapon. "I'm sorry I didn't get up here faster. I'm so sorry."

Chapter Twenty-Three

SERGEI USED HIS CELLPHONE to make a quick call to the police and then turned his attention once again to Pia. Her eyes were fixed on Jack Cleary's body. Blood from the wound in the center of his chest had spread across the front of his shirt. Sergei brushed the hair back from Pia's pale face, pulled her to her feet, and led her down through the house to the kitchen. It wasn't long before three police cars with sirens screeching pulled up in front. Less than a minute later, a fourth vehicle driven by Morton arrived.

The detective's day had been awful from the start and now she was worried it was about to get worse. First thing that morning she'd called forensics to see if there were any DNA test results for the materials picked up from the burka. Blair Mackenzie, the lab chief, promised her a report by dinner time. That seemed like good news so she went off to court in a decent mood. She wasted all day there waiting to testify at the murder trial of two gang members accused of shooting a rival at a downtown club. She knew from experience that they would lie and obfuscate and suffer from bouts of severe memory loss. But before she had her chance to testify and do her bit to expose them as vermin, court adjourned for the day. Morton went back to the station expecting Mackenzie's report on her desk. Instead, there was a voice-mail message with more promises of an evening delivery.

It was just after nine-thirty when she finally finished her paperwork. She was about to give up and go home when her telephone finally rang.

"You know, I don't get overtime for this sort of thing," Mackenzie said in a voice exhausted by long hours and too many cigarettes. "But anyway, I've got your answers and more, so pay attention."

Before Morton could say a word, he plunged on. "After I got my test results I called my buddies south of the border to cross check them with what they have in their data bank and bingo: we got a match for hair and saliva from inside the hood of that thing you gave me. The burka. They tell me that the guy who wore that burka is one JJ Claremount, age thirty-seven, wanted for murder in Boston. Killed a sixty-two-year-old guy, some kind of art expert, Norville Merivale. The victim was one of the go-to guys for people who want to find out if their paintings are the real thing. Anyway, your guy Claremount is apparently quite an artist."

"Did you say he was called JJ? – JJ Claremount?" asked Morton. She recalled the "JJ" who had turned up repeatedly in Wilson Scott's daybook.

"Yeah, initials JJ. The story is that about seven years ago he turned up in Boston, put his firm young flesh at Merivale's disposal in bed, and persuaded the old guy to let him copy the odd expensive painting that came through his hands to be authenticated. Merivale would then give the forgery to the unsuspecting owner and tell them that their treasure was a quality fake. Too bad, so sad, that sort of thing. The two scamsters, meanwhile, would sell the original to the sort of folks who don't mind keeping their most prized possessions in hiding."

"So where's the murder part?" Morton was impatient. Her alarm bells were ringing.

"Merivale got busted after some savvy owner realized he'd been shafted. But it was all handled very discreetly. The old guy was offered a break if he would rat on his artsy partner. I don't know if Merivale accepted the offer or was just considering it but it doesn't really matter because he was found dead in his apartment before the case got any further. The cops down there still talk about it because the killer really enjoyed his work – victim's hands on the burning stove element, one eye poked out with a pen, and lots of knife work on living flesh. Really sick stuff. Their lucky break was that Claremount apparently really got off on this sort of thing. There was semen all over the dead guy's body that matched DNA samples taken from young JJ's apartment."

"Blair, is there a photo of Claremount?"

"I've e-mailed it to you. Check your inbox."

She pressed a few keys on her computer and then cursed viciously as the image unfurled before her. There was no doubt about it. JJ Claremount was Pia's artsy-fartsy buddy Jack Cleary. Morton went back to the government website just to be sure. She grabbed the telephone and tried Pia at home and on her cell. No answer. Morton thought for a moment, did a quick search for a phone number, and made another call.

"Margaret, we've never met, but I'm Detective Nancy Morton with the Toronto Police. I urgently need to find Pia, but she's not answering her cell. Do you know where she might be?"

"She was having a drink with Jack Cleary at a pub downtown earlier this evening. I dropped her off myself around seven. What's going on?"

"Christ! I'll call you back later."

Morton checked Cleary's address and was already headed for the Danforth when the first 911 call came in. Neighbors in the area were reporting a single gunshot. Then somebody phoned from Cleary's house to report a shooting death. She turned on her siren and stepped on the gas.

Dread turned to relief when she pulled up in front of the house and saw Pia Keyne being helped out of the house by a fierce-looking older man.

"That's my girl," she said quietly before getting out of the car to do her job.

Chapter Twenty-Four

JACK CLEARY HAD BEEN right about one thing, Pia thought as she sat in her backyard two weeks later, contemplating the evening shadows and patting Winston, who was curled up on her lap. Killing a man wasn't something she could file away under "to be forgotten" – even if the man was a monster. She worried about the white, blinding anger that compelled her to pull the trigger. Most of the time she didn't regret pulling the trigger. But sometimes in the dark of the night, she woke up wondering if maybe there had been alternatives that she'd chosen to ignore.

Things felt even more complicated during those few days when she thought she might be pregnant with Jack Cleary's child. The idea made her nauseous, prompting her to think that perhaps she had morning sickness. Pia threw herself on her bed and cried with relief when it turned out to be a false alarm.

Morton and Sergei had assured her she'd had no choice but to use the gun. And Gabriella Garcia was being helpful. Pia had hesitated before calling her. She had canceled a string of appointments with the psychologist earlier in the month because she didn't want to discuss her decision to sleep with both Martin and Jack. To her relief, she hadn't been fired as a patient, despite her truancy. Dr. Garcia, after hearing Pia out, talked about the primal urge to survive and what happens to people when they are cornered. It helped a little but in the end, Pia suspected, nothing would help a lot.

In the meantime, she was taking some time off work to regroup. The *Gazette* went crazy over the Cleary story when it broke, running with it on the front page for three days straight. Pia, after the drugs she'd consumed had cleared out of her system, wrote a first-person account of what had happened.

Work by other reporters revealed that Jack Cleary, alias JJ Claremount, was really John Binkle, born to an alcoholic mother and an unknown father. He became a Crown ward when he was five and was subsequently adopted by Eugene and Edna Binkle of Vancouver when they were in their early forties. Young John Binkle revealed his artistic talents early on in school, but his adoptive father disapproved of such things. He wanted his son to follow in his footsteps and become an auto mechanic. Throughout high school, the younger Binkle labored after school and on weekends in his father's garage. Then one Sunday morning, when just the two of them were trying to catch up on some work, the hoist in the garage failed. John Binkle said at the time he'd gone out to buy some gum at the nearby corner store and returned to find his father crushed to death under the black Cadillac he'd been working on. Investigators never could figure out what went wrong with the hoist. His mother sold the garage and used the proceeds to pay for her son to study fine arts, first in Toronto, then in some of the best schools in the United States, Italy, and France.

"After he finished school ten years ago, he forgot me," Edna Binkle told a *Gazette* reporter when she was contacted in a retirement home in Kelowna, British Columbia. "I got a postcard a few years ago, but that was it. The boy broke my heart. Now when you tell me he did these evil, evil things, it's breaking all over again."

Doctors at the Hospital for Sick Children announced that young Tariq had emerged from his coma and would be just fine after a period of recuperation. Pia rejoiced, went to see him, and promised a steady supply of pizza. She also put some money into a fund for his education down the road. She couldn't bring back Mohammed, but she could try to make the world a little less awful for the child who had survived.

It was getting chilly outside on the deck, so Pia pushed Winston out of her lap, picked up her empty wineglass, and went into the house. She toyed with not answering the doorbell when it rang. Louise Lutkin had been pressing her to start the book about Gatway, Scott, and Cleary, and it was quite possible the agent had come to make her case in person. When she went to the door, however, Pia found Martin Geneve on the step.

"I tried calling a few times but kept getting your answering machine," he said. Pia smiled at him uncertainly.

"I needed some time to myself. But I am glad to see you." As soon as the words were out of her mouth, Pia realized she meant it. "Come in. I'm just about to throw together some pasta. I'll make enough for two."

He followed her into the kitchen and handed her the package he'd been carrying. When she opened it, Pia found the Gina Petrus drawing she'd admired the night they attended the Fine Arts Ball. To her dismay, her eyes filled with tears.

"You don't like it?" Martin said lightly while she tried to get herself under control.

"No, no, I love it. It's just that you do these nice things for me, and all I've done is suspect you of the worst possible behavior."

"Would you care to elaborate?" he said, taking charge of the wine bottle, filling first Pia's glass and then the one she'd set out for him.

"I thought at one point you might have killed May Gatway because she was going to make it harder for you to hang on to those two Egon Schiele drawings. The two that Rose Arnberg says were taken from her family."

Martin froze, his wineglass half way to his lips. "That's why you started giving me the brush-off?" He paused to digest the information before continuing more slowly "And let me guess, you were showing Julieta photos of Wilson Scott because you suspected me of murdering him too?"

Staring down at the tabletop, Pia nodded miserably. Any moment now she expected to hear the sound of the door closing after him.

"Pia?"

She looked up and saw he was smiling.

"Let me tell you about Rose Arnberg. There's never been any serious dispute about what will happen to those drawings. When Rose's lawyer first approached me, he made it clear her intention was to recover the drawings and to donate them to a French museum. I did my homework and realized she had a legitimate claim. I told her lawyer I wasn't about to put up a fight. She decided to fly over here to see the drawings and to meet me. We had lunch and bonded, and the next thing I knew, she proposed that the pieces be shared by two museums, one in France and one in Canada. This has required some sorting out, but I think we're almost there. We made a pact that neither of us would talk about the arrangement until it was finalized, so that's why I didn't say anything to you when you saw the drawings at my place. A huge mistake on my part, I see that now.

"As to being Wilson Scott's homosexual lover turned murderer, well, I obviously didn't make much of an impression on you the times we've been in bed together." He paused, then reached out to pull Pia toward him. "That's a situation I'd like to rectify."

Pia closed her eyes as she felt the heat of his body against hers. Then she reached up and wound her arms around his neck. Faced with a choice between life and death that night in Jack Cleary's studio, she'd chosen life.

She was curious to see where it would take her next.

Acknowledgments

I want to thank the Ontario Arts Council for financially supporting this project. I also would like to express my gratitude to Margie Wolfe, Carolyn Jackson, and the team at Second Story Press for taking a chance on a first-time author and making this book a reality. If there are any errors or shortcomings, the responsibility is all mine. Finally, this is an opportunity to publicly acknowledge those who encouraged me to keep writing and to say that their support was much appreciated. Joy Crysdale, Antonella Artuso, and Gillian Kerr were constant in their enthusiasm, honest in their critiques, and unwavering in their faith. Rob Benzie made me believe getting *Headline: Murder* published was possible. Anatoliy Mostepanenko insisted I translate my dream into words on paper – yet another reason to love him.

APRIL LINDGREN has worked for more than twenty years as a journalist, editorial writer, and radio and television political commentator. Her last "beat" – and the inspiration for this, her first book – was covering provincial politics at the Ontario legislature in Toronto for CanWest newspapers. She now teaches at Ryerson University's School of Journalism in Toronto, where she lives with her partner Anatoliy.